A Stolen Kiss

Heat burned Elena's cheeks. "If you're not enjoying yourself, you can go on without me and do whatever it was you had originally intended."

She knew she sounded like a petulant child, but somehow Lord Black had a way of jabbing at her emotions and making her behave in ways she'd never act otherwise.

Suddenly he pulled her against him, so fiercely that her breasts crushed into his chest.

"I don't want to go on without you."

Her heartbeat raced. Everything she had been feeling—the irritation and impatience—went into a complete reversal at his touch. He gazed down at her with sensual, almost intimidating intensity. She still heard the voices of the museum visitors in the next room.

Lord Black kept his voice low and discreet. "I want to kiss you. To drag you off like the cretin you just vilified and ravish you behind that partition."

There was an earnest, raw tone to his voice that thrilled her to the core. Gone was his emotionless façade. Her guidebook fell to the floor, forgotten, as she grasped his forearms and instinctively leaned into him, boldly matching her hips against his.

She gasped as he seized her by the waist.

He murmured, "Do you see why I have stayed away?"

"So, you were avoidin

"What is the alternativ

She peered up from be

net. "Kissing me again."

everything, darling me," she accused softly

the curve of her bon-

NIGHT
Falls
DARKLY

A NOVEL OF
THE SHADOW GUARD

KIM LENOX

A SIGNET ECLIPSE BOOK

SIGNET ECLIPSE
Published by New American Library, a division of
Penguin Group (USA) Inc., 375 Hudson Street,
New York, New York 10014, USA
Penguin Group (Canada), 90 Eglinton Avenue East, Suite 700, Toronto,
Ontario M4P 2Y3, Canada (a division of Pearson Penguin Canada Inc.)
Penguin Books Ltd., 80 Strand, London WC2R 0RL, England
Penguin Ireland, 25 St. Stephen's Green, Dublin 2,
Ireland (a division of Penguin Books Ltd.)
Penguin Group (Australia), 250 Camberwell Road, Camberwell, Victoria 3124,
Australia (a division of Pearson Australia Group Pty. Ltd.)
Penguin Books India Pvt. Ltd., 11 Community Centre, Panchsheel Park,
New Delhi - 110 017, India
Penguin Group (NZ), 67 Apollo Drive, Rosedale, North Shore 0632,
New Zealand (a division of Pearson New Zealand Ltd.)
Penguin Books (South Africa) (Pty.) Ltd., 24 Sturdee Avenue,
Rosebank, Johannesburg 2196, South Africa

Penguin Books Ltd., Registered Offices:
80 Strand, London WC2R 0RL, England

First published by Signet Eclipse, an imprint of New American Library,
a division of Penguin Group (USA) Inc.

First Printing, October 2008
10 9 8 7 6 5 4 3 2

Copyright © Kim Lenox, 2008
All rights reserved

For Jon and Tristan,
the best office assistants a writer ever had

ACKNOWLEDGMENTS

The pursuit of authorship is no simple endeavor. *Night Falls Darkly* would not have become a reality without:

Eric, the keeper of my heart, my "hero worth waiting forever for." Even if you don't read my books.

My parents, who support me in everything. If I jumped off a cliff, they'd probably jump too, and I love them for it.

Kelly, my brother—my earliest storytelling partner. You are a true modern-day warrior and an inspiration in all that you do.

Author Cindy Miles, whose heartfelt friendship, zany humor, and care packages truly (*truly*) got me through the dark times. There just aren't enough words.

Kim Lionetti, my very talented agent, and the person who set me on the path to this book.

Laura Cifelli, my editor at NAL. You made me think bigger and better, and I thank you for it. And also Lindsay Nouis, who always had an answer and a smile. You both made the publishing process a true pleasure.

Kimberly Gardner and Julia Templeton, two writers I've known since "the beginning." Thank you for the lightning-fast final reads and camaraderie. Life is better with friends like you.

William Simon of Abberline Investigations, my very
own Ripperologist. Thank you for all the friendship,
knowledge, and documentation you shared.

I am also very grateful to Lee Jackson, who created, and
continues to compile sources for *The Victorian Dictionary*,
which everyone can enjoy at www.victorianlondon.org,
and also the phenomenal resource *Casebook: Jack the Ripper*, at www.casebook.org, Stephen P. Ryder, executive
editor. Many thanks to the staff at the Hirsch Library,
Museum of Fine Arts in Houston, and to the members
of NWHRWA, WHRWA, and Hearts Through History chapters of Romance Writers of America, whose
support and encouragement have always meant so
much.

Prologue

Spitalfields slums
London
April 1887

"Come out, Mr. Winslow." Archer stepped out from the stairwell onto the dark tenement roof. "It's your time to die."

Wind, biting and ruthless, sent the tails of his greatcoat snapping behind him. He wove between crumbling chimneys and piles of rubbish, avoiding the sagging tar paper and rotted beams that might collapse and send a more careless being into the black oblivion of the abandoned building below. He pulled the leather gloves from his hands and tucked them into his hip pocket. Another gust twisted his long hair about his shoulders. Inhaling deeply, he savored the scent of fear on the air.

"How rude of you to run and hide, when I've traveled all this way *just . . . to see . . . you.*"

This was his favorite part of the hunt, the exquisite, slow torture of his prey right before Final Reclamation. He could choose to darken into shadow and make quick business of things, but no—a deviant like

Winslow deserved to be terrorized on a much grander scale.

Archer closed his eyes and summoned the quickening. Heat seared his skin and fluxed through his veins. When he opened his eyes again, he knew they were no longer gray, but wholly black. He spread his palms at his sides. Eight claw daggers hissed out, nearly to his knees, their blades formed of equal parts fire and primeval silver.

A crumbling stack of bricks stood at the south end of the roof. Though the fog was dense and the sky held no stars, he required no light to discern even the minutest detail. The air fairly quivered around the bricks. With a growl, he leapt the distance and leveled them with one blow.

Winslow reeled into the open. Though he was Herculean in stature, his scream rang as high-pitched as a child's. Unexpectedly, he dragged with him a tempest of woolen skirts, slender limbs and pale hair. Archer bit out a curse, his pleasure in the hunt instantly soured. He had sensed no other presence but Winslow's. How could this be? Never before had he made such a grievous mistake. With a scowl, he advanced.

"Wot the 'ell are you?" Winslow gaped, his eyes fixed in terror, first on Archer's claws and then his eyes. Scarlet furrows scored one cheek, evidence of his captive's mettle. "A demon, or the devil 'imself?"

Winslow dragged the girl toward the far ledge.

"Let . . . me . . . *go!*" She cuffed his jaw. Her lower lip was bruised and swollen. One of her sleeves gaped open, torn and flapping in the wind.

Archer hissed. How was he to Reclaim his target without sacrificing the life of the girl?

Winslow's heel pierced a weak spot in the roof. Both went tumbling. Recovering quickly, he clamped one arm around her chest, the other in a high choke hold against her neck, and hauled her backward onto the ledge. Behind them the slum lay blanketed in sooty darkness. Heedless of the danger, the girl flailed her arms and kicked at the beast's shins with her bare feet.

"Stop fightin' me, bitch!" Winslow ground out between yellowed and broken teeth. He struggled for balance atop the narrow ridge of crumbling mortar.

Archer halted. Any fall would be fatal for both. He cared not about Winslow—nothing could save the bastard now—but he would not be held accountable to the Primordials for the death of an innocent.

"I hope he kills you," the girl shouted, clawing at the meaty hands, trying to pry them away. "Kills you for what you did to me. For what you did to the others."

"Shut your mouth." A jealous animal guarding his claim, he wrenched her hard against his body. The ledge shifted. Bits of brick and mortar splintered out. "I'll jump before I let 'im cut me wi' them wicked blades, an' I'll take you wi' me."

"Then do it now, coward!" challenged the girl, her voice a defiant sob. "Jump!"

Archer searched the darkness of his mind and found her name there.

Elena, he commanded in silence. *Stop.*

She froze. Her arms and legs eased in their tension until the tips of her toes almost touched the muddied cuff of Winslow's boots. She rasped, fighting for breath, and with visible effort, tilted her face to stare wide-eyed and disbelieving at Archer.

What odd eyes she had. Brave eyes, one blue and one brown. Time, which usually rushed past him with the speed of a tumultuous, engorged river, almost stopped. His pulse—or hers?—beat in his ears, a dark cannonade. Beyond her tears he saw dignity and strength, and a reflection of himself as she saw him.

Cruel. Violent.

Beautiful.

His mind reeled to another existence, to a time when he had lived and loved. Dreams or memories? He couldn't be certain anymore.

"Do what you will," she whispered to Archer.

Winslow spewed blasphemies, his face a mere blot against the background of the night.

Archer stared at Elena, puzzled that he could not break the connection he had put into place between them. How could it be that with only a glance and a few words, a woman—a mortal woman at that—could penetrate him so completely? He felt all tangled up with her, something his mind rejected, but his soul craved.

Unnerved, Archer looked away, and into the eyes of something he understood better. "It's time we brought this dance of ours to an end."

"Go ahead," Winslow warned, wrenching the girl's head higher against his shoulder. "But she'll die too."

"You think it all ends with that?" Archer whispered. "With death? I'm afraid not. You can't escape, so let the girl go."

"She stays with me!" bellowed Winslow. His beefy fingers pressed into the pale flesh of Elena's throat.

Throughout time, Archer had always hunted with the dispassionate precision of a wolf, but now rage welled within him, so black and intense he felt he would disintegrate from the inside out. He cursed the limitations of his power, wishing he could slay by mere glance. Instead, left with no other choice, he darkened into shadow. With a frantic gaze, Winslow shouted and searched the rooftop. He sidled along the ledge as if to escape.

Mortar crunched, then slid and crumbled. The girl screamed.

Archer retracted his claws and lunged for her, but too late. A flash of petticoat, and she disappeared with Winslow over the edge.

Frantic to save her, he fell against the bricks and thrust out his arm, his only reward a brush of fingertips and her terrified stare locked onto his as she spiraled out of reach.

Chapter One

September 29, 1888

Elena grasped the girl's wrists. With the weight of her body and every bit of her strength, she pinned the young prostitute to the table.

"Bastards!" Lizzy shrieked, and heaved herself up with such force she nearly threw Elena off.

"Shhhh, shhhh," Elena soothed. "He'll make sure it goes fast."

With a *pop*, the bone slid into place.

"Success," announced Dr. Harcourt.

"You see?" Relief coursed through Elena, along with an electrifying charge of pride. "That wasn't so bad, was it? I told you he was good."

She eased off Lizzy, but carefully. In her brief time on the ward she'd learned one could never be certain of a patient's response. Some reacted with gratitude, others with a strike to the jaw. Glancing down, she saw twin rivers of tears streaming over Lizzy's temples and into her bright red hair. The girl's pallor nearly matched the white enamel of the table beneath her. Smelling salts might be in order.

"Lizzy?" Elena smoothed an unruly curl off a

freckled forehead. The girl was very young and clearly alone in the world. "Are you all right?"

Suddenly slender arms seized Elena in an embrace so fierce her feet rose inches off the floor.

Lizzy sobbed, "Oh, thank y', miss. Thank y' for stayin' wi' me. I ain't never been so scared in all me born days."

Her patient smelled of tobacco and gin rather than soap and flowers as a young girl should, yet Elena felt sympathy for her and admittedly, a sort of kinship. Who could say she wouldn't be living on the street and doing *anything* to survive if fate hadn't handed her a different set of circumstances?

"You've been so brave through all of this, Lizzy." Elena gave her a squeeze. Stepping back, she slipped a hand into her apron pocket and pulled out a handkerchief. "Two days ago I watched a grown man fall to pieces when faced with the same procedure."

"Truly?" Lizzy gave a sheepish smile and gratefully accepted the folded square of linen. She dabbed at her eyes.

In the corner of the tiny room Dr. Harcourt gave instructions to the young medical student who had assisted with the procedure. Elena listened as well, hungry for any bit of knowledge, be it simple or complex. They would employ a wood splint and sturdy bandaging to ensure the girl's knee remained safely aligned for the next several days. His instructions given, the doctor strode toward the door.

"Wait, Doc," Lizzy called out, raising herself onto an elbow. Her threadbare waistcoat stretched across narrow shoulders.

Dr. Harcourt paused, a shock of blond hair tumbling over one eye until he brushed it aside. "Yes, Miss Harper?"

He wore a physician's smock and trousers, an understated uniform for the highborn second son of one of England's wealthiest and most influential families. He was tall and athletic of build, and the top of his head nearly met the upper frame of the door.

Lizzy blurted, "I'm ever so sorry to 'ave called you a bastard." She glanced toward the student. "You too, sir. So very sorry."

Harcourt flashed a warm smile, the one Elena saw him employ often with his patients. Unlike many of the older physicians on staff, he had a way of putting his subjects at ease. His gaze lifted to Elena for a brief moment before returning to the girl. "Don't think of it again. I'm pleased to have been of assistance."

With that, he disappeared into the hall.

Lizzy's grin revealed a row of crooked teeth. "Lor', if the doctor ain't the most 'andsome man I ever seen. 'Ow can you even stand workin' with 'at one?"

Elena laughed softly but offered no response. Harcourt *was* a handsome man, but he had been her personal physician in the months following her accident. Now he was her mentor. Though over time they'd become something like friends, she didn't think of him in terms of attractiveness.

Oh, *bosh*. That was a filthy lie if she'd ever told one.

But she did take her position at the hospital very seriously. Only out of desperation had Harcourt dropped his insistence that she devote herself to "pursuits more appropriate to her station" and granted her a probationary role among the nurses. The proximity of the vicious Whitechapel killings to the hospital infirmary had inspired a wave of panic amongst its female employees. A number of nurses had resigned their posts, leaving the London sorely understaffed. It had been a full three weeks since the last murder, but in that time the authorities had made no firm arrests, and a thick pall of fear hung heavy across the district.

Elena wasn't afraid of the killer—not here on the actual premises of the hospital—and she'd do anything to stay.

She helped Lizzy into a seated position and arranged the girl's woolen skirts discreetly at her knees. "All that remains is for this good gentleman to bandage and splint your leg. I'll go to the dispensary and see about getting you a pair of crutches. Have you anyone to see you home?"

"Oh, I won't be goin' 'ome again. . . ." Her voice faded into melancholy silence.

"No?" Elena hadn't pressured the girl to explain the circumstances of her injury. The ladies who came here for charity services rarely admitted to being the victim of a brutish "old man" or customer. She kept her voice light. "Where will you go, then?"

"Me good mate Catherine'll be waitin' for me in the ward—Catherine Eddowes. She's like me ma, you see." Lizzy nodded, and smiled bravely. "She stays at a nice place, real regular, on Shoe Lane. Maybe I can stay wi' her. . . ."

"I'll fetch her, then."

"She's wearin' a black straw 'at and a coat with some fur on the collar."

Two slats of wood in hand, the student scooted his stool closer to Lizzy's injured leg. He and Lizzy eyed each other warily.

"You're certain this one knows wot he's doin'?"

"He's had the very best teacher," Elena assured her as she left the room.

Nurse James, the head nurse, swept past, balancing a tray of rolled bandages. "Dr. Harcourt asks that you see him in the chemist's laboratory."

"Thank you, ma'am."

Elena did not miss the sharpness of Nurse James's tone. For the most part, the nurses on staff were much older than she, and of modest backgrounds and means. They resided in the on-premises dormitory and lived little of their lives outside the hospital walls. Though she'd made her share of friends, a good number of the women had not taken kindly to her intrusion into their ranks—she with her fine Mayfair address, private carriage and driver, but she'd held her own. Not wishing to appear to hold herself above the rest, Elena had recently taken to spending two to three nights a week in the dormitory as well.

She smoothed her apron and hurried a few doors down. There she found the doctor scribbling out an order at the chemist's desk, his spectacles low on his nose. Ointment pots, glass carboys and stoneware jars dotted the shelves behind him. The air held the distinct tincture of camphor.

"You require my assistance, Dr. Harcourt?"

"Miss Whitney. Thank you for coming. I wish to speak with you about an application that arrived on my desk this afternoon."

Suddenly, the room seemed much smaller, its walls and ceiling, closer.

Elena straightened her shoulders. "Yes, sir."

He wore a professional, but pleasant, expression. She could read nothing in him that would lead her to believe he would grant or deny her request.

"You have managed to surprise me yet again, Miss Whitney."

"How, so, sir?"

"Most young women of your privileged means wouldn't deign to drive down the street in front of this hospital, let alone work in its charity ward. And now I hear you have engendered the admiration of our resident human oddity."

"I wasn't seeking anyone's admiration, Dr. Harcourt. Truth be told, my first visit with Mr. Merrick was completely accidental. It seemed only polite that I should stay and chat for a moment."

Just days before, one of the other nurses had thought to chase Elena off the job by having her carry a tray of beef tea into the room of a "private patient," only for Elena to discover the man was Joseph Merrick, a former sideshow attraction vilified in the papers as the Elephant Man. It would be a lie to say his appearance hadn't startled her, but after introductions were made, they had spent the better part of a half hour conversing on all manner of subjects.

"He wishes you to know he enjoyed the books very much."

To be certain Mr. Merrick knew she had not been repelled by his deformation, and that she had truly enjoyed their visit, Elena had made a point to return the next day, bringing him several of her favorite selections from the library at Black House.

"I am glad."

The doctor considered her for a long, silent moment. Elena resisted the urge to clasp her hands, or adjust her apron.

"With regard to your application—"

"Yes, sir."

"The path you seek is one fraught with difficulty, and unfortunately, much prejudice against your sex."

She attempted an easy smile. "I have put much thought into my decision, even before my time here at the hospital began."

"I know you have." He nodded, removed his spectacles and slipped them into the pocket of his smock.

"But what about marriage? Children? As you know, Lord Black left instructions that if you should wish to marry, he would bestow a generous settlement."

Her lip twitched. "Yes, Lord Black has been quite generous."

Indeed, her mysterious guardian—a man she could not recall ever having met—had left her mistress of his Mayfair residence, an opulent, expansive manse worthy of the queen herself. She also had at her disposal a ridiculously large allowance, and accounts at all the finer establishments.

Why was it so hard to understand that she needed more? She needed identity. Purpose. Somehow, this felt *right* and true to the person she must have been before. Elena glanced at her apron, at a smudge in the shape of a child's handprint. Her fingertips brushed over the precious bit of filth.

"Nonetheless, Dr. Harcourt, my interests lie outside the home."

"And you wish for me to write a letter of reference?"

"Only if you believe I would make a competent physician."

Slowly, the corner of his lips took on the curve of a smile. "Of that, I have absolutely no doubt."

"Thank you, Doctor." Elena exhaled, stunned and flattered by the uncharacteristic warmth of his words.

"I will write the letter—"

"I shall be forever grateful."

"—on one condition."

"Yes, sir. Anything. I shall scour bedpans or—"

"Not bedpans, Elena."

Elena flushed at hearing him speak her given name. He had never employed such a familiarity before.

"Mother's birthday fete is tonight."

Anxiety speared through her stomach. "I received the invitation. Regretfully—"

"I know it is difficult for you to move amongst society, and to suffer the inevitable questions about your past."

An understatement, to be sure.

"It's not only that, Dr. Harcourt. I now work under your supervision."

"And so your attendance would be inappropriate? Nonsense. We are neighbors, and Lady Kerrigan adores you. She was quite disappointed to receive your note declining."

Dr. Harcourt's mother had made several visits to Black House during Elena's recovery. Likely, the countess had simply been curious to get a good look at the reclusive Lord Black's amnesiac ward, but all in all, the lady's blatant nosiness aside, they had gotten along exceedingly well.

Harcourt pushed back his stool and stood.

"With the adjournment of Parliament, most everyone has left for the country, so the event should be a rather small affair."

How could she refuse him? He had already done so much for her, and now that the esteemed physician had agreed to write her letter of recommendation, she was assured of acceptance into the London School of Medicine for Women.

"You have convinced me," Elena capitulated, and smiled despite her dread of the impending evening. "Please tell Lady Kerrigan I would be pleased to attend."

"Excellent." His voice warmed with pleasure. "Then you must return to Black House at once, as I doubt you've a suitable gown amongst your things in the dormitory. And a few hours of rest, doctor's orders. You've been on your feet since dawn. Lady Kerrigan would be highly offended if you came to her party only to nod off in a corner chair."

"Thank you, Doctor. I'll just finish up with Lizzy. Do you think one of the cart drivers could see her and her companion to their place of lodging? One of the casual wards on Shoe Lane, I believe."

"Yes, certainly. We shall look forward to seeing you tonight, then." He smiled as she pulled the door to, behind her.

With a quick glance at the timepiece pinned at her waist, she scurried down the corridor and into the crowded reception rooms. She didn't bother a glance toward the left, for that space would be filled only with men—sailors, factory workers and other male laborers. Instead, she steered right.

"Mrs. Eddowes?" she called. "I'm looking for a Mrs. Eddowes."

Coughs and moans punctuated the lively murmur of the large, ill-lit room. A few faces turned in her direction, but quickly looked away. Women and children milled about or sat on wooden benches. Some slept on the floor or in corners. The air smelled like sickness and human filth. The unfortunate ladies who surrounded her were bundled up tight, most wearing every piece of clothing and miscellany they owned. Each face told a different story through its scars or wrinkles, its expressions or missing teeth. She could not explain, even to herself, why she felt more at ease in this gloomy ward than at afternoon tea in the sumptuous drawing rooms of Mayfair. Likely the answer lay hidden in her past.

Elena circled round toward the back of the room. "Mrs. Eddowes?"

Two young boys, fists swinging, tumbled into her path.

"I'm the Knife, boy! I'm going to cut your guts out an' leave you for the dogs ta' eat."

"Help! Police!" bellowed the other, falling to the floor at Elena's feet.

"You two stop that," Elena ordered in her best imitation of the hospital matron's authoritative voice. She helped the boy up by his arm. "No horseplay or out you'll go. Whom are you here with? All right, then. Take your seats by your mum, there against the wall."

She gave one last call, "Mrs. Eddowes?"

No one raised a hand or stood. Elena prayed Lizzy had not been abandoned, not when she so desperately needed the constancy of a friend. She retraced her steps to the center of the two reception rooms where the day porter sat behind his desk.

"Mr. Morgan, I know chances are slim, but I'm desperate to find a woman wearing a black hat and a coat with a fur-trimmed collar. Might you have seen her?"

The porter nodded wearily. "Oh aye, I remember *'at one*. Got 'erself into a bit of a row with the big-mouthed tart on the front bench." He hooked his thumb in the direction of the doors. "She took off about a quarter hour ago."

"Damn," muttered Elena, curling her hands into fists.

He gave a phlegmy laugh. "Lor', but aren't you startin' to sound like a Whitechapel gel!"

Elena shot him a rueful smile as she pushed through the large paneled doors, to stand upon the covered portico that ran the length of the hospital. Vaulted archways provided a dim view of White-chapel Road. Though the afternoon hadn't fully surrendered to night, the shadows were long, and a wispy, gray fog hovered all around. An old man in a dented hat and patched coat sat on the top step, smoking a cheroot. Beyond him, a hansom clattered past, its side lamps illuminated by orange flame.

"Sir," she called. "Was there a woman here, waiting?"

He nodded, and pointed rightward, in the direction of Raven Row.

"Thank you, sir."

The air carried an uncomfortable chill and a faint chorus of voices from one of the nearby dramshops.

"Ta-ra-da-boom-di-ay, ta-ra-da-boom-di-ay . . ."

Elena crossed her arms for warmth and traversed the length of the walkway. A low wind caught at her skirts and twisted them about her legs. Reaching the end of the portico, she circled the final column but saw nothing besides fog and shadows. She frowned. It seemed there was nothing to do but tell Lizzy Mrs. Eddowes had left without her. Besides, she didn't want to remain out here any longer. She wasn't one to claim odd feelings or premonitions, but there was something discomfiting about the moment, something that teased the vulnerable, exposed skin on the back of her neck and made her want to hurry back inside.

Just then she heard a woman's laughter, low and flirtatious. The sound was close, yet difficult to place as far as direction. Though she could easily see a stone's throw all around, fog muddied anything beyond.

"Hello?" She descended the steps and continued along the sidewalk until she came to stand beneath a towering lamppost. She peered up toward the source of its comforting glow, only for the gaslight to waver as bright as a guttering candle and be extinguished.

A chill scratched up her spine.

Though the hospital's façade loomed above, stalwart and filled to its chimneys with all manner of science and humanity, she suddenly had the feeling of being utterly cut off.

A sound echoed about her, a breath or a gasp. She twisted, searching the gossamer wall around her. The hair on her arms and neck rose up.

Someone watched her. No one she could see, but she *felt* the presence—its intensity and malice—as certainly as if the person's rancid breath dampened her skin.

Footsteps met her ears, heavy and purposeful. A man's boots.

"Who is there?"

Fragments of newspaper accounts surfaced in her mind.

. . . throat cut from ear to ear . . .

. . . the abdomen had been ripped up . . .

. . . murder in its most horrible form . . .

Elena dashed toward the stairs. The toe of her shoe snagged in her hem, and with a hard strike to her knees, she fell. The steps came closer.

Just a person, walking along Whitechapel.

No, a *killer.*

The boots picked up pace, and from the corner of her eye she saw a dark shape lunging toward her. She parted her lips to scream—

Only to realize the person who wore the man's boots also wore skirts. Blue with red flouncing, to be precise.

A woman said, "Oh, *luhhv.* Did you fall? The fog's a terrible sort tonight, isn't it?"

A firm hand helped her up by the elbow. "*Soooo* good to see you breathing. At first . . . well, you know what I thought. Thought the Knife had gotten you." The lady chuckled a bit nervously. She wore a straw hat upon her russet curls, and a fur-trimmed collar framed her narrow face.

"Mrs. Eddowes?" Elena gasped.

"Aye. Oh, dear. Did you come out here looking for me? *Sooooo* sorry. Had to step out for a bit." Though her words were tellingly slurred, Mrs. Eddowes's careful speech revealed the faded polish of an educated woman. She considered Elena with shrewd, glassy eyes. A small green bottle peeked from her hip pocket. "Lizzy all right?"

Together they climbed the steps, and Elena led her toward the infirmary doors. She glanced, just once, over her shoulder, to be certain no one followed.

"The doctor was able to repair her knee. Thankfully she suffered a simple misalignment, nothing broken." Elena spoke carefully, still working to calm the panic in her veins. How foolish of her to have frightened herself to such a degree.

"I can take her home, then?"

"Lizzy told me she can't return home. Can I trust you to find her suitable lodging for the next few nights?"

Mrs. Eddowes's laugh held a defensive edge. "What do you mean, can you *trust* me?"

Elena glanced pointedly toward the bottle.

The woman sighed heavily and rolled her eyes. "I've only had a touch, to take the edge off my aching head. I didn't expect to sit in this charity ward all damn day."

They crossed through the wooden doors into the noisiness of the waiting room. The warmth and bustle eased Elena's tension immeasurably.

"I'm certain Lizzy appreciates your concern."

Mrs. Eddowes's expression softened. "She reminds me of my own dear daughter. I was planning to go to Bermondsley to see my Annie this afternoon, you see. I stopped by to see if Lizzy wanted to go as well, but I found the poor girl like that. Her bugger of an old man had thrown her down the stairs, he had."

Elena bit down on her lower lip and frowned. No one deserved such violence, especially a gentle soul like Lizzy.

"No." Mrs. Eddowes shook her head resolutely. "I won't be taking her home. She can stay with me, only I've got to come up with eight pence for our bed, else we'll both be eating skilly at the poorhouse tomorrow morning."

"Mrs. Eddowes—"

The woman waved her off. "I'll come up with the money. I always do."

Elena knew what that meant. It meant venturing into a dark alley with a stranger, at the risk of disease or death, all for a paltry coin or two. Such an endeavor was dangerous enough without the added peril of the Knife stalking women like Lizzy and Catherine on these very streets. They left the reception rooms and entered the quiet of the central corridor.

"Wait." Elena placed a hand on Mrs. Eddowes's arm and brought her to a stop. She looked about to be certain no one would see. The seamstress had sewn a small pocket inside the band of her apron. She withdrew a few coins and pressed them into Mrs. Eddowes's thin hand. "Take these, for you and Lizzy."

Elena prayed she wasn't making a mistake. She'd been warned by the other nurses against offering personal charity. They told her she'd only be disappointed with the outcome. But for some reason Lizzy had touched a deep chord within her, and Mrs. Eddowes truly seemed to care.

"Such an unexpected kindness." She stared, disbelieving, at the coins in her hand. "Lizzy will be so
grateful."

"Don't tell her they came from me. Let the kindness be your own."

For the first time, their gazes truly met. Suddenly,
the woman's expression changed into one of realization. "Heavens, dear, I know you from somewhere,
don't I?"

"I've been working at the hospital for three weeks
now. Perhaps you've seen me here?"

Mrs. Eddowes frowned. "I've come here a time or
two for my Bright's, but no. It was that common
house on Berner. I'm certain of it. Remember? Filthy
place, and overrun by rats. I'm glad to see you've
gotten out of there, and found respectable work for
yourself."

Elena smiled and shook her head. "I'm afraid not.
I grew up elsewhere and only arrived in London—
well, not so very long ago. Since then, I've resided
at only one address, outside of Whitechapel."

A simple explanation for a complicated span of
months.

"Odd. I could swear you were the girl, one and
the same." Mrs. Eddowes scrutinized her face. "I remember those eyes. One brown and one blue. So different. I'd never seen anything like them before."

Elena's smile faded. She'd never met anyone else
with eyes like hers either.

But Mrs. Eddowes had to be mistaken. Elena had
grown up on the Ivory Coast with her widower father, a missionary physician. She had traveled to
London only after his death to live under Lord
Black's guardianship.

Not that she remembered any of that firsthand, of
course—not since the carriage accident that had cru-

elly stolen her memories. She simply knew them to be true because . . .

Lord Black had told her so in his letter.

Archer crossed the narrow gangplank. Water, black and fetid, slapped against the embankment below, a reflection of his dark mood. Behind him, a dense wall of storm, tangled up with the night, bore down upon the Thames, moments from engulfing the city.

Impatience left him ill-tempered. Another Reclaimer's incompetence had forced his premature return to England, when he ought to be on the far side of the earth bringing his own assignment to a successful end.

His dark-skinned captain stood beside the custom-house officer, the *Corinthian*'s leather-bound logbook in his hand. "I shall await word at Tilbury, my lord."

"Two to three days, Charon. A week at the most."

He stepped down, onto the dock. A discarded newspaper rolled toward him and wedged against the narrow toe of his boot. Its headline read, THE WHITECHAPEL MURDERS. The first few drops struck the cobblestones and dampened the shoulders of his greatcoat. Archer closed his eyes and breathed in the amalgam of scents from the city. Too dirty. Too complex. Rain would cleanse the air and quicken the hunt.

The other members of his party waited off to the side, amidst twining strands of fog: his secretary, Mr. Leeson, and Selene, with her raven's-wing hair rippling over her shoulders. Their umbrellas spread above them like large, black toadstools.

His town coach rolled into view, its silver, artisan-hewn harnesses boasting four black, perfectly matched Hanoverian geldings. Powerful muscles bunched beneath their gleaming coats. A footman leapt down to open the door. Leeson marched forward, his eye patch a dark spot against his skin. His arm extended toward the vehicle, an invitation for Archer to proceed.

Lord Black, he bellowed in silence, in a tongue so ancient that even if overheard, no one but Archer would understand. *Welcome home to England.*

Chapter Two

Rain drove against Elena's third-floor windows in pulsating waves. Although a chill hovered in the dark corners of the room, Mary Alice had lit a warming blaze. Elena thought wistfully of Lizzy and Mrs. Eddowes. It didn't seem fair she was here, not only safe and warm, but surrounded by sumptuous comfort, while they spent another night in the worst of human conditions. At least she could feel better knowing they wouldn't be on the street tonight, not with the money she had given them.

On any other night at Black House, she'd just be settling in to indulge in the stacks of medical and physiology texts, on generous loan from Dr. Harcourt's personal library, scattered about her room. Yet to her surprise she truly looked forward to an evening out. Perhaps she had allowed the afternoon's frightening episode outside the hospital to affect her mood too greatly, for she really didn't wish to be alone tonight.

She seated herself on the upholstered bench in front of her dressing table. She wanted to wear her locket, but couldn't see jabbing its rusted pin through the lovely peacock blue silk of her gown. The round front plate had been dented in the accident, but the delicately etched piece remained her most treasured possession. While she had no memories to confirm the belief, she suspected the locket had once belonged to her mother.

Mrs. Hazelgreaves, the society matron retained by Lord Black's solicitors to act as her companion, had explained to her that nearly everything else had been stolen by ruthless street thieves in the moments after the omnibus crashed into her hired hansom. The accident had occurred as she'd been traveling to Black House from St. Katharine's Pier, where her steamship from Africa had docked.

She opened the locket's tiny metal clasp and peered into the eyes of the man memorialized inside in ambrotype: Dr. Phillip Whitney.

"Wish me luck tonight, Father."

Odd, how the face of a veritable stranger could give her such reassurance. She missed him terribly—even though she couldn't recall what, exactly, she missed about him. There were odd chunks of memory . . . impersonal things such as a knowledge of medicine, languages and music, but as of yet, her mind refused to recall the more personal details of her life.

Dr. Harcourt assured her that one day soon her remaining memories would return in a blazing rush of color and detail. She clung to the hope, but as of yet that hadn't occurred. Her work at the hospital had provided a very welcome distraction, and she looked forward to the exciting months ahead when she would begin her more intensive training at medical school.

Elena slipped the locket into its faded velvet pouch and placed the small bundle in the drawer of her dressing table. There, her glance touched upon the letter—the only letter she'd received from the Marquess Black in all these months. She ran her fingertips over her name, *Miss Elena Whitney*, written in his dark, precise script. The envelope was stamped Cairo, and dated a full fifteen months before.

Not a single portrait of her guardian hung upon Black House's walls. Mrs. Hazelgreaves assured her most Mayfair families kept family portraits in their country homes. Unfortunately, when she tried to picture him in her mind, her subconscious inevitably substituted the same image she saw in the locket—that of her father. Without any true remembrances of either man, her mind continually attempted to merge them into one. Partly out of respect for her father, she wished with a burning fervency that Lord Black would return to England and provide her with a clearer definition of himself.

She had written letters to him, and even dispatched telegraphs, hoping additional details about her circumstances might trigger something within her. But between St. Petersburg and Burma and the other foreign locales, her communications had apparently never reached him. Eventually she'd given up trying, and approached Harcourt about a position at the hospital. There came a time when one must carry on.

A knock sounded on her door.

"Yes?" she called.

"Mrs. Hazelgreaves asks that you meet her downstairs, miss."

"Thank you, Mary Alice. I'll be right there."

The clock on the mantel chimed a quarter to ten. She took one final look into her gilt-edged mirror. Two different colored eyes peered back at her. In June, as she'd stood in St. James's Palace in her elaborate court dress, waiting with forty-some other young women to be presented to Prince Albert Edward and Princess Alexandra, she'd overheard a whispering matron describe her eyes as "peculiar." Her tittering companion had agreed, adding the descriptor "unnerving." Elena had to admit that, despite her "peculiar" and "unnerving" eyes, she felt rather pleased with her appearance tonight. With a hot curling iron and a handful of pins, Mary Alice had transformed her mane of streaky-blond hair into an elegant coiffure.

As Mrs. Hazelgreaves had declared, peacock blue just might be her color.

Gathering up her black lace shawl from the settee's rounded bolster, Elena left her room. Gilt wall sconces in the shape of upturned acanthus leaves lit the narrow hallway. Though the manse boasted thirteen private bedchambers, only two of them were presently in use. Until recently, Mrs. Hazelgreaves had occupied the room beside hers, but upon September's arrival she had pronounced the chambers drafty, cold and "an affront to an old woman's rheumatism," and had ordered her belongings moved to a set of rooms at the far end of the hall.

As she passed the pillared doorway of the master suite, she paused. The door was open. Other than the rooms utilized by herself and Mrs. Hazelgreaves, the rest of the manse lay shrouded in dust cloths, except during routine cleanings by the skeleton staff employed in his lordship's absence. Inside, two housemaids pulled dust cloths from the furniture. The scent of lemon oil emanated outward. Elena stole a glimpse of the cavernous room, filled with hulking, dark furniture, and continued on.

At the center of the house she descended the staircase, a massive marble structure that twisted up from the earth like a gleaming black leviathan. A flash of lightning illuminated the shadows through the domed skylight above. Reaching the ground floor, she looked about, but Mrs. Hazelgreaves was nowhere to be seen. Neither was the chamberlain, Mr. Jarvis. Indeed, the hall lay shrouded in darkness as if the staff and the house had long ago been put to bed. Only a pair of small lamps, at either side of the wooden doors, lit the cavernous hall. She hoped Mr. Jarvis hadn't forgotten they were going out tonight. She walked to the bay window and pushed the curtain aside to see if, by chance, the carriage might have already come around from the mews. The long, circular drive extended toward the street, empty and wet.

Odd, but the high iron gates were open. Usually the staff kept them fastidiously locked.

A cool draft permeated the panes and sent chill bumps over her skin. She drew away, intending to summon Mr. Jarvis with a ring of the table bell, but a glimmer of light caught her eye. A narrow shaft speared out from an antechamber that preceded the study. The room had never been in use since she'd lived at Black House. Indeed, she had never seen the interior because the door had always been locked. Perhaps she would find Mr. Jarvis or even the hall porter therein. She crossed the anteroom, careful not to bump into any of the darkly upholstered furniture. . . .

Furniture normally covered in ivory linen.

She knocked. "Mr. Jarvis?"

No answer. She pushed the door a bit, just enough to see inside.

On the far side of the room blazed an immense and intricately tiled fireplace, tall enough for a man to walk through without bumping his head. The fire's warmth touched her face. There were trunks and cases everywhere, some of them open, some still bound with leather straps. A soft shuffling of papers sounded from within. Her heartbeat quickened.

A traveler had come home.

A large potted palm obscured her view of the desk. She ventured inside. True to her prediction, a man sat at the desk.

Lord Black.

She clasped trembling hands together. He was everything she'd hoped he would be, and blessedly, very different from the picture of her father. Elegant, mustachioed and gray, he pored over a ledger with a frown of concentration and a critical eye. Yes—an *eye*—for the other was covered by a black patch! Fascinating. She could not wait to hear the story of how he'd lost it—perhaps to Bahamian pirates or a tribe of unruly natives.

For eighteen long months, she'd waited for this moment. Finally, her curiosity would be satisfied. Finally, her questions would be answered. She took a deep breath and approached.

"Lord Black?"

He did not move. He merely continued to ponder the documents. He even took up a pen to scribble a quick notation. Could it be that her guardian was hard of hearing? She searched the desktop for an ear trumpet, but saw nothing of the sort.

"Lord Black," she said a bit louder.

This time, the man looked up. A perceptive, intelligent eye perused her up and down. He smiled.

"Your lordship." She smiled warmly and sank into a curtsy. "I cannot tell you how pleased I am to finally make your acquaintance."

He continued to smile.

Thunder boomed above, and wind rattled the expanse of windows that formed the far wall of the room. After a rather *extended* period of smiling and staring, Elena began to feel altogether foolish.

"Lord Black, I—"

"He is not Lord Black," a man's voice announced from behind her, so low and smooth that the words brushed against her skin like a lover's breath.

The older gentleman's amused gaze rose up to a space above and beyond where she stood.

Elena turned. Her eyes widened.

Flickering lamplight revealed the outline of a man standing in a small alcove off the study. A tall, *naked* man, save for the narrow swath of linen he clasped against a tightly corded hip. His skin glistened damp and golden, except for the defining shadows that clung to each tautened sinew. Behind him sat an enameled hip tub.

A sudden vision assailed her, that of a dark angel poised for terrible violence. The image disappeared from her mind, forgotten as quickly as it had appeared.

"I am Archer, Lord Black."

If she had been drinking tea with Her Majesty the Queen at that very moment, she would have spewed a mouthful across the carpet.

"Oh . . . indeed?"

"Indeed."

"Welcome home, your lordship."

"Thank you." He leaned against the door frame, a move that brought him into the light. Humor lit eyes that she suspected might, under other circumstances, appear a cool and distancing gray.

Mortified, Elena found herself pinned to the spot. He, on the other hand, did not appear the least bit mortified. The barest hint of a smile teased the corner of his sensuous lips.

From what she had been told, her guardian

claimed no direct heirs. Surely she would have received a letter, or some sort of formal notification if *her* Lord Black had perished in his travels during the past year and left his title and estates to a distant and *younger* relative. Yet how could this be her Lord Black?

"You are not at all what I expected," she managed to say.

"What did you expect?" Dark hair was slicked away from his face, emphasizing the masculine slant of his cheekbones. Though she could not perceive its exact length, it appeared unfashionably, and intriguingly long.

"I—ah, had assumed you would be much older."

"Oh, yes?" A narrow stream of water glimmered upon his skin, drawing her eye as it descended in a slow, teasing path down his neck, collarbone and chest.

"And I did not expect you to be so . . ."

She couldn't stop herself. Her gaze drifted even lower, down the lean and well-defined length of his body.

"Naked?" Smoky eyes contemplated her with such intensity, she felt as naked as he.

"That too," she whispered, dry of mouth.

Heat swirled up from the pit of her belly, and curled in delightful tendrils through her entire body. She felt the urge to fan herself with her hands, or better yet, to run out into the rain to allow the downpour to cool her skin, peacock blue silk be damned.

Instead, she tore her gaze away. "I am truly sorry. If I had known you were here, I wouldn't have imposed."

"I thought that was precisely why you imposed. Because you knew I was here."

Again, their eyes met. "Yes, but only when I saw

you . . . I mean *him*, there, at the desk. With his clothes on."

Their conversation, while riveting, grew more absurd with each passing moment, but she had a thousand questions to ask him. Already her mind placed each one in queue, the first being how he had known her father.

The slightest shift in stance, and the muscles of his abdomen flexed. "I'm afraid I neglected to telegraph ahead, so my traveling party and I have caught the staff completely unawares. Chambers are only now being prepared, yet I've somewhere to be tonight and didn't wish to go smelling like the Thames."

Elena nodded. "I should go." An understatement, to be sure. "We can talk when you are not—"

"Otherwise occupied?" a woman's voice interrupted.

Elena twisted toward the sound. An elegant brunette in a rich, garnet-colored gown stood in the doorway, framed by shadow. She stared at Elena with mocking, catlike eyes.

The blood drained from Elena's face, and the thrill of meeting her guardian summarily evaporated.

"Archer," the woman said, "perhaps you should introduce us?"

Her words carried a slight, but noticeable accent, one of Mediterranean origin if Elena were to venture a guess.

Lord Black's expression transformed into a scowl, and he strode toward one of the open trunks, leaving a trail of damp footprints on the carpet. In an ill-humored tone, he muttered, "Introduce yourself, why don't you?"

Archer snatched up a precisely folded shirt from the collection of others within the trunk and shook out the creases. He had not remembered Elena to be so intriguingly lovely. That night—a mere blink in time ago for one of his immortal existence—she had been pale with terror, bruised and thin, nearly unrecognizable from the young woman who now stood at the center of his study, her face aglow with vivacity, and her platinum-streaked hair twisted into a glossy mass of curls.

He had known many beautiful women. There was something different about Elena. Something warm and luscious and intoxicating that radiated from her person, from her very soul, that captured and held his attention. The same elusive "something different" he had sensed on the roof that night, and forced himself to forget.

"Lady Black—" She smiled, too brightly.

Archer clenched his eyes shut. What an altogether unfortunate assumption, one that he knew would feed Selene's vanity immensely. His ward continued on with her misguided greeting.

"Welcome home. I must apologize for this intrusion on your collective privacy. I had not realized—"

One of Selene's silky dark brows arched up. "Don't apologize to me."

"Pardon?" Elena's cheeks flushed.

An irrational urge to touch her luminous skin, to soothe the heat away, seized him with unexpected force.

"She's not Lady Black," he interjected.

Selene's gaze shifted possessively toward him. "He's a tad stubborn that way."

The older man at the desk chuckled. Suddenly the whole exchange took on a tawdry hue. He could only imagine the sordid conclusions Elena must be drawing.

"*Miss.*" Archer reclaimed her attention. He clutched

his towel, unable to release it as long as she stood in their midst. "I beg only a moment, so that I may dress."

In those few moments he could interrogate Leeson and extract an explanation for her unexpected presence at Black House. But with a glance, he could see the damage had already been done. Despite the brave set of her jaw, her remarkable eyes glimmered with tears.

"I wrote you a number of letters," she whispered. "Did you receive them?"

Archer cast an intense glance at Leeson, who responded with a sheepish shrug and shake of his head.

"It appears not."

"What about my telegraphs?"

Another glance. Another shrug.

"I received no telegraphs."

She nodded curtly. "Why must you look to him for every answer?"

"Because Mr. Leeson handles my correspondence and obviously does an awful job of things, Miss— Miss—"

Damn, he had stepped in it now. He knew her name to be Elena, but could not, for all the sinners in hell, recall her surname.

Leeson mumbled the answer.

Archer blurted, "Miss *Whitney*."

Elena gasped, her eyes widening in realization. "You don't even know who I am."

"I know who you are," he barked, furious with his secretary for speaking the answer out loud, when silent communication would have been the obvious choice. Realizing how harsh he must sound, he attempted to redeem himself in a subtler tone. "I simply could not recall your name."

Tense silence held the room.

He uttered, "If I could just put on my shirt and trousers, we could—"

"Perhaps tomorrow." The girl straightened her shoulders and raised her chin. Her eyes no longer met his. "I am obligated elsewhere tonight and fear I am already unforgivably late."

"Miss Whitney—"

"A pleasant evening to you all."

To his dismay she set off toward the door where, her arms crossed, Selene stood, a petulant gatekeeper. She offered no leeway, and as Elena passed through, their skirts brushed heavily.

"Don't do it, Selene—" Archer warned.

But Selene's hand already gripped the edge of the door.

Elena's head pounded with the same intensity of the door that had just slammed behind her. All this time, she had lived in Lord Black's home and appreciated his generosity, believing he was a man to be respected, that he had bestowed his guardianship upon her out of kindness, and out of respect for her deceased father. She had waited for him to return to England, craved his company and imagined him to be some sort of surrogate family, or at least a friend. Someone who might answer her questions, or provide the key to unlock her memories.

Now she realized he was none of those things, and devastatingly, she was nothing at all to him. He was simply a rich profligate, too involved in himself to remember her name, let alone be concerned with her past or future. Had he even written the letter?

She waited until she'd reached the hall to ease her shriveled lungs with breath.

"Good evening, Miss Whitney," a voice trilled from above.

Two footmen carried Mrs. Hazelgreaves down the staircase, step-by-careful-step. Velvet straps bound the elderly woman into her favorite chair. "My apologies for being so late, dear. I forgot my wrap, and as usual Mary Alice was nowhere to be found. These young men were kind enough to carry me back up."

Mrs. Hazelgreaves wore a pale pink gown—pink was her favorite color. The faces of the footmen had surpassed pink. They were red with exertion, and their liveries were soaked through with perspiration. A few more steps and they settled her diminutive, gray-haired companion to the floor. If Mrs. Hazelgreaves were aware of Lord Black's return to England, she gave no indication.

Elena considered sharing the news, but decided on silence. Mrs. Hazelgreaves, who had never met his lordship either, would certainly insist on making his immediate acquaintance.

"What is it, dear? Are you ill? You look piqued." The old woman sighed heavily. "I warned you about working with those unfortunates in Whitechapel. Filthy and diseased, they are."

"I'm not ill."

Not in the way Mrs. Hazelgreaves meant anyway.

Mrs. Hazelgreaves continued to hold out hope Elena would change her mind about working in Whitechapel, or working at all for that matter. For that very reason, Elena hadn't yet shared the news of her application to medical school.

Elena knelt beside the chair and unfastened the straps with frantic hands. It was only a matter of time before the new arrivals would venture out from the study, and she had no intention of greeting them again.

"I've said it before, and I'll say it again: Young

ladies of privilege aren't intended to take employ-
ment. I dread what Lord Black will say when he
finds out."

"Perhaps you should write him a letter," Elena bit
out from between clenched teeth.

She presented her arm and assisted Mrs. Hazelgreaves out of the chair. Servants appeared, bearing
long cloaks that they draped over the ladies' shoulders. The main doors of the house flew open, and a
footman swept in, his cloak dripping onto the marble
floor. He lifted an enormous umbrella, even though
a generous porte cochere would offer them due protection from the downpour.

"Careful, girl," her companion warned. "Don't let
the rain cockle your gown."

Elena was no longer concerned about her gown.
Instead, it was her sanity that was now in serious
danger of becoming cockled.

Archer thrust each button through its correspond-
ing hole. "I don't like surprises."

"My apologies, your lordship." Mr. Leeson grasped
up a leather case and riffled through its contents. "I
just don't understand. . . ."

Selene huffed across the room and flung herself
onto the chaise, pouting as she always did when they
spoke the ancient tongue, a language that at only
nineteen hundred years of age, she did not understand.

"I asked you to take care of her."

"I did take care of her, sir."

"I meant for you to take her to a *hospital*." Archer
arranged his silk necktie with practiced expertise.
"And then perhaps arrange for her to attend one of
those girls schools."

Leeson's eye narrowed, and he thrust his barrelchest outward. "You told me to use my judgment."

"Something I shall not ask you to do again."

Amaranthine Reclaimers hunted. They did not intervene. By sparing Elena's life that night on the roof, Archer had revealed a dangerous weakness within himself, one he still did not understand and had ruthlessly striven to purge ever since. That she had appeared tonight, in his very sanctuary, when he had considered her to be a forgotten part of his past, left him highly unsettled.

Mr. Leeson appeared to find that which he searched for. He set the case aside and sifted through several thin booklets.

"Here we are. Listen carefully." Opening to one dog-eared page, he read aloud in an affected voice, *"With a generous dower from her uncle, a dressing room full of exquisite Worth gowns, and invitations to the Season's most exclusive balls, Minerva was assured of betrothal to a wealthy suitor within the passing of three months' time."*

Archer snatched the volumes away and sifted through them. *"Minerva Fairchild's Love Story? His Lordship's Hidden Heart?* You made your decisions regarding Miss Whitney's future based upon penny dreadfuls?"

Mr. Leeson stiffened. "These *novelettes* are an accurate reflection of modern culture and ideals. Even so, things haven't changed much over time. Mortal women have always required two simple elements to achieve happiness: a wealthy husband and babies."

"Surely you jest."

Archer couldn't claim to know what might please a mortal woman. Although necessity required him to move amongst them at times, he took care to keep himself distinctly apart. The few he had passed time with had seemed to enjoy sex an inordinate amount.

"No, it's *true*," Mr. Leeson assured him. "You know of my interest in mortal behavior. I've gathered many sources besides these."

"You don't say."

"I thought to myself, why shouldn't we give the girl those things? We had no intention of returning to England for at least another decade. During that time the house would remain fully staffed, and the carriages would sit unused. Heaven knows you've enough wealth to last a thousand mortal lifetimes. Better that Miss Whitney benefit than no one at all."

"You should have warned me. I didn't even know her name, for God's sake."

Archer closed his eyes, trying to forget the look of betrayal she'd thrown him just before leaving the study.

Leeson bit his lower lip. "Miss Whitney's appearance was as much a surprise to me as to you. Your London barristers were to submit requests for additional funds if the girl depleted those I . . . er, *you*, originally allocated, including a generous lump-sum settlement if she were to become betrothed to a suitable gentleman, the details of which would, again, be handled by a committee of your barristers. I never received a request, and so naturally, believed her to be successfully wed."

"What of the letters and telegraphs she mentioned?"

"I never received any."

"Why would she claim to have sent them, if she did not?"

A dark realization swept over Archer. He glared toward Selene, who lounged on the chaise, twining her long hair around her fingers.

"Selene, do you know anything about the letters and telegraphs that were sent by Miss Whitney?"

"Hmmm," she sighed heavily, and crossed her ankles upon a tufted cushion.

"No doubt burned to ash," muttered Mr. Leeson.

More likely, Selene had eaten them. A bibliophile of immortal proportions, she suffered a quirky, fetishlike hunger for the written word—a hunger of the most *literal* sort. She devoured all varieties of letters, newspapers and books like an indulged child might gobble down sweets.

"I have no patience for this," Archer growled, thrusting one arm, and then the other, into its coat sleeve. "Not tonight when there is so much to be done. But Selene, please know you and I will discuss this matter further, and in *excruciating* detail, when I return tomorrow morning."

"We're going out?" Selene shot up, dropping her guise of languor. "I'll fetch my mantle."

He grasped her by the arm as she swept past. She twisted, pressing herself and all her womanly attributes against him. With smiling lips and direct gaze she sought to provoke, and to tempt, but he felt nothing for her, no spark of their former passion. He never forgave a betrayal.

"Understand this," he uttered quietly, "because I will not repeat myself. We don't work together. We will *never* work together again."

Selene jerked away, a deep flush claiming her cheeks. "I'm a Reclaimer, damn it, just like you. We've two targets, working in ridiculously close proximity to each other. It only makes sense we unite our efforts."

"I've already got your damned errant brother to deal with. I don't need you underfoot as well."

"That's not fair." Her fists curled into the silk of her skirts.

"You don't think so?"

"Of course not."

"You're right. I've changed my mind."

"You have?" She stepped forward, her expression easing into hopefulness.

"You won't be going out at all tonight."

She froze. *"What?"*

"That's right. Drink wine. Play cards with Leeson." Archer narrowed his gaze into hers. "Eat some books. But you are forbidden to leave the premises of Black House."

He strode from the room, firmly shutting the door against her shriek of fury.

In the hall, he grasped the wooden handle of the brass bell and gave it a stiff ring. Footsteps sounded from down the hall. Mr. Jarvis appeared.

"Yes, my lord?"

Archer glanced at his pocket watch. "I'll need the coach again."

"Very good. I'll inform the mews." The man bowed, then retraced his steps.

"Mr. Jarvis," Archer called after him.

"Yes, Lord Black?"

"I wish to be taken wherever Miss Whitney has gone."

Chapter Three

"The stuffing in this cushion is too soft. It is only a matter of time before my back begins to ache." Mrs. Hazelgreaves scowled and gripped the pommel of her cane.

Elena and her companion had only just arrived at Lord and Lady Kerrigan's Curzon Street house. After they'd made their way through the receiving line, Mrs. Hazelgreaves had been all too eager to find a place to perch.

"Please, take my chair." Elena stood. "It's rather firm, and the arms are padded as well. May I get you some lemonade?"

Lady Kerrigan's "small, casual affair" had turned out to be neither small nor casual after all. Guests thronged about from one opulent room to the next, admiring the family's extensive collection of sculpture and gilt-framed art. On the far side of the gallery the carpets had been rolled back, and a small orchestra played Strauss.

"Perhaps later, dear. For now, I simply wish to sit and take everything in."

Still shaken from her unexpected introduction to Lord Black, Elena agreed, more than content to attend to her elderly companion and act as nothing more than drapery for the remainder of the evening. Besides, her feet ached from her long day at the hospital.

Like most of the great Mayfair houses, the Kerrigan manse had not been refitted for modern gas illumination, but a chandelier grand enough for any Parisian opera house hung from the center of the gallery's paneled ceiling. The Venetian fixture boasted a cascade of crystal tears all around, and no less than a hundred burning tapers. Candelabrums and mirrored wall sconces provided additional light along the periphery of the elegant room.

Mrs. Hazelgreaves reached out to clasp Elena's hand. "Oh, lovely. Here comes your Dr. Harcourt."

"Please don't say that."

"Say what?"

"That he is my Dr. Harcourt. You make it sound as if I have a *tendresse* for him."

"Well, you ought to."

"I most certainly ought not. He is my supervisor at the hospital."

"He shouldn't be."

"Shhhh." As discreetly as possible, Elena wedged her blank *programme du bal*, which listed the order of dances for the evening and twenty blank spaces for the scheduling of partners, between her seat back and cushion.

"Mrs. Hazelgreaves. Miss Whitney." Harcourt beamed his golden warmth upon them. He first reached for the older woman's hand and kissed the backs of her fingers. His eyes met Elena's before he bent to do the same with hers. "I am so delighted you were both able to come."

"We're honored to share in her ladyship's special occasion." Mrs. Hazelgreaves beamed.

Harcourt glanced aside. "Here comes the queen of Curzon now."

Lady Kerrigan glided toward them, a vibrant, pale-haired jewel in green silk. Elena straightened in her seat. Dr. Harcourt moved to stand at her side.

"Miss Whitney," announced Lady Kerrigan. "I vow you look so lovely tonight it makes my heart absolutely *weep* with admiration."

Elena did not miss the manner in which Dr. Harcourt's beautiful mother examined her from head to toe.

"Thank you, Lady Kerrigan."

"Charles tells me you've settled into your duties at the hospital splendidly."

"I've enjoyed every moment I've spent there."

"*Wonderful.* The service of London's deserving poor is such a worthy cause. Me, I prefer the shops of Bond Street."

"Much to my father's woe," chuckled Dr. Harcourt, eliciting a laugh from everyone. In truth, her ladyship's activism in a number of charities was well-known to all.

Lady Kerrigan's face assumed a more solemn mien. "Seriously, Miss Whitney, I would be remiss if I did not make mention of my fear for your safety. The murders of those women—"

Dr. Harcourt interjected, "Not a single one of which has taken place upon the grounds of the hospital."

"But only a few streets away!" Lady Kerrigan clasped a hand upon his arm. "Too close for my comfort."

"I have repeatedly voiced the same fear." Mrs. Hazelgreaves gave a feathery sigh.

Harcourt shook his head. "I assure you both, upon my honor, Miss Whitney is in no danger whatsoever—not unless she takes to wandering the streets and alleys of the East End alone in the hours after midnight."

Elena added, "It's true. I've never feared for my well-being while at the hospital."

Whatever had occurred in the fog outside the hospital that afternoon did not count, of course, because she'd only frightened herself.

Lady Kerrigan pressed her lips together. "I won't make mention of it again, not tonight anyway, because I'm not going to allow that ghastly *beast* to ruin my birthday. I simply wanted Miss Whitney to know how I felt."

"Thank you for your concern, Lady Kerrigan."

Her ladyship nodded before moving closer to Mrs. Hazelgreaves's chair. "On another note, Mrs. Hazelgreaves, I have so much to tell you. Mother has written from Venice. . . ."

Elena knew from prior conversations that, decades before, Mrs. Hazelgreaves and Dr. Harcourt's paternal grandmother had been debutantes together.

Harcourt extended a hand. "Let us dance while they share news."

"Yes, dance," urged Lady Kerrigan. To Mrs. Hazelgreaves, she murmured, "Beautiful young people. How I envy their youth."

Reluctantly, Elena left her chair. She had no desire to dance, but she did need to speak with Dr. Harcourt privately.

"Miss Whitney," Lady Kerrigan called after her. She waved a white card. Elena's heart sank. "Don't forget your *programme*. I expect to see the remaining spaces filled by midnight. Several eligibles have already made inquiries."

Elena retrieved the card. "Thank you, your ladyship."

With the end of a quadrille, the orchestra quickly transitioned into a *valse à deux temps*. Dr. Harcourt led her toward the dance floor where couples paired off.

"If we hurry, we can step in with this one."

"Doctor—"

"*Charles*. Call me Charles tonight, and I, in turn, shall call you Elena." He widened his eyes a bit, in feigned incredulity. "Shocking, I know, but we're here to enjoy our evening, and we're friends after all, aren't we, Elena?"

"Yes, we are. Charles." She gave a small, self-conscious laugh. "But if it's all right, I'd rather sit this one out and . . . perhaps we could just talk."

"Please don't disappoint me." He grinned persuasively and drew her by the hand toward the floor. They attracted the interested gazes of many who stood along the way, including their Lordships Drayson, Bernard and Thackston, each of whom had called upon Elena at Black House after her presentation at court, and her half-hearted appearance at several society events, only to have their efforts politely rebuffed.

Charles continued. "Truth be told, I've been waiting to dance with you ever since you started to walk again. Call it my vanity as a physician, but I'd like to believe my expertise played a part in your recovery. Besides, I'm certain if I don't claim my waltz early in the evening, my old school chums will get a look at you in that lovely dress, and I won't have another chance."

Elena bit her lower lip. "Thank you for trying to make me feel more at ease. It is just that—"

They neared space where carpet gave way to polished parquet. Elena felt the vibration of the stringed instruments through the soles of her slippers. She adored music and would love to dance.

"What is it, Elena?"

"If I knew how to dance before the accident . . ."

"Tell me."

"I don't remember how any longer."

Immediately, he halted his gentle abduction. "I see."

"It's true. I can rattle off the chemical properties of quinine"—she waved an anxious hand—"but I can't recall a single dance step."

He glanced toward the floor. "They are not so difficult."

"Yet I don't wish to learn before this audience."

"Perhaps private lessons are in order?"

"Mrs. Hazelgreaves has suggested the same. . . ." Elena's voice drifted off. She couldn't imagine returning to Black House and undertaking anything so ordinary as dancing lessons, or even breakfast for that matter. She recalled Lord Black's handsome face, scowling over her forgotten name. Nothing would ever be the same. In truth, she had no home.

"I meant that I should teach you."

"That would be lovely," she answered, barely registering his words. "Dr. Harcourt?"

"Charles."

"Charles." Elena flushed. "May I speak to you about something?"

His face grew serious. "I hope you know you can speak to me about anything."

"Might it be possible for me to move into the nurses' dormitory on a more permanent basis?"

His brows drew together. "You heard my mother and Mrs. Hazelgreaves over there. I'd never hear the end of it. Besides, why would you want to do such a thing?"

"It would only be until my courses at the college began."

"Is Mrs. Hazelgreaves pressuring you to resign? Should I speak with her privately or write a letter to Lord Black?"

"A letter. Hmmm, no. Let it only be said that I don't wish to remain at Black House any longer."

"There must be a reason, Elena. What has happened?"

A shout went up from the reception area, claiming their attention. There, servants clung to two massive carved doors. Despite their efforts and seven pairs of dragging feet, the panels groaned inward upon their hinges. A frigid gust swept the room, snuffing the life of every candle. The orchestra dwindled to silence.

Harcourt's hand moved protectively to the small of her back. "It's only the wind."

Nervous laughter tittered everywhere.

The closure of the doors reverberated through the room, and the majordomo held up a lantern. He shouted, "Stand aside, for the chandelier must be relit."

Nearby, servants removed a panel from the wall, and hand-cranked the enormous fixture to the ground. Dim shapes rushed forward, bearing lit tapers. Elena watched in fascination as each candle burned anew—only to perceive, on the far side of the shimmering heap, a pair of gray eyes trained intently upon her.

"Heave," bellowed the majordomo.

The crank sounded, and the chandelier jerked upward with a musical jangle.

"Heave."

Slowly, the masterpiece of faceted crystal lurched higher and higher until the weighty mass trembled above, leaving an unoccupied expanse of carpet that no one dared yet cross.

No one but Lord Black.

*   *   *

When the man touched Elena—claimed her so presumptuously for all the world to see—Archer's vision went unexpectedly black. The urge to destroy, a deeply imbedded instinct, snarled up from within.

"Lord Black," Elena blurted, her eyes growing wider with each step he took toward her.

Suddenly, an overabundance of thoughts, sounds and expectations reeled toward him, turning the moment into something ugly and surreal. Voices whispered, murmured and even shouted his name. Not out loud of course, but in the minds of those who took note of his presence.

"Lord Black?" A woman in green led the pack of mortals who suddenly thronged about him. Her cheeks flushed bright with excitement. "Forgive my bold introduction, but we are neighbors after all, are we not? I am Lady Kerrigan. What an unexpected pleasure, to have you grace my little birthday soiree."

"The pleasure is . . . all mine." Archer did his best to smile, when inside he could only curse himself for having brought this attention upon himself, when he had wanted none. A sudden, searing pain shot through his left eye. He had never done well in crowds when all the attention was focused upon him. Seeking surcease from the cacophony inside his head, he stared at Elena's lips, and saw her form the words, *No Charles, I am not mistaken. That is my guardian, Lord Black.*

Charles. Why did she not refer to him by Lord So-and-So, or Mr. Someone? Why so familiar? Charles's hand still pressed against her back.

With due effort, he kept the growl from his voice. "If everyone would excuse us, I would like to dance with Miss Whitney."

The dance floor was the only place he could think

of where no one would follow them, and talk, and talk, and talk.

Lady Kerrigan's eyes widened, as if slightly shocked. She glanced to Elena. "Certainly."

"Miss Whitney?" Archer extended his hand.

Elena bit her lower lip, but after a moment, said, "Of course."

She placed her hand into his larger one. As etiquette dictated, she wore gloves. Archer did not.

Charles protested, "But you don't know how."

Archer removed his top hat, and handed it to him. "Would you mind?"

Without waiting for an answer, he shouldered his way through the crowd, drawing Elena behind, his thumb pressed against the underside of her wrist. Their heels sounded against the parquet. Feeling more ferocious with each passing moment, he took the printed card from her hand and released it to fall in a zigzag descent to the carpet. The members of the orchestra ogled them, their various instruments poised in hand.

He drew Elena to his side, deliberately placing his hand in the exact spot where Charles's had been, over the row of tiny buttons that traced the length of her spine. He glanced down, only to find himself entangled in her gaze. He had expected anger, confusion or fear. He deserved any one of those reactions. Yet she peered back as calmly as an Egyptian caryatid.

"I understand," she said plainly. "But I don't know how to dance."

"Yes, you do."

Her breasts crushed alluringly against her bodice with her sharp intake of breath. Her eyes flared with sudden challenge. Three couples eagerly took the spaces beside them, and the orchestra leapt into a lively quadrille.

He bent his head low, and murmured, *"Le Pantalon."*

With one hand, he guided her off to the right. Together they walked the circle, weaving in and out of the other couples, touching each hand as they passed. Soon, they had returned to the place where they'd started, and once again stood side by side. She threw him a look of wide-eyed astonishment.

He quietly announced the next stage of the dance. *"L'Eté."*

Always, his attention remained fixed upon her—her hair, her face, her lovely neck. By concentrating on her, he filtered out the rest. There was only the music, and Elena. The pain in his head subsided. Soon enough, they touched again.

Eyes bright with tears, she whispered, *"La Poule."*

They carried on through *La Trenise*, and eventually, *Le Finale*. The orchestra paused, and the other couples separated. Archer stood beside Elena. Cards flashed, and partners changed. The gathered assemblage hovered along the edge of the floor, watching. *Waiting.* Charles stood amongst them, his eyes dark and his jaw set. Once again, the orchestra raised their instruments, signaling the onset of the next dance.

He heard Elena say, "Thank you, my lord."

She took a step as if to walk away. The first strains of a waltz, softly ardent, drifted over the ballroom. Archer caught her hand and brought her back against him. Gasps sounded all around. Despite the layers of wool and silk between them, he felt her rapid heartbeat against his chest.

Tentatively, she rested her hand against his shoulder, her fingers curling into his hair.

Already, he led her into the first steps. She moved against him, sylphlike and sweet. Only then did Archer concede to himself what a grave mistake he had made in coming here tonight.

A short time later, Elena stared out over the night-shadowed gardens, but she recognized nothing—not a tree, a fountain or a shrub. Instead, every fragment of her being fixed on the man who stood in darkness, a few feet behind her.

When the waltz had come to an end, they had escaped to this small unlit gallery off the dining hall where tables of food and drink had been laid out for the guests. The faint light of the garden lamps shone through the windows. On the other side of the doorway, voices laughed and conversed. Crystal clinked.

He broke the silence first.

"Are you all right?"

"I'm still just a bit warm from the dance."

Her gloves lay on the windowsill. She removed her palms from where she'd pressed them against the cold panes, and held them against her cheeks.

The dance. What had happened between them out there? Somehow, his words or his voice had unlocked a memory buried deep within her. Not only that, but she had experienced such a mix of emotions. Afterward, she had felt most unsteady on her feet. She reminded herself she'd spent a long span of days on the hospital ward. Likely, she merely needed rest. Lord Black had brought her here to recover.

"I wish to apologize for what happened earlier this evening, in my study."

Elena laughed softly, lowered her hands and turned to face him. "You didn't know my name."

"I did not."

She couldn't see him very well but somehow knew he did not return her smile.

"You didn't even know I lived in Black House, did you?"

"No."

She laughed again. "Somehow the darkness makes it easier to ask you these questions."

"Then I'm glad we are here." He came to stand beside her. She tensed a bit, but he merely mirrored her stance, resting his palms against the horizontal window frame behind them and easing back against it. Now only a fraction of space separated them from touching.

"I have so many questions for you."

"Ask anything you like." Here, beside the window, midnight painted his features blue. He was a beautiful, masculine male, from the high cut of his cheekbones to the firm set of his jaw. With his impeccable clothing and his unbound hair he appeared elegant and wild all at once. Her breath snagged in her throat each time she dared a glance.

"I suppose my foremost question is how I could be under your guardianship for eighteen months and you not know a thing about me?"

"I do know a thing or two about you, Elena. More than you might believe. But I suppose at times I rely too heavily upon Mr. Leeson to manage the more obscure details of my life."

"I don't know if I ought to be offended," she teased, determined to keep things light between them. After all, it wouldn't do to take him too seriously. She had no real experience in matters of romance—at least not that she could remember. She suspected he was the sort of man a woman could fall in love with, hopelessly so, only for him to destroy her heart. "I'm quite certain I've never been called 'obscure.' "

"You're not obscure, not anymore. I made a mistake. Forgive me."

"I might." She couldn't think, not with him looking at her lips. She could barely string two words together. She sidled a few steps away. "Tomorrow, perhaps."

"Leeson assumed you would be married by now."

"Married?"

"Why do you laugh?" Now he did smile, just a little.

"You and I *do* have much to talk about."

There was something agonizing and exhilarating about his nearness. In her mind, she imagined what it might be like for him to bend down and kiss her. She'd never entertained such thoughts, not even about the charming Dr. Harcourt. Just the idea sent her pulse leaping. He was her *guardian*. She twisted away from him.

"What are you doing?"

"Trying to open this window, just a crack." She struggled with the latches and prayed the frame had not been sealed shut. "It's so warm in here. I'm sure it's the heat from the kitchen ovens on the other side of that—"

His arms came around her, rich dark wool over muscular heat. He didn't touch her anywhere but her hands. There was only an excruciating nearness, the brush of material against her arms, her bare shoulders and back. Long, elegant fingers moved beneath hers where they curled upon the metal handles. Gripping them, he easily lifted the window a few inches.

"Better?" His breath touched her cheek and her neck.

Oh, yes, even better than the kiss she'd imagined. *Everything* tingled—her body, her skin. Since awakening after the accident, without memories, she'd felt the absolute necessity of control. Controlled emotion, controlled thoughts, so she wouldn't succumb to the panicked realization she was completely and utterly alone in the world. Now everything within her screamed abandon.

"Thank you."

"Elena . . ." His jaw brushed against hers. His clean, spicy and very male scent enveloped her.

"Yes?" she murmured, dazed.

A rap sounded and simultaneously the door flew open, washing the narrow space in golden light. Elena broke free of Lord Black's embrace and moved to stand several steps away. Lady Kerrigan and Mrs. Hazelgreaves pushed inside, an army of two in pink and green. Both smiled tightly.

Lady Kerrigan held two glasses. "Would either of you care for some refreshment?"

Archer leaned back against the window frame, in a pose of nonchalant grace. "No, but thank you."

Mrs. Hazelgreaves waggled her cane at him. "She's not really asking if you want lemonade. What she's saying is that you're being *conspicuous*. Everyone's talking. Or at least whispering. And whispering is worse than talking."

Lady Kerrigan pressed a glass into Elena's hand, and then into Lord Black's. "After traveling in such exotic locales, it must be difficult to return to the more stringent rules of polite society."

Elena's first instinct was to leap to Lord Black's defense, but he appeared not the least bit abashed. In truth, neither was she. She sipped her lemonade.

Archer responded quietly. "Miss Whitney felt fatigued. I merely brought her here to recover away from the excitement and the lights. I'm her guardian—should I not be concerned for her welfare?"

Lady Kerrigan gave a nervous laugh. "There are different definitions of 'welfare.' Please take this as a compliment, your lordship, but this society matron has never seen a guardian quite like you. I must warn you, the proximity of your ages alone will inspire talk."

Mrs. Hazelgreaves thumped her cane against the carpet. "And talk, like whispering, is something I simply will not abide. It's why your solicitors retained me as companion to the girl, is it not, Lord Black? To ensure her character is above reproach."

"Yes, indeed." He glanced at Elena. Amusement lit his eyes.

She bit her bottom lip, so as not to smile.

"On that note," announced Mrs. Hazelgreaves, "I am weary and wish to return to Black House."

Elena protested softly, "We've only just arrived."

Lady Kerrigan implored, "You'll miss Eddy."

Mrs. Hazelgreaves sniffed. "The *Court Circular* has him at Balmoral."

"Only this afternoon he indicated in a telegraph that he might travel down by train, just for the night."

A grimace twisted the older woman's lips. "Eddy's a dullard."

"Nonetheless," whispered Lady Kerrigan, with a glance over her shoulder to be certain no one would overhear, "that dullard might very well be our future king."

Mrs. Hazelgreaves's lips flattened into a thin, white line. "It's nearly midnight."

"Of course." Elena nodded. "If you are weary, we should go."

Lord Black straightened to full height. "I shall arrange for your carriage to be brought around."

Elena murmured, "Thank you, Lord Black."

Mrs. Hazelgreaves narrowed her eyes upon him. "Miss Whitney *will* be accompanying me."

His dark brows lifted. "I did not doubt that."

Archer strode across the crowded gallery, his gaze fixed on the exit. The voices and thoughts of those in the room around him reverberated uncomfortably in his head. Damn it, if half the population of West London wasn't hatching plans to call upon him at Black House tomorrow afternoon to welcome him home.

When he was almost to the doors, something changed—he passed through a tangled cluster of thoughts that made him pause. Immortal thoughts were, by the natural order of things, protected. He would not be able to read Leeson or Selene's thoughts—or the thoughts belonging to the immortal apparently mingling here amongst the Kerrigans' guests. However, a number of women presently entertained fantasies about someone he easily recognized. He searched and quickly found a fair-haired gentleman standing head and shoulders taller than the cluster of beautiful women gathered around him.

"The elusive Lord Black," the blond Amaranthine lauded, lifting his crystal glass in salute. A close-cut beard framed the mischievous slant of his smile.

A host of female gazes alighted upon Archer. They were mature women—the choicest widows in attendance, and likely a few adventurous married ladies as well. A surge of interest rippled through them at Archer's approach. Marcus Helios, Lord Alexander, sensed it too. His smile grew instantly frigid.

"Alexander," Archer acknowledged with a shallow tilt of his head.

"What a shock to see England's most reclusive peer out and about amongst us lowly mortals."

A private immortal jest, one in which Archer found no humor whatsoever. Unlike him, Mark had always enjoyed dabbling in the social affairs and the beds of humans.

"No less a shock to see you here. Certainly you have much to prepare before your departure?"

A unified protest went up from the ladies, and they vehemently shook their coiffured heads.

Mark scowled. "I'm afraid you've been misinformed. I've no plans for travel." He settled his glance upon one young woman, and then another, the smile instantly returning to his lips. "Perhaps only for a house party in Yorkshire or a hunt in Kent."

The females tittered delightedly.

"You and I will talk."

Mark raised the glass to unsmiling lips. "I have no doubt of that."

"Good evening." Archer bowed to the ladies, and pivoted on his heel to resume his travel toward the doors.

"Black," Mark called after him.

Archer paused, feeling the young immortal's regard strike him like a wall of ice. "Yes, Alexander?"

"Your ward is ever so lovely."

Mrs. Hazelgreaves scowled out the carriage window, fixing Elena and Lord Black in her suspicious gaze. The air held the scent of rain. Beside them, the door of the vehicle creaked open in the wind, and the stairs hung down. The footman stood at a respectful distance. Additional conveyances arrived to collect members of the raucous and well-dressed crowd gathering atop the steps, while others were just arriving.

"Will you be returning to Black House as well, my lord?" Elena asked, not ready for the evening or her time with her mysterious guardian to end.

"Not yet."

She could not help but wonder where he would go. Did Lord Black belong to a club like the other gentlemen of his class? Did he gamble, smoke or drink?

"I still have so many questions for you." She grasped the opening of her cloak against the night chill. His gaze settled there, against her hands, then swept upward to her lips.

"I'll answer all your questions in the morning." He lifted his hand, then touched her cheek with his fingertips. Excitement danced low in her stomach.

A hard tap sounded on the pane beside them.

"I suppose I should go," she whispered. Regret weighed her voice.

He withdrew his hand slowly, smiling. "Good night, then, Miss Whitney."

His hand moved to her elbow, and he helped her inside.

A half hour later, Archer's carriage trundled off the Strand onto Whitehall. Though the time was just after midnight, London's streets thronged with traffic and the more restless creatures of the night. When the columned façade of the Admiralty came into view, Archer closed his eyes and altered to shadow. His vehicle clattered off into the distance.

He hovered in the dark street, surrounded by rain-slicked cobblestones. Cloaked by darkness, he swept beneath the archway of Number 4 Whitehall, and slipped between the door and its frame.

He followed the discordant notes, the teasing

blackness and the stench of his prey, like a black sonata on the wind. Along the way he passed a sergeant and three uniformed police constables.

Finally he came to a small, windowless room off the assistant commissioner's office. Inquest reports, photographs and empty cups covered the tabletops, but of most interest to Archer was the box of letters.

He lifted the first, with its accompanying envelope, and scrutinized each stroke for angularity and width, tension and control. He smelled the paper and the ink, and tasted its peculiar bitterness upon the air. Soon, there were two stacks before him, authentic and false. With jaded eyes, he sifted through the images, those of Polly Nichols and Dark Annie, two women who could not have deserved the gleeful savagery the Whitechapel Killer had inflicted upon them.

Archer had seen enough. In his vaporous retreat he brushed against Inspector Abberline on his way in. Twisting low, he skimmed along the tiled floor and exited to the street.

There, he inhaled and drank deeply of the darkness. He summoned the turning, the terrifying predator within him that he would never allow Miss Whitney, in all her renewed innocence, to see again.

Chapter Four

"Miss Whitney, I trust you enjoyed your evening out?" Mary Alice emerged from the distant end of the hallway, her smiling face a startling contrast to her black maid's garb, which blended seamlessly into the shadows. She carried a brass coal bucket.

"I did, thank you, Mary Alice," Elena replied.

She'd enjoyed a perfectly *scandalous* evening if one were to interpret Mrs. Hazelgreaves's demeanor on the carriage ride home. Despite Elena's attempts at conversation, there had been only silence and scowling. As the footmen carried the old woman up the stairs, she had slumped dramatically in her chair and demanded a tonic be rushed to her room.

Perhaps now that Lord Black had returned, there would be discussions as to her future. She rather hoped the formality of a companion could be dispensed with, as she had no desire to advance herself in society, or attract the interest of a wealthy or titled suitor. She had danced around the issue with Mrs. Hazelgreaves for months, citing her lack of memories as her reason for avoiding the afternoon calls and myriad of social events to which they had been invited, but truly, once her medical education began, she wanted to devote herself completely to her studies. She and Lord Black had gotten on . . . so well. Her cheeks flushed. He seemed the sort of man in whom she could confide her aspirations, and she looked forward to easing that burden from her mind.

Mary Alice turned as if to accompany Elena to her room. "I've just added coal to your grate, so your room will be toasty and warm. Let's take down your hair and I'll help you undress."

"Thank you, Mary Alice, but it's late. I can manage myself. Please go on to bed." Truth be told, Elena couldn't wait to be alone to savor the thrilling events of the evening. Even now, the intense attraction she'd felt with his lordship seemed a seductive dream.

The brown-eyed maid hesitated, gripping the handle of the coal bucket with both hands.

"What is it, Mary Alice?"

"There was something else I wished to tell you, but I can't seem to remember what."

"I'm sure if it's anything important, you'll remember and tell me tomorrow."

After another moment's rumination, the servant shrugged good-naturedly. "You're right, of course. Good night, Miss Whitney. You have only to ring if you require my services."

"Sleep well."

Elena continued on alone into the darkness. The wall sconces had been dimmed and provided only the faintest light. Before tonight, the corridor had always felt ominous, like a tunnel of some forgotten catacomb—much like the rest of the vast structure. With Lord Black's arrival, each richly carpeted stair, each hallway, seemed infused with his powerful presence. She couldn't wait until morning, when they would meet again, and all her questions would be answered. At the same time, she wasn't ready to close her eyes on what had been an unexpectedly wonderful night. She had remembered how to *dance*. Perhaps other memories would soon follow.

"*L'Eté.*" She spun around, remembering his voice and his touch. Her skirts whirled out, darkly vivid, to whisper against the wood paneling. She turned the brass knob and entered her room.

Yet disturbingly, she wasn't alone. Indeed, the person she least wished to encounter bent shoulder-deep inside the open doors of her wardrobe. A garnet-hued bustle wiggled about, giving away the intruder's identity.

Elena crossed toward her bed, and laid her shawl against the coverlet.

"Good evening," she said.

A hollow *thunk* sounded from inside, pate against wood.

Lord Black's traveling companion backed out, touching long, elegant fingers against the back of her head. Her luxuriant hair fell free about her shoulders and shone like mink in the lamplight.

"Hmph," she sniffed, visibly irritated to have been interrupted. She didn't appear the slightest bit ashamed to have been discovered foraging in another woman's belongings.

"I'm sorry. I don't know exactly what I should call you. We were not properly introduced this evening."

"I am Selene, the Countess Pavlenco," the woman announced. Pride sparked in her dark eyes.

Why would the countess travel with Lord Black if they were not married? Were they lovers, or did they share some other relationship?

With that curiosity burning in her mind, Elena continued their introduction with a question. "Forgive my boldness, but is there a . . . er . . ."

"A Count Pavlenco?" Her ladyship assumed a doleful, entirely unbelievable expression. "I grieve his loss to this day."

"My sympathies."

"You are too kind." She leaned casually into the V of the open wardrobe and rested her arm along the top edge of the door. Rich, faceted gems shimmered on her fingers. "Obviously, I have carried on."

"Is there something I can help you with?" Elena seated herself on the velvet coverlet at the end of the bed.

"I find myself in need of a night rail."

Elena kept the look of surprise from her face. A night rail? So personal a garment? What woman did not travel with several?

"I see," she responded carefully. "Your trunks have not arrived?"

"Of course they have."

"And you do not have a night rail amongst your things?" It wasn't good manners to be so blunt in one's questioning, but neither was it polite to dig around in another person's private belongings. At least they were on an equal footing of sorts.

Full lips curved into the most cutting of smiles. "Not one, I'm afraid." Her teeth gleamed brightly. "I forgot how prudish Archer's English servants could be."

The countess certainly dropped enough hints that she and Lord Black were involved in some sort of romantic affair. Common sense warned Elena, like a wet slap in the face, to forget her attraction to his lordship, and keep herself as far away from him and his peculiar associates as possible. In all likelihood he would not remain in London long, and any dalliance, emotional or otherwise, would end only in pain.

Elena said, "To your left, in the middle drawer. I

prefer the one on top, but you may borrow either of the others."

Selene disappeared into the shadow of the wardrobe, and Elena heard the rattle of the tiny silver handles. After a moment, the countess twisted round with the garment plastered against her front. Her eyes narrowed with displeasure above the prim, high collar. The hem hung at an awkward length between her knees and ankles. The sleeves fell short as well, giving her a distinctly Amazonian appearance.

She smiled tightly. "I hadn't realized you were such a *child*."

Elena wasn't really all that petite, but statuesque did not begin to describe the countess.

"I can only offer more of the same. There is a matching robe behind you. Certainly tomorrow you can visit the shops and find something more suited to your tastes. Lady Pavlenco, are you cold?"

The countess tossed her head. "I'm famously hot-blooded. Why do you ask?"

"Your lips." Elena leaned forward, squinting. "They're . . . blue."

Not really blue, but smudgy and dark.

"Oh, hmmm." Selene licked them and swiped a thumb across. The smudginess disappeared, almost as if it were ink. Blinking rapidly she announced, "Likely his lordship has returned by now. I ought to go to him before I am missed."

Elena answered without thought, "He won't be back until later."

The countess stiffened from head to toe. "And how would you know that?"

"We found ourselves at the same social event this evening, and he indicated he would not be returning directly."

Selene paled. She took a few steps toward the bed,

the wadded night rail clasped against her breast. Her shoulders convulsed, and she pressed a hand against her mouth.

"Des phénomènes relatifs . . ."

The words burst from her lips almost as if they had been belched. Such a familiar phrase, still Elena couldn't place it.

"My lady, are you all right?" she asked, now feeling a twinge of regret for the woman, for obviously her emotions and passions hinged very much upon his lordship. A warning alarm sounded off inside Elena's head. Was Lord Black such a dangerous man to admire?

Selene dropped to the coverlet beside Elena. All confidence and fire appeared to have abandoned her. Another spate of words burst from her lips.

"A la polarisation rotatoire des liquides . . ." She struck a balled fist against the center of her breasts.

Elena stood. "I'll call for some tea. Sometimes that settles the—"

"I'm fine," Selene growled, grasping Elena's forearm and pulling her back down beside her.

A rap sounded on the door.

"Yes?" Elena called.

Mary Alice stepped inside, the coal bucket still hanging from the crook of her arm. "I thought I heard voices."

She bobbed shallowly before extending an envelope.

"Your ladyship, a message has arrived for you."

Selene leapt up and snatched the missive. With her thumb she broke its red wax seal. Feline eyes scanned the card within.

"Huzzah!" she exclaimed. Her gaze skimmed over Elena dismissively. "It appears I won't require your little doll dress after all."

With a grin, she tossed the night rail to the bed. Brushing past Mary Alice, she dropped the note into the bucket and disappeared into the corridor.

Elena and Mary Alice considered each other, until at last Elena spoke. "Earlier, when you said you'd forgotten something, was it that you'd seen the countess in my room?"

"Surely not . . . ," the maid murmured faintly. "I would have remembered her, wouldn't I? She's rather the memorable sort."

"Indeed she is."

Mary Alice hovered for another moment before saying, "Well, then. Good night, miss."

"Good night."

Mary Alice pulled the door closed behind her.

Elena bolted from the bed and yanked open the door.

"Mary Alice!"

But Mary Alice hadn't gone far. The young woman stood on the other side of the threshold, squinting at the smoldering card that she held pinched between her thumb and index finger. Shamefacedly, she offered it to Elena.

"I won't tell if you won't, miss."

Gray smoke arose in tendrils between them, scenting the air with ash.

"Agreed."

Elena claimed the card, careful not to touch the blackened edge, and again retreated to solitude. Drawing near the lamp on her escritoire, she bent to read the message:

Come to me.

Her chest tightened. A lover's summons? She frowned, hating the curiosity that compelled her to open her desk. Within moments, she'd laid the card and the Cairo letter side by side. Was the handwriting the same? She couldn't be certain, due to the brevity and slapdash penmanship of the note. Certainly, both were written by a masculine hand.

Stung by the whole exchange with the countess, and the likelihood of her relationship with his lordship, Elena hurriedly pulled the pins from her hair and changed into her night rail. She folded the one Selene had discarded and returned the garment to the bottom of the drawer.

Far too distracted to sleep, she selected a medical text from the top of her reading stack and settled onto the window seat. She tugged a blanket over her legs for warmth, all the while trying to blot out the lingering memory of Lord Black's arms around her, and the intensity of his gaze upon her mouth. A movement along the edge of the courtyard caught her glance. She wiped the gathered condensation away to see more clearly. A carriage, nearly obscured by fog and shadows, raced around from the mews and toward the front of the house—certainly to take Selene to meet the writer of the mysterious summons.

Burrowing her shoulders into the pillows, Elena cleaved open the book to the section she'd last left off reading.

She found only a jagged gap.

The entire section of Pasteur's germ theory, in its original French translation, had been torn from the binding.

St. Botolph's immense steeple speared upward into London's night sky. Archer leaned against the cool concrete, staring down into the labyrinthine maze of the East End. The ledge beneath him, and the air all around, vibrated with the sonorous crescendo of the church's pipe organ, a wakeful clergyman's entreaty to the cadre of prostitutes who even now circled the church's sidewalks, calling to strangers with offers of illicit pleasure.

The stalls of Aldgate had closed hours before, but the smell of fish, cabbage and blood still lingered. Gas lamps dotted the thoroughfares, too dim and widely spaced to provide more than faint illumination. Once, this place had been nothing but endless fields, and later, a battlement. Since then the streets had seen the parade of kings and popes, not to mention pestilence, executions and fire. And always, there had been the ever-burgeoning population and crime borne of abject poverty.

He trained his silver-black gaze upon a rat scuttling along the gutter below, and a shadowy excitement rippled through him.

How can they catch me now? one of the Ripper's letters had taunted.

Perhaps they couldn't. But Archer would.

How had he forgotten, if even for the space of an hour, what he was? Although he preferred the solitude and comfort wealth could provide, he belonged here, amongst the lowest of the low. He was no mannered suitor. No guardian, lover or friend.

He was a hunter. A killer.

He owned the night.

Odd that at a time like now, when he felt most removed from humanity, *she* should linger in his thoughts. He closed his eyes and savored the sensation of the wind lifting his hair from his shoulders, away from his heated skin. Elena was a golden glimmer of sunlight to a creature who had spent his immortal life in darkness—and an alluring temptation for one who had grown dissatisfied of late, restless and searching for something above and beyond the boundaries of his existence.

And so with marked irony he stared with high expectations into the decay of the vast wasteland. For the first time in a very long while he felt the hunger to stalk and to Reclaim, because Jack the Ripper—as the killer had so aptly named himself in his most recent letter to the authorities—was different. Archer had sensed the same on the docks the moment he had arrived in London, and confirmed his suspicion in the evidence room at Scotland Yard. Might he actually be in for a challenge?

Could Jack be moving toward Transcension?

It had been so very long. He smiled faintly and, in shadow, stepped off the ledge. Clinging to the bricks, he descended to the street and proceeded upon a northerly path along Houndsditch.

Like a phantom fisherman, he cast out his enormous mental net, capturing only the most wicked of thoughts. Words, emotions and other nebulous remnants clung like spiderwebs to his psyche. Despair. Envy. Greed. He shrugged them off, for they did not belong to the one he sought. His prey would distinguish itself by a void of conscience, and a disposition to evil that defied the darkest of insanities.

"Looking for some company tonight?" a woman called from a narrow alleyway.

She appeared nothing more than a narrow shadow in a dingy apron. Raindrops fell around her, plunking into the puddles that had accumulated on the pitted street.

"I'm the girl for you, yes I am."

The solicitation wasn't intended for Archer, but rather for the three young men who clipped along the sidewalk in front of him, backs straight as soldiers, doing their best to look as if they belonged on these rough streets—just boys really, from respectable homes, here in the district on a dare to one another. They walked a bit faster now.

As he drew closer, his nostrils flared. An inordinate amount of malice tainted the air. He assumed shape and crossed the cobblestones toward her, pulling a pair of dark-lensed spectacles out from his pocket. He quickly lowered them onto his nose to cover the residual gleam of his eyes.

Seeing him, the woman stiffened, obviously perplexed by the manner in which he'd appeared so suddenly out of the darkness. She apparently soothed her confusion away, for a smile returned to her lips. Somewhere in the distance a badly out-of-tune dulcimer struck up a melody. They were just off Commercial Street, a populated venue even at this hour.

"What about you, gov'na'?" She chuckled thickly, a drunken attempt at seductiveness. "What's a handsome gent like you doing alone tonight?"

"Good evening, madam." He tipped his top hat, drawing to a stop before her.

"I'm Kate, luv, and *youuu* must be the most *handsome* bloke I've seen all night." She swayed toward him and pressed a flirtatious hand against his shoulder, smelling as if she'd bathed in gin. The movement revealed something on the brick wall behind her, something pale, like chalk. Given the shadows, the mark would have gone unseen by any mortal eye; however his radiant conscience revealed it in stark relief: N.

A bit of graffiti or a scratch left behind by a barrow in the crush of the daily throng? Archer reached over her shoulder. She flinched.

"My apologies," he said.

He brought his whitened fingertips to his nose and inhaled the faint, yet distinctive stench—the same one he'd experienced in the evidence room while examining the letters. Sulfur mixed with putrid decay. His blood vacillated distinctively, an indication the soul he hunted might be near.

"That's all right, *gohhv-na*. We're all a bit edgy these nights." She smiled broadly; yet her hand, pressed in a defensive gesture against her throat, gave her nervousness away. "Can't forget there's a madman about."

"So I've been told."

"Do you think they'll catch him before he kills again?" Her gaze wandered toward the darker shadows across the street.

"I have no doubt. Perchance do you know who left this mark on the wall, behind you?"

She glanced over her shoulder. "Hmf! I thought he scribbled something."

"Who?"

"Another gentleman, dressed smart like you. Pulled something from his pocket, he did, and scratched at the wall, but *yooou've* far better eyes than me, even with those dark glasses, if you can make out what he wrote."

"It appears to be an N."

She shrugged. "Makes sense, I suppose."

"How so?"

"N for Mr. Nemo." She waved a limp hand. "That's what he told me his name was. As you can guess, I meet *scooores* of Mr. No Ones out here on the street."

"Had you ever seen this gentleman before?"

"If I have, I don't remember. Odd fellow, but good-looking enough. Told me to wait here for him, that he had to go tend to some *business*, and he'd be back." She snorted sardonically, swaying again toward Archer. "Empty promises, I've heard them all before. His loss, eh, *luhhv*? What do you say you and I spend some time together? Anywhere you like. This alley behind me is nice and private, and cleaner than most."

Archer steadied her by the arms. Enabled by the contact, he scoured her recent memories. There were shadows . . . a drunken view of the inside of a jail cell . . . several alleyways and passersby . . . and finally, the faintest image of cold eyes.

Should he stay here with Kate, in shadow, and lie in wait on the slim chance Mr. Nemo might reappear?

Not a chance. If he lingered here, he might lose the trace altogether. His target was close—close enough to catch. Besides, as Kate surmised, Mr. Nemo's promise to return was likely an empty one, the sort a harried passerby would offer to an aggressive shopkeeper hawking cheap wares from an open doorway.

He propped her against the wall. "I must be getting on."

"Ah, hell, that's the story of my life." She scowled. "Come back if you get lonely. I'll be here awhile longer."

Wisping into shadow, Archer left her. He'd traveled only a block when he saw the T scrawled across an advertisement placard. He coursed over the cobblestones, mentally scouring every crevice and shadow.

He saw the S traced against a warehouse wall mural.

A T against the side of a wooden water trough.

And an O on the chest of a drunk, slumped in a doorway, so fresh the miniscule bits of powdered chalk still slid free of their original mark.

NTSTO.

Obviously the letters had been left as a message to

someone—the police, Archer suspected, if they were observant enough to find them. Such daring confirmed the arrogance of the Ripper, an arrogance that would lead Archer on a direct path to his target.

He continued on. The air grew heavy, and he tasted the tang of metal on his tongue. Hunger slid through his veins, quickly consuming him—as well as the faint disappointment of knowing the hunt would conclude all too quickly, when he had expected something more.

A blur spiraled out of the darkness, slamming him sideways into a wall of brick. His concentration shattered, Archer took shape and whirled round to confront his attacker.

A thin-boned female swaggered along the far sidewalk. Under her arm she carried a large placard reading REPENT OR BE DAMNED. By her look, she was one of the Salvation Army lasses who spent their days and nights on East End street corners, boldly preaching their message of salvation to the lost.

Archer leapt the distance, landing square in front of her.

"Lor'!" she gasped, sinking against the wall. "Be this a demon before me?"

"You tell me." Archer seized the placard and sent it spinning into the darkness. She darted off in an attempt to flee, but he grasped her by the shoulders of her woolen coat and lifted her off the ground. With a hiss, he slammed her against the wall.

"Please no!" she sobbed, her face crumpling with fear. "I've done nothing to deserve such violence!"

Archer slammed her against the wall again. And again. With each blow the façade of femininity cracked and disintegrated, until her thin shape filled out, grew heavier—and a familiar face glared back at him above broad shoulders.

Archer growled, "Your disguises need more work, *boy*."

He released the younger Shadow Guard.

Mark's boots stamped heavily against the pavers. He cursed, blue-eyed and furious, and pushed away from the wall. He'd discarded his evening coat and necktie, and wore only a white linen shirt, braces and trousers.

"This is my hunt, *old man*. Go back to whence you came."

"You've been called off."

"Likely at your behest."

"Sorry to disappoint. I don't betray my peers."

"Neither do I, teacher, regardless of what you've chosen to believe."

Archer saw something over Mark's shoulder—a jagged P scratched into the dark dado of the far warehouse wall.

NTSTOP.

A reminder he had no time for this.

"I didn't come to trade pleasantries. I came to complete a failed Reclamation."

"I haven't failed," Mark growled. "Though I know you wish it."

"The Ripper's continued defiance is an affront against us all. Not only you, Mark, but every Shadow Guard. And now your refusal to answer the summons of the Primordials has cast you into disfavor."

"They want me to leave in the midst of a hunt. I won't do it." Mark leaned in, eye to eye and nose to nose with the immortal who had once been his mentor and greatest champion. "I just need a bit more time."

Hidden deep in his gruff assertion, Archer heard an earnest plea. He wavered in his anger. Once, he and Mark had been something like friends.

"You say you need more time?" He shook his head. "Time for him to dishonor the Shadow Guard even further? Time for him to kill again?"

The muscles in Mark's neck corded visibly, in response to his clenched jaw. "It's been weeks since his last victim. He's gone into hiding."

"You're a Shadow Guard, Mark. You hunt him down, drag him kicking and screaming out of whatever hole he's hiding in and you send him to hell. Quickly and efficiently. That's your job."

"This one's different, Black. Different than anything I've ever experienced."

Archer remembered how he, too, had at first believed the same thing.

"Yet he is here. Now. Close by."

Mark's eyes narrowed. "Impossible. If you sensed him, so would I."

The shrill keen of a whistle broke the silence of the night.

"Murder!" interrupted a distant shout. *"Murder!"*

Chapter Five

Archer's head whipped around. A wave of fear slammed into him, the magnitude of which could only be generated by a crowd. Forgetting Mark, he evanesced to shadow and raced toward the source. Countless mortals, men and women, clambered toward a narrow alley wedged between two tall buildings. High wooden gates rattled against the walls as the throng pushed through. Shouts of "Police!" and "Murder!" filled the night in the myriad languages of the district. Archer did not miss the flamboyantly scrawled M on the outer wall. He, too, delved inside.

In the small courtyard, candles and lanterns bobbed about. Their meager light did not reveal Archer in his shadow form, or the tall Amaranthine who followed. A pony, harnessed to a costermonger's wooden barrow, shied nervously as Archer passed. He sidled through the crowd, forcing his way into the epicenter of fear. Then he saw her. A woman lay on her left side, her face turned away from the crowd.

"Stay back," Archer growled to Mark, casting a warning glance over his shoulder, only to see Selene slip through the crowd to stand beside her twin.

Archer crouched beside the victim. She lay in a puddle of rainwater, a corsage of red rose and maidenhair fern pinned primly to the breast of her jacket. A number of sweet cachous lay spilled about her, their narrow envelope still clutched in her hand. Heat exuded faintly from her body, but her mortal life had ended, and savagely so.

He had known there would be one more letter, and he spied the mark through the bloodied rainwater: A tiny E, scratched against the cobblestone at the peak of her bonnet, as coy as a wink.

NTSTOPME.

Archer's hands tightened into fists. The message was clear. You can't or won't stop me. A taunt to the police, as he'd earlier believed, or might there be another possibility? Unease rippled through his veins. Could the Ripper be taunting the Shadow Guards who hunted him?

"Move aside. Move aside," a voice commanded, imperious but underscored by dread. The concentrated beam of the constable's bull's-eye lantern pierced Archer through.

He stood, every muscle attuned to the hunt. Was the Ripper here, even now, watching? His trace was everywhere—*everywhere*—so thick it crowded Archer's nostrils and throat. He examined the crowd, soul by soul, opening his mind to any evidence of abnormal deterioration. He sensed only fear.

Sometimes he hated himself for how jaded he had become. Murder was common amongst the mortal population. Because of his recurrent exposure to such crimes, he felt more regret about failing the Guard than failing the dead woman at his feet.

He had been so damn close. A hackney scuttled through the gate and officers spilled out, immediately working to disperse the crowd. Archer broke free and strode toward the street.

Mark's voice challenged from behind. "I won't be held accountable for this death. If not for your interference—"

Archer halted and pivoted, grinding the heel of his boot into the ground. Rain began to patter down around them in heavy, snapping drops.

"My interference?" he seethed. "How many times must it be said before you accept the truth? You've botched this Reclamation and will remove yourself from it."

"He approaches a state of Transcension. You can't deny that."

"Because of you. You let things go too far while you attended your balls and your routs. While you gambled and whored."

Mark hissed, his eyes wavering from blue to black. "As if you didn't suffer your own bit of distraction tonight."

Archer struggled to tamp down the dangerous fury searing his veins. He'd taken such care to be certain his immortal peers did not learn of Elena's existence. But something that infuriated him more was that he agreed with Mark' accusation. He should never have gone to that ball tonight. He had made a mistake in deepening his involvement with Elena.

That did not change the issue at hand.

"I told you that you weren't ready for a Reclamation of this complexity. Not yet."

"I am more than ready," Mark countered fiercely. "And I'll prove my abilities to everyone, given the chance."

More onlookers, attracted by continuing clamor and the shrill alarm of police whistles, rushed past, oblivious to the towering immortals who sparred in the center of the street.

Selene circled them, a shadowy admirer. Moving close, she clenched a possessive hand on one shoulder of each Reclaimer.

She laughed, low in her throat. "So nice to have us all together again."

Archer shrugged her hand off. "Don't pretend we were some sort of team."

Shadow Guards were notoriously mercenary, renowned for their ruthlessness and solitary natures. They rarely cooperated on anything. Indeed, they usually went out of their way to avoid crossing paths with one another. Yet, when the world's deteriorated mortal fringe grew out of hand, the Primordials recruited additional immortals into the ranks of the Shadow Guard. Archer had found himself tasked with an unwanted mentorship—at least at first. He'd come to believe Mark and Selene held unparalleled promise. He had trusted them, as he had trusted no one before.

Until Paris.

Mark growled, "It was only an experiment—a forced experiment at that."

"One that failed."

"Miserably."

Archer tipped his head to his adversary, smiling coldly. "At least we agree on one thing."

Selene shook her head, her hair shining like agate. "We were good together. Better than good."

Archer leveled a cold gaze upon her. "I gave you explicit instructions to remain at Black House."

Mark shouldered in. "She doesn't take orders from you. Not anymore."

"I can defend myself, brother," Selene snapped.

"Ah . . . it's all coming back to me now," mused

Archer, a twisted smile on his lips. "How we were *so very good together*. Alas, I have had enough reminiscing for one night. Selene, you will concentrate your efforts on your own assignment. Proximity does not make us partners. Keep to the Thames. Mark, consider yourself relieved of duty. If the order displeases you, petition the Primordials, for the decision to remove you came from the Inner Realm. In other words: Stay out of my way. There's no reason I should come across either of you in the East End again."

He turned on his heel and moved to rejoin the shadows.

"Don't walk away." Mark pursued him. "We're not finished here."

Lacking patience, Archer waved the palm of his hand and slammed a focused wall of air and ultimately Mark to the ground.

"Archer, *no*!" Selene fell to her knees beside the powerful Shadow Guard, who lay nearly paralyzed, gasping for breath.

As Archer turned the corner he heard Mark gasp, "Damn. I wish I knew how he did that."

Archer rapidly distanced himself from the twin immortals. His mind played a recurring image—that of a drunken prostitute wearing a skirt patterned in Michaelmas daisies.

NTSTOPME

Told me to wait here for him—he had to go tend to some business, and he'd be back.

NTSTOPME

His shoes struck the cobblestones with a rapid pace, the reverse path of his earlier steps. Eventually he arrived at the spot where Kate had stood, but he found the alleyway deserted. Perhaps at the return of the rain, she had sought shelter for the night.

A constable appeared out of the darkness, his bull's-eye lamp in hand. He walked briskly, scouring the shadows of what was likely his customary beat.

Archer followed a few paces behind in silence, his instincts leading him in the same direction. High walls lined the walkway on both sides of Church Passage.

A pale line dissected the right wall, midway up, as if someone had dragged a piece of chalk beside them while they walked.

A familiar stench rose up around him, already fading. . . .

Damn it. *Damn it.*

At the end of the passage lay a small, darkened square framed by condemned, empty houses and a warehouse marked in large white letters as belonging to KEARLEY & TONGE. Here there was no crowd, but only night shadows and the smell of fresh blood.

A moment later the beam of the constable's lantern swept over Kate's body, revealing to the officer what Archer had already seen. His frantic footsteps echoed throughout the square, and the warehouse door swung inward.

"For God's sake, man," the constable shouted to a startled night watchman, dozing just inside. "Come out and assist me. Another woman has been ripped open."

The black town coach clattered through the darkened streets of Mayfair. Night still claimed the earth, but morning would arrive soon. Already the refuse wagons trundled from one great house to the next, removing the insufferable reality of filth before their privileged occupants awakened from their comfortable beds.

Archer sat rigid against the velvet cushions. Word
had spread quickly through the slums. Two more
mutilated victims. A maniac still at large. Even
though he was able to find evidence of the Ripper's
trace crisscrossing through the streets and alleyways
of the district, the intensity of fear and panic seizing
the area clouded the air, making it impossible to latch
on to any specific thread. He had roamed the East
End until exhaustion twisted his thoughts and weakened his powers. Although no longer fully transformed, he was trapped at a torturous point in
between, a sickness of sorts brought on by having
come so close to his target, only to fail at its Reclamation.

What he needed now was solitude, and time to
return to his natural state.

The carriage raced through Black House's open
gates. Two huge iron lamps, crafted centuries before
by Tibetan artisans into twisting, garnet-eyed drag-
ons, flickered on each side of the grand doorway
while the remainder of the manse slept in darkness.
The vehicle rolled to a stop.

With shaking hands, he pulled the dark spectacles
from his coat pocket, and thrust them onto his face.
The carriage door swung open, casting a beam of
wavering light from the lanterns across his shoes. A
creak of metal, and the stairs went down.

A long moment passed.

"My lord, do you require assistance?" the young
footman inquired from without, not daring to en-
croach upon his lordship's privacy.

"No," Archer growled.

He tugged the brim of his top hat lower on his
forehead and turned the collar of his greatcoat high.
It took all his discipline to climb down and walk

past the liveried footman and the two sleepy-eyed
doormen without lashing out at them in an absurd,
punishing rage.

Rage at Jack for escaping, but most of all, rage at
his own failure. He had craved a challenge—not a
bloody rout. He forced himself to cross the expanse
of gleaming, night black marble, and took the stairs.

God, curse him, his mind still scoured everything,
irrationally seeking some trace evidence of his prey—
even here, in his sanctum. He paused midway up
the staircase and pressed a fist to the center of his
churning head.

Yet all he could sense was *her*.

Elena. His mind reached for her, twisting and seeking, a thousand ravenous black vines yearning to
claim her and seize her close until she became part
of him. He shoved his hands through his hair. His
top hat fell to the stairs behind him.

A warning sounded in his mind, one that told him
he still hunted, and that his mind no longer had the
ability to distinguish one prey from the other. If only
he could make it to his chambers and lock himself
away until the effects passed . . .

On the third-floor landing, he gripped the banister,
blinded by confusion. Where the hell *were* his chambers? Where the hell was Leeson when he needed
him?

Everything around him, the carpet and the stairs
were familiar, yet entirely *unfamiliar*, as if each detail
had been rearranged by mischievous sprites. From
above, the skylight glared down like a black Cyclo-
pean eye, in damning accusation. He snatched the
glasses from his face. The rims, normally cool and
smooth against his skin, abraded him beyond bearing. The glass crunched as with shaking hands he
thrust them into his pocket.

Visions of the young woman who had gazed at him with such quiet trust only hours before tortured him. His body demanded her and shouted—as it had that night two years ago on the rooftop—that she would make the confusion and pain go away.

When he hunted, he lost himself to sensation and impulse. . . . Time passed in shattering fragments of excitement and light. . . .

No one need tell him where her bed lay. Even from this distance, he could smell her. He could hear her heartbeat and feel the sensuous warmth of her breath against his skin. The scene before him altered.

Her room was filled with shadows.

She lay on the window seat, propped up on tufted pillows, looking like a medieval beauty bespelled into a thousand years of sleep. His ravenous gaze moved over her pale skin and luxuriant, unbound hair. Before, she'd been laced into layers of wool, silk and linen, and even then, while sane and in complete control—he'd barely been able to keep his hands off her. Now she wore only a peasant-style shift.

Whatever curiosities he'd had about the authenticity of the shape and curves of her body were answered by the sheer nature of the delicate garment. The cambric bodice gathered over her high, round breasts, with a pale green ribbon tied beneath. With interest, he noted a dark band around her wrist, a tattoo in the shape of a twining serpent. The mark would have been hidden tonight under the long sleeve of her glove, and only served to inflame him more deeply, for it added a forbidden, sensual dimension to her innocence.

His body tensed. Ached. He wanted her.

Goddamit, he *craved* her like a raving addict craved opium.

His teeth locked on a growl. His gaze shifted to

her face. He prayed for her sake that her eyes would open, and that she would stare at him in such horror he'd go and never come back to harm her. But she slept on, unaware of the beast in her presence.

That night in Spitalfields, he had tried to save her, but once she'd spiraled out of his reach, he had let her fall. He'd forced himself to remain on the ledge, telling himself her death was out of his control—intended to be.

Reclaimers hunted. They did not intervene to spare the fleeting lives of mortals, no matter how unjust the circumstances. He was a killer, not a savior, and was expected by those he protected to be quite single-minded about his role within the Guard. He'd never encountered the slightest temptation to stray from his destined path before.

But after he'd descended from the roof, he had made the mistake of standing on the cobblestones beside her and looking down into her beautiful eyes. Still clenched in the arms of the beast who had murdered her, she had stared up at him and gasped for her dying breath. But it hadn't come. She'd been suspended in the torturous, despairing place between life and death, and the ice around his cold immortal heart had shattered.

Just as he hadn't been able to stop himself from touching her then, he could not stop himself now.

Gently, he lifted her from the seat. Her head lolled against his shoulder, and she sighed. He inhaled her breath, savoring her life essence. Her skin was cool where it had been exposed to the night air, but warm and velvety beneath the blanket draped over her legs. He'd taken only a step when a book thumped down to ride atop the blanket's long tail. He tensed, certain she'd wake and scream at him, at his unnatural eyes and skin. And indeed, her eyes opened.

"But I can't dance," she murmured.

Did she see him? Did she see the glow of his eyes and the naked hunger on his face?

"Yes, you can," he whispered, paralyzed by her heavy-lidded stare. God, he wanted nothing more than to hold her tighter, to press his mouth against hers. She sighed and closed her eyes again. He nearly groaned in relief. A few more steps and he lowered her to the bed.

Weakened by failure and exhaustion, he sank to his knees beside her. Some fragment of his surviving conscience shouted that he crossed a forbidden line, but his craving grew too out of hand. It had been so long since he'd been close to someone. Close enough to feel their heartbeat. Slowly, he lowered his cheek against the gentle slope of her breast. As he had somehow instinctively known, slowly, the pain and confusion subsided.

He lost all conscious thought. Selfishly, mindlessly wanting more, he spread over her, blanketing her with his shadow.

"Archer . . ."

Had she whispered his name? Drunk on her skin, her hair and her scent, he twisted around her, embracing her in his heat, more man now than shadow. Bit by blessed bit, his mind returned to center. She moved restlessly against him, twining her hand into his hair.

"Yes," she whispered, shifting her legs, her thighs, inviting him closer.

"Elena."

She nuzzled his jaw with her lips, searching. He pressed his mouth against hers, daring to explore inside with his tongue. His hand moved to her breast. She sighed again, moaning softly.

Suddenly she froze and, with a cry, shoved her arms and fists through his quickly shadowed form.

"*Archer*!" she gasped, pushing herself up from the bed.

He retreated to the far corner of the room, pulse thundering. Her hair fell wildly about her shoulders, and she seized the sheet to her breast. Her stunning eyes, wide-open and fully aware, stared so intently into the place where he'd gone. Did she see him?

Gingerly she touched her swollen lips.

After a long moment, she groaned softly and speared both hands through her hair. She lowered herself to her elbow, then collapsed into the pillows.

Even now he wanted to go to her. He battled primitive urges, so base and rampant he despised himself for feeling them. She was everything he wanted, everything beautiful and innocent and good—

And everything he could never have.

With a silent roar of fury, he twisted in upon himself and escaped through the narrow crack beneath her door.

Three hours later, Archer brooded out the window of his study, his mood as black as a dirge. Last night he had failed, and devastatingly so, on every level. This, after century upon century of perfection.

In the garden, little birds flitted from tree bough to tree bough. Rotund clouds lumbered across the sky. The crisp report of footsteps sounded in the hall as servants rushed to and fro to complete their morning duties. The earth continued to turn. Lives moved on.

Not his.

Who will catch me now? You didn't, Reclaimer.

A taunt created by his own tortured conscience,

but at this point it really didn't matter. Every fragment of his being, down to his immortal marrow, demanded revenge. He grasped the draperies and pulled them together, sinking the room into darkness.

Unlike the night before, his mind was crystal clear; it had returned to perfect, cold sanity. He refused to allow logic to attribute the near-miraculous recovery to Elena and what had transpired in her room—or afterward as he'd pleasured himself to a stunning release in the shadowed privacy of his chamber, closing his eyes against the reality of his hand and surrendering himself to the fantasy of her.

Elena. Goddamit, he couldn't believe he'd gone to her room. He rubbed his forehead, trying to banish the sensual memories. She had shown him nothing but admiration and trust, and he had betrayed her.

He glanced at the folded parchment on his desk and the triangular black seal he'd broken just an hour before. He could delay no longer in answering the summons.

A fire crackled at the center of the enormous hearth, which was bordered by ancient terra-cotta tiles painted with lotus flowers in red and black. He swung his desk chair around and drew it as close to the punishing heat as possible without igniting the upholstery. Taking his seat, he stared into the orange and red flames, and imagined himself burning there as penance for all he had done and not done throughout his existence. He closed his eyes and cleared all thought from his mind.

Soon the flames took on a purple hue, and a low hum spread through the room. A voice emerged—three distinct tones entwined into one. The heat grew as cold as frost, and the faintest image of a face took shape in the flames.

"Two more atrocities . . ." The voice did not taunt; it merely stated a fact.

Nonetheless, Archer's hands curled around the thick wooden armrests, as if he were a boy called into the schoolmaster's office for a reprimand.

"The soul evaded me. It will not happen again."

The face blurred, fluctuating between the characteristics of the three Primordials who governed the Inner Realm and the Shadow Guards who protected the fragile boundaries of that immortal domain. "Does the marked soul approach Transcension?"

Only fully Transcended souls had the ability to cross from the mortal world into the Inner Realm and wreak destruction and murder against its immortal inhabitants. The Shadow Guard prevented such incursions. Until last night, Archer had found the rare soul working toward Transcension to be a challenge to his skills as a Reclaimer.

"His trace is distinctive, but not always clearly discernable due to the dense population and turmoil of the city. Having only just arrived yesterday, I would like more time to decide the true level of his deterioration."

"Let there be no chance of his crossing over."

Archer's brow went up. "My honor would not allow it."

Archer stared into the flames. He had never received any sort of reprimand, no matter how slight, from the Primordials, and the words stung.

"Ancient . . ." Already the voice grew faint. Soon the portal would close.

"Yes?"

"The girl."

Those two words revealed everything. Despite his efforts to keep his indiscretion private, the Primordials knew about Elena. How? *Mark*?

The Primordials would not allow their most powerful warrior to be diverted from his eternal purpose. They did not act out in malice, but with the emotionless precision necessary as rulers of a threatened world. If they believed Elena to be of any hindrance to him, they might choose to end her existence.

"She is not a distraction."

"Make sure that is so."

Chapter Six

The purple flames climbed high and returned to orange. Heat once again scorched his skin. Archer shoved the chair back a space and rubbed a hand against his forehead.

First things first. He would not be able to concentrate his undivided attention on the crisis at hand until he dealt with Elena. Damn, but he was loath to hurt her.

He should have been a bastard from the start. The sooner this farce of a guardianship came to an end, the better for everyone involved. Crossing the carpet, he yanked open the door. He strode to the hall to set his unhappy mission into motion.

Just then, the grand entry doors opened and Selene swept inside, releasing one of her devastating smiles upon the footman. The young man stared, stupefied by her boldness until he saw his scowling employer. With a quick bow of his head, he quickly accepted the mantle she handed over to him and disappeared into the darkness of the far hall.

"Why have you returned to Black House?"

"Why else?" she answered dryly, her eyes narrowing. "To spy on you. Besides, you know my brother prefers common lodgings. I want a hot bath.

I smell like death. I've just spent the last two hours examining an arm."

"An *arm*?"

"It seems my Thames murderer is in a dismembering mood again."

With that pronouncement, she gripped the banister and, in a dark froth of skirts, ascended the stairs.

Just then Mr. Jarvis pushed out from a door under the staircase. In his hands he carried two small table lamps, which he had presumably refilled with oil.

"Mr. Jarvis."

"Yes, your lordship."

"Please tell Mrs. Hazelgreaves I wish to speak with her in my study as soon as she is available."

"Right away."

Returning to his desk, he snatched up Leeson's leather case, and after a few moments of rummaging, settled at his desk with a fistful of the old man's "novelettes."

"Miss Whitney?"

"Oh—" Porcelain clanked against porcelain, Elena's teacup falling against its saucer. She immediately lifted the cup again to see if she'd chipped either piece. In the process she sloshed black coffee, which she preferred to tea, onto the pristine white tablecloth.

She sat in the enormous breakfast room. Life-size statues of Greek gods and goddesses—Lord only knew which one was which—stood on Corinthian pedestals, artfully dividing the broad expanse of windows. Silver chafers steamed on a large mahogany buffet, and the fragrance of sausages and kippers wafted about. Normally she breakfasted with Mrs. Hazelgreaves, but the older woman hadn't yet come down. Hopefully she wasn't still overcome by the

"scandalous" events of the night before. Mrs. Hazelgreaves was capable of holding a nasty grudge.

"My apologies, I didn't mean to startle you," Mr.
Jarvis said from the arched doorway.

"My fault entirely." She blotted the tablecloth with
a napkin. "I was so intent upon the morning papers."

Newspapers were one of her vices. Each morning
she poured over stacks of them: the *Times;* the *Pall
Mall Gazette; Lloyd's;* and *Reynolds.* Because she'd
slept at the hospital dormitory on Thursday and Fri-
day night, they'd accumulated a bit, unread. She
didn't like to read out of order, so this morning's
Sunday papers had been placed at the bottom of
her stack.

Not that she'd even glanced at them—not with last
night's fragmented dream of Lord Black still so vivid
in her mind. Just the memory sent heat pooling in
her cheeks again.

She hadn't seen his lordship this morning and
hoped she could get her nerves under control
before—

"Lord Black asks to see you in his study."

Her fingertip snagged the edge of the cup. Coffee
spilled across the table, blackening the corners of several papers before she could snatch them up.

"Oh, damn!" she blurted, leaping up.

Mr. Jarvis hurried forward, averting his gaze, but
looking altogether shocked.

"No cursing. Not here," she chided herself beneath
her breath for the unfortunate habit, picked up at the
hospital. "I'm so sorry, sir."

"Don't give it another thought, miss. I'll tend to
things here." He waved over a maid—a maid Elena
did not recognize—who had come from the kitchen,
bearing a fresh pot of tea for the sideboard. It ap-

peared that with the arrival of his lordship, the household staff had multiplied overnight.

"Thank you, Mr. Jarvis." Elena clasped the papers to her chest and hurried out of the room. Once beyond the chamberlain's view, she backed against the wall and took a steadying breath. She mentally upbraided herself.

Lord Black was her guardian, and there were matters that needed attending to, including her receiving answers to some very important questions about her past. Obviously last night's dance, and the brief time they'd spent together afterward, had inspired in her mind a sort of subconscious infatuation, brought about by some dream man who likely didn't even exist.

Who could blame her subconscious, really? Physically, Lord Black was quite simply nonpareil.

But daylight brought the stark reality of their legal relationship into focus, as well as the matters at hand between them. There was no justification for the ravenous blush creeping up her neck and such flashpoint nerves.

Save for that lovely dream.

She pressed her fingertips against rebelliously smiling lips. Truth be told, she didn't want to forget the images, his imagined touch or the kiss. Not ever.

But dreams were dreams, and reality was reality, and she was, if anything, a realist. Within days, Lord Black would certainly leave England and resume his travels—with the countess, who was very likely his lover—and Elena would find herself in the same position as before, a young woman without memories, doing her best to forge a meaningful path in life. Better to get this over with quickly. She had a confession to make, and now was likely the most opportune time to share it.

She hurried across the foyer, squaring the newspapers into a neat stack and depositing them on a japanned table just outside the study.

At the closed door she smoothed her hands over her hair. She could not deny having dressed carefully this morning. She'd chosen a rich plum-hued dress, believing the color and the careful tailoring of the bodice flattered her figure, accentuating her trim waist and making the most of her rather average bust. Instead of twisting her hair into its customary chignon, she'd left it long, and had allowed Mary Alice to turn a few carefully placed curls with the hot tongs. Flashing an inane smile into a nearby gilt mirror, she felt ever so thankful she still had all her teeth.

She planted a brisk knock at the center of the door.

"Come in, please," called a masculine voice.

His voice. Instantly she remembered the sensation of his jaw brushed against hers, and the way he'd murmured her name in the darkness of the gallery the night before. Her legs turned into something the consistency of marmalade. Yet she stepped bravely in and pulled the door closed behind her.

"Good morning, your lordship."

He sat behind the desk, undeniably magnificent. His hair had been drawn back from his handsome face into a loose queue. He wore a white dress shirt and a perfectly turned black silk necktie.

But his expression . . . oh dear, his expression . . .

"Good morning," he answered in a low voice.

Gone was the sensual man of the night before. His silver gaze moved over her in a passionless assessment, and his lips—well, they appeared as if they'd never felt the warmth of a smile.

To her surprise, Mrs. Hazelgreaves sat before his

desk in a high-backed chair, looking decidedly imperious.

"Good morning, my dear."

"Good morning, Mrs. Hazelgreaves."

Obviously, Mrs. Hazelgreaves had spent time with Lord Black this morning. She could only imagine what they had discussed. A feeling of breathlessness came over her.

"Your gown, dear."

Elena glanced down. Only then did she realize dark streaks marred the skirt, coffee from the earlier spill. Suddenly she felt altogether clumsy and unkempt.

"I'm afraid I spilled my coffee just now, in the dining room, but I did not wish to keep his lordship waiting."

Mrs. Hazelgreaves's lips drew into a tightly condensed moue. Just wait until Mr. Jarvis reported the unfortunate slip of her tongue to the old warhorse. And he would. No matter how much she liked the man, he was one of *them*—what she had ruefully termed months ago in her mind as *the Society for the Policing of Miss Whitney's Good Manners*, of which Mrs. Hazelgreaves was the Grand Vicereine, and Mr. Jarvis her faithful Lord Lieutenant, along with other various and assorted tattling underlings throughout the house, Mary Alice excluded.

"Please sit," instructed Lord Black over slender, steepled fingertips.

She lowered herself into the chair beside that of Mrs. Hazelgreaves.

Lord Black eased into his seat. "As you know, while I keep my primary residence in London, my interests demand I remain almost exclusively abroad."

"Yes, my lord." Whatever those interests were. No one had ever explained, and she wasn't about to ask him with his face looking like that.

"I will not be in London long," he continued briskly. "Therefore certain issues must be addressed and expediently attended to."

She nodded. "Of course."

"One of those issues being the matter of your future."

Elena gave a weak smile and flicked away a bit of lace at her throat that had taken to scratching against her skin. "I agree."

She glanced between her guardian and her companion. The smug expression on Mrs. Hazelgreaves's face did not bode well for the impending discussion.

"Mrs. Hazelgreaves tells me you never had a proper coming-out."

Elena blinked. She'd thought she was beyond all that, having safely maneuvered the prior London Season with minimal involvement. "I was presented to Their Royal Highnesses Prince Albert Edward and Princess Alexandra in June."

"Yet you declined to have a come-out ball, as is customary for all young ladies of your station."

Elena cleared her throat uncomfortably and glanced toward Mrs. Hazelgreaves, who offered her nothing but a level stare. "I did."

"Might I ask why?"

Why dance around the truth? She'd always prided herself for her forthrightness. "Because I didn't want one."

"Nonetheless, I have instructed Mrs. Hazelgreaves to assist you in preparing for such an occasion. Now that I have returned to London, I think it appropriate I present you to all of society as my ward."

Elena blinked rapidly, trying to make sense of

what he had just said. Her fingers curled around the upholstered armrest of the chair. "A come-out ball? For me? It's the first of October. It would go against all protocol to announce such a thing so out of season."

His gaze narrowed. "When you are as rich and influential as I, Miss Whitney, you set the protocol, and others scramble to follow suit."

She responded. "Of course, my lord."

"I am pleased you agree."

His cool demeanor chafed Elena. He obviously sought to intimidate her into doing as he wished, which, after their pleasant accord the night before, just didn't seem right. She couldn't help but feel the sting of betrayal.

She straightened in her chair and lifted her chin high. "Might I ask, sir, why it is so imperative I be presented at such an event?"

"How else are you going to attract an offer of marriage?"

"Marriage?" The word struck like a kick to the center of her tightly laced, ribbed corset.

"Yes, Miss Whitney. *Marriage.*" He enunciated the word carefully, as if he were explaining a common concept to a provincial bumpkin—she, of course, being the bumpkin. "Marriage is what young ladies of your station and good fortune *do.*"

Elena blanched and sat silent. Yes, every other unmarried debutante to whom she had been introduced over the past months grew pink-cheeked and giddy at the mention of betrothal to an esteemed nobleman or wealthy financier. Their thoughts centered on trousseaus, St. George's Church and wedding gifts.

Elena didn't begrudge them that. She simply had other plans. Distinct, well-thought-out plans. Should she reveal her aspirations of becoming a doctor to his lordship now? Her stomach twisted. She had hoped to ease into her confession over a comfortable and *friendly* course of conversation. Last night he had seemed so different, like someone she could talk to about anything. Something had changed. This morning he radiated cold tyranny, and his face appeared carved of stone.

At her silence, he prodded, "Have you something against the institution of marriage, Miss Whitney?"

"No, of course I don't," she answered a bit too sharply.

Marriage was perfect for other people. People who wanted to be married. But she'd suffered a loss of memories. How could she think of devoting herself to another person when she didn't truly yet know who she was? On the other hand she was crystal clear about her desire to serve the poor community of London through medicine.

"Then it is settled. You will make yourself fully available to Mrs. Hazelgreaves, and all the necessary arrangements will be made for—"

Elena flushed in consternation. Things went too far. She had to say something, and say it now.

"Your lordship," she attempted to interrupt. "If I might . . ."

"—a date within the next two weeks."

"Two weeks!" she blurted.

Certainly Mrs. Hazelgreaves would protest. No event of her caliber could be prepared in such an abbreviated window of time. Yet Mrs. Hazelgreaves's penciled brows went up, and a pleased smile curved her thin pink lips.

"*Lovely.*" She clasped her blue-veined hands in delight. "I'll make arrangements with Gunter's to cater—pork cutlets and lentil pudding, of a certainty. And a florist. We'll have flowers *everywhere*. Darling girl, we can't possibly get Worth to design a gown on such short notice, but there's still Madame, who is every bit *de rigueur*—"

Elena lurched up from her seat. "I have something to say. Something important."

"Yes?" Lord Black practically growled, one brow raised, a dark slash of sin.

She didn't like him *growling* at her. She wanted the other Lord Black back—if not the man of her dreams, then at least the man he'd been the night before. The fire on the hearth flamed high behind his chair, making it seem as if she had the audience of the devil himself.

"Don't look at me like that—as if I've done something wrong." Her voice rose an octave with each word. "I wrote you. I telegraphed you. I *needed* your counsel."

Mrs. Hazelgreaves gasped. "My girl, don't speak to his lordship so."

They both looked at her as if she were a misbehaving child. But she was a woman—an intelligent, independent woman with dreams of her own.

Lord Black scowled, his eyes fixed darkly upon her. "You must understand that—"

Every bit of hurt she'd experienced over the past months flew straight from her heart into her mouth. "Oh, yes. I understand. I understand you were too busy for me. That I have no place in your life. But if you think, dear guardian, that you can just sweep into *my* life after nearly two years of absence, after two years of not giving a *damn*—"

A moan went up from Mrs. Hazelgreaves's direction.

Lord Black's gaze wavered. "Mrs. Hazelgreaves. Are you all right?"

"She's fine," Elena answered for the old woman.

"She has *fainted*," he argued accusingly, pushing back his chair to stand.

"She's *pretending*." Elena moved closer to the desk. "She's done it before whenever I've behaved in a manner she found abominable, only I've never confronted her about it."

He eyed the old woman. "She's pretending?"

"Yes. She did the same thing when I told her I'd taken the nursing position at the hospital."

His gaze returned to Elena. "How often do you behave 'abominably'?"

"I am normally very well behaved, when not exceedingly provoked. And as I was saying, you can't just sweep into my life after all this time and expect to troth me off within a week or two." She planted her hands at the edge of his desk and leaned toward him. Elena knew she was acting the hoyden, and to her surprise, she found it not such an appalling place to be. "But, yes, now that I consider the matter further, please do your best."

She had never favored dramatics, but she had tried so hard since awakening after the accident, to balance the demands placed upon her by the society she'd found herself amongst, while preserving the validity of her own dreams.

She tried not to look at Lord Black's lips, tried not to remember the way she'd wanted him to kiss her the night before.

"Do my best?" Archer planted his hands against the desktop, and met her nearly nose to nose, a mistake, because as soon as he got close to her he wanted nothing more than to press a kiss against her beautiful, nonsense-spouting lips. "Are you challenging me? The man who is legally in control of your very existence?"

"I'm quite certain none of the gentlemen you could

dredge up on such short notice would want me for their wife."

"That's not true." Archer did not care whether she saw the angry, twisted admiration on his face. She was beautiful, intelligent and spirited. What mortal man in his right mind would not kill to have her? "Why would you say such a thing?"

Peripheral vision enabled him to see Mrs. Hazelgreaves straightening in her seat. The old woman rolled her eyes and muttered, obviously conscious. Dammit if a smile did not tug at his lips.

Her eyes dropped to his mouth, and back to his eyes. Tension snapped like electricity between them.

"I told you," she whispered.

"So you did," he whispered back.

Elena cleared her throat. "Has it occurred to you that I have a life of my own? That in your silent and unresponsive absence, I might have made decisions for my own future?"

Whatever humor he'd managed to find in the moment summarily evaporated.

"Such as?" he demanded.

Something inside him bristled, a thousand pointed needles aimed into his heart. If she told him she'd already accepted a proposal from someone, and that her future husband's name was Dr. Charles Harcourt, he would lift up the desk and smash it against the wall.

"These men you hope to entice into marrying me—"

"Yes?"

"Would be horrified at having a doctor for a wife."

"A *doctor*?" gasped Mrs. Hazelgreaves.

"That's correct." His ward crossed her arms over her high, delectable breasts. "I've applied to the London School of Medicine for Women."

"Impossible." He shook his head. "You would have to sit for—"

"Examinations. Yes," she agreed with obvious satisfaction. "I've passed them."

"And arrange for—"

"A letter of reference. It has been written, and submitted."

"By whom?" He already knew, of course, but wanted to hear the blasted name from her lips.

"Someone who apparently believes in me."

"And so?" he demanded quietly. Coldly. "What now?"

"I shall continue to work as a nurse at the hospital, as I await my formal acceptance."

His gaze skimmed over Mrs. Hazelgreaves—then staggered back to her. "*Bloody hell.* I think she's truly fainted this time."

Elena threw him a disbelieving look, but upon assessing her elderly companion, whose mouth gaped ajar and whose features had relaxed into a mask of one who was truly unconscious, she grasped her skirts and hurried to respond.

"Mrs. Hazelgreaves?" Kneeling, she took up the old woman's wrist and held a finger to her pulse. "Oh, dear."

"Perhaps you've killed her," Archer suggested darkly.

Mrs. Hazelgreaves's eyes fluttered open and after a moment, her watery gaze fixed upon Elena. "Someone please tell me I've awakened from a terrible dream."

"Everything's going to be all right," Elena soothed.

"What will everyone say?" her companion warbled. "You might as well have joined a traveling circus. And don't think I haven't seen that ink marking on your wrist!"

Elena smiled wanly. "I think she's coming around."

Mrs. Hazelgreaves pressed a hand to her forehead. "Summon one of the downstairs housemaids. Have them bring me a tonic!"

Moments later the maid arrived, a discreet silver flask in hand. Mrs. Hazelgreaves pushed up from her chair and clutched on to the girl's arm.

Elena reached to assist. "Are you all right to walk?"

"Of course I am." Mrs. Hazelgreaves swatted her hand away. "I'm not *decrepit*."

"Perhaps some time in the conservatory would restore you," Elena suggested, wanting to spare her a trip up the stairs.

"Yes, the conservatory. I need time alone to recover from the shock of this announcement." Mrs. Hazelgreaves muttered to Archer, "Unless you can convince her to abandon her ridiculous quest, our list of eligibles has just been shredded to bits."

Elena watched her companion go. As she turned, her lips twitched into a mirthless smile. "Aren't we a fine pair?"

"What do you mean by that?" he answered curtly.

She laughed ruefully. "You the endearing guardian, and I your obedient ward. It's like one of those awful penny dreadfuls gone rampantly awry."

"You oughtn't speak to me like that. So casually."

He strode to the window and glared out. He radiated frustration, and she realized he didn't have any idea how to deal with her. Was she so different than other young women?

It stung that he couldn't even face her. A sudden wave of loneliness weighted her spirit.

"In two weeks' time you'll have departed London, and I'll be on my honeymoon with some aristocratic wastrel who married me only because you threw a ridiculous amount of money at him. What will it all matter then?"

She didn't want to hear his response. Instead, she swept from the room, pausing only to claim her stack of newspapers, if for no other reason than to give her shaking hands something to grip on to.

He was right. She shouldn't have spoken to him in so bold a manner. Her cheeks burned with mortification. What had come over her? Perhaps she sought to provoke him, to demand whatever attention from him he hadn't given her before. That just didn't seem to fit with the Elena she had come to know in these recent months.

She didn't know! She only knew the whole exchange had made her miserable.

She had worked to hard to discover her true self, and simplify her complicated life, for everything to be turned completely upside down by his arrival in London.

Mary Alice rushed toward her from the direction of the kitchens. "Oh, miss. I've been waiting for you to come out of his lordship's study so I could tell you. Have you heard the terrible news?"

Oh, yes. She'd heard the terrible news. Her guardian, the man legally in control of her life, would likely demand she abandon everything that mattered, and marry into a loveless marriage, all for his own selfish convenience. But something told her the girl's face wouldn't be ghost-white over such news.

"What is it, Mary Alice?"

"There were two more murders in Whitechapel last night."

Chapter Seven

"No!" gasped Elena, instantly forgetting her own problems. "Two? Two women?"

The maid's head bobbed in confirmation.

Lizzy and Catherine, her mind morbidly supplied. No, certainly not. Most likely they were safe somewhere, and even now drinking a morning pint at their favorite local pub.

"Are you sure? Or is this merely rumor?"

"It's certainly true, miss. Mr. Watkins, the footman, told me, and he's never been one to jest."

"Would this be in the morning papers already?"

She dropped her stack to a nearby table, and spread them out, scouring the dates. "Here's this morning's *Lloyd's.* Let's see . . . oh, my. Yes. An extra-special edition, and look at the headline. *More East End Tragedies.*"

"So it's true," Mary Alice whispered.

"I'll read the details. *This Sunday morning, atrocious murder of a woman in Aldgate. The victim . . .* oh, dear—"

Elena closed her eyes against the words she'd just read. Throat slashed. Mutilated. Disemboweled.

She shook her head. "The details are too terrible to be read aloud."

Mary Alice shuddered, wrapping her arms about herself. "God bless their souls."

Elena read further into the article. "They describe the killer as *diabolically cunning*. They must certainly be correct. What sort of person could do such things to another human being? He—or she—must certainly be mad."

Mary Alice mused, "There's some that believe those women deserved what they got because they are"—she lowered her voice—"*ladies of easy virtue* and of an *oversexed nature*."

Elena scowled at that. "Ridiculous. I work with 'those women' at the hospital. They are just like you and I, only they have fallen on terrible times and have been abandoned by society. They have no other way to provide for themselves."

Mary Alice nodded solemnly. "It could happen to any of us, I suppose. Poor souls. Speaking of falling on terrible times, I don't wish to lose my own position. I'd best get back to my duties before Mr. Jarvis discovers me here speaking to you."

"I understand. Thank you for telling me about this, Mary Alice."

After the maid had gone, Elena read on, searching for the names of the victims. There were no such particulars, but the deceased women were discovered in two different locations a shockingly short distance apart—only about a quarter of a mile. A double event, allegedly exacted by the same murderer! The idea was staggering. It was almost as if the killer were flaunting his horrible sanguinary skills to the authorities, and indeed, to the world.

To her surprise, in a separate article just below, there were details of another recent incident. Earlier in the month, a woman's severed arm had been found floating in the Thames near Pimlico. Now, a second arm had been discovered in Southwark. An uncomfortable chill trickled down her spine. Really, what was the world coming to?

Elena returned her attention to the article about the Whitechapel killings. One of the victims was described as being between thirty-five and forty years of age, the age she would estimate Mrs. Eddowes as being. There was no such estimation for the other victim.

Elena folded the newspaper into her lap. She was being foolish. It was outlandish to fear that two women she'd met only yesterday had become victims of the most horrific murderer in London's history. There were thousands of such women on the streets of the city, at all hours of the night, unprotected. The victims could be anyone.

Standing, she walked to the window and peered out to the street. Shining phaetons rolled past, boasting the world's wealthiest men and most beautiful women, no doubt on their way to promenade through Hyde Park or pursue some other equally lighthearted diversion.

They didn't know what it meant to pass the night sitting upright in a squalid alleyway, with only a wet newspaper for a blanket. Neither did she, for that matter. She couldn't get Lizzy's brave smile out of her mind.

Surely Lizzy and Catherine wouldn't have spent the money she'd given them on something other than shelter.

"Good morning, madame," a man's cultured voice greeted from the door of the conservatory. "A lovely day, is it not?"

Surrounded by orchids and palms, Belinda Hazelgreaves sat in a large rattan chair, pondering the profusion of gray feathers on her pink silk parasol. She had purchased it in Paris nearly fifteen years before, and it still looked perfectly new, a testament to the quality money could buy. Three canaries chirped in a large gilt cage beside her. The silver flask containing her tonic sat on a small, metal side table, and beside it, an empty sherry glass.

Tall and golden, and perfect in every way, he quite simply took her breath away, and that hadn't happened in a very long time. By her experience, the most handsome men were usually dangerous. She, being a wealthy widow, had to be careful of wolves in sheep's clothing. Still . . . clothes said a lot about a man, and men who wore impeccable, finely tailored clothes, gold watches, and boots as fine as this gentleman were normally very rich themselves. He held his top hat in his hand, and idly tapped the brim against the side of his leg.

He tilted his head toward the manse. "I am early for my appointment with his lordship. I hate to be rude and present myself early. Might I sit with you a while to pass the time?"

She narrowed her eyes at him. "I suppose."

He entered, ducking—for he was impressively tall—to walk beneath the threshold. Once before her, he bowed at the waist. "I am Alexander."

"Ah . . . Lord Alexander?" She extended her hand. He bent to claim it, brushing his lips over her knuckles.

"Indeed."

"I am Mrs. Hazelgreaves."

"Hazelgreaves . . . ," he mused. "Any relation to Ibbot Hazelgreaves, the cabinet member?"

She tilted her head. "I am his widow."

"A very important man. It's true what they say.

Every successful man has a great woman behind him. You must be that great woman."

Belinda smiled, for he spoke the truth. Ibbot had achieved great things, both politically and socially, because of her. So would her rebellious charge, whether she wanted to or not. She refused to allow Miss Whitney to be a black mark on her perfect record. She had been patient with all the nursing foolishness, but the announcement about medical school had gone quite over the line. Judging by his lordship's reaction, she felt certain he believed the same.

"You and his lordship are friends?" she asked.

He leaned over the arm of the chair, gregarious and confiding. "Lord Black and I go a long way back. What about you, dear Mrs. Hazelgreaves? How do you find yourself here at residence at Black House?"

"I am companion to his ward, Miss Elena Whitney."

"Ah, I see." He flashed his perfect white teeth. "Miss Whitney. I believe I caught a glimpse of her at the Kerrigan event last night."

"You were there?" She beamed. "Miss Whitney is a lovely girl, is she not?"

"Stunning."

"I expect, though, I'll soon be returning to my son's estate in Wilshire."

"Oh, yes? Why?"

"His lordship wishes for Miss Whitney to marry, or at least to have entered into a suitable engagement, before he departs London again."

"Interesting."

"What about you, Lord Alexander?" She smiled suggestively. "Are you . . . attached?"

"Why, Mrs. Hazelgreaves." His eyes glinted with mischief. "I am not."

"Well, then, I am very pleased to make your acquaintance."

"She's gone!" Leeson charged into the library.

Anxiety radiated from him, something rare enough to command Archer's attention. His secretary normally moved through his immortal existence with the unflappability of a bovine. The old man produced a handkerchief from his waistcoat pocket and mopped it across his brow.

Archer hadn't been able to read Elena's thoughts since that first night on the rooftop. Unfortunately, there were some rare exceptions to every rule. It was simply that way with some souls. Those souls simply left a different sort of trace, or trail behind in the wake of their movements. As such, he had sensed her absence as soon as she'd stepped off the premises of Black House. Perhaps, like him, she needed time alone to recover from their unpleasant exchange. Things had not gone at all as he'd wished.

"She, who?" Archer responded coolly, jabbing his ink pen into its berth.

His secretary's eye narrowed. "The only woman in this house you give a damn about."

Leeson paced the length of the library and waved an arm in an uncharacteristically dramatic gesture. "I saw her walking out to the street, but I couldn't stop my driver quickly enough to intervene."

"I'm sure she's simply gone to the park for a walk."

"She's gone out alone, without a suitable escort or companion, and young English ladies from Mayfair are *not* supposed to do that. From all I've read and observed, it's not considered seemly."

In his green coat, he looked like a red-faced, one-eyed leprechaun. "Not only that, but she took off across the side yard like a common housemaid. *Dressed* like a common housemaid. And she summoned a hackney. A filthy, hired vehicle driven by a stranger. Why would she do that, when every luxury has been made available to her from the start?"

All at once Leeson went stiff. He shot a glare toward Archer. *"What have you done?"*

"Watch yourself, Leeson, or I'll have you reassigned."

Leeson fumed. So did Archer. He had vowed to the Primordials Elena wouldn't be a distraction, but that was exactly what she had been from the moment he'd laid his ancient, jaded eyes upon her. He ought to just let her go, but the idea of her wandering about unescorted and unprotected left him uneasy.

Jack was out there somewhere, and "somewhere" was too close when Elena was concerned, even in this churning city of millions. Goddamit, he had to Reclaim the bastard quickly.

Archer drummed his fingertips atop the desk, and tersely confided, "Miss Whitney made it clear this morning that our current arrangement is not to her liking. I believe—though she did not specifically say so—she would prefer her independence."

While pondering the appropriate course of action he glanced aside, into the garden. Moments before, Mrs. Hazelgreaves had been sitting in the conservatory, but he saw no trace of her now. Her open parasol, pink damask trimmed with gray feathers, lay open on the flagstones, fixed in place by its handle. He would dispatch one of the servants out to collect it, for she must have left it behind.

Leeson commandeered his field of vision. "Independence? You can't allow it, your lordship. Our precious girl oughtn't be out on her own in that city *any* day, let alone this one. News of the double murder has spread, and the city is in absolute turmoil."

Archer closed his eyes, and wearily rubbed the narrow bridge of his nose, having expected to hear the same. Leeson collapsed into an upholstered mahogany chair.

"There are mobs in the streets, calling for blood. People are behaving like lunatics, suspecting everyone of murder and madness." He leapt up again. "I'm going to find her and bring her home where she will be safe from all the wicked bastards ruling the streets out there."

"I'll go," Archer interjected, standing.

If he left now, he would still be able to pick up her trace. Besides, now that his senses were returned to center, he needed to submit himself to the tangled confusion of the city. Total immersion would ensure the deadly precision he sought. "You stay here and finish your review of the books."

Leeson waved his hand. "There's time for the books. I'll go with you. Who knows where or how far she's gone by now We can split the city between the two of us."

"Finish the books, Leeson. I will bring her home."

A quarter of an hour later, Archer descended the concrete steps into the Baker Street station. Travelers milled about on the platform, awaiting the next train. Nearly all of their thoughts were consumed by the morning's horrific news.

A newspaper boy circulated, shouting,"Ripper kills again. Two murdered, just last night."

The papers were snatched from his hand, one after the other, almost faster than he could collect payment.

Archer found Elena standing off to one side, near two older ladies, in a proximity he assumed was intended to give the impression to strangers that she companioned them in some way, either as a poorer relation or a maid. She didn't see him, of course, because he'd followed her in shadow. As Leeson had reported, she had garbed herself as a lower-class female, wearing a shabby, black straw bonnet decorated with a cluster of black flowers and a faux cardinal, a threadbare black coat and striped gray skirt. All had likely been purchased at some second-hand, street-market stall. A faded patchwork purse hung from her wrist.

Screeching metal, piercing light and billowing steam announced the arrival of the eastbound train. Archer followed Elena onto the second-class car, where she flashed her token to the conductor and took a seat on the bench beside the two women. Archer situated himself in the aisle before her. As the train lurched into motion, she pulled from her bag a small book, bound in blue linen. He glimpsed the title as she parted the pages to begin reading. *The Bacterial Theory.* He could not help but smile at that.

His smile dropped, though, realizing several male passengers stared at his ward, obviously as intrigued as he. Though she kept her head tilted forward, so that her hat obscured much of her face, her lush, pink lips were clearly visible. And worse, a stray tendril had escaped her bonnet to rest upon her shoulder.

A pale, glossy tendril. Goddess hair. He could still remember the delicious scent and feel of it. But he could not allow himself to act upon impulse. Not again. He would do what was honorable by her and ensure the security of her future, even if she despised him for it in the end. Curse him, but somehow, in this short bit of time he'd come to care deeply for her.

She did not get off the train at either the King's Cross or Farringdon Street stations with the two older ladies. She did not tuck her book away until the conductor called out "Aldgate."

When the doors opened, he shadowed her off the train into a churning crowd. His young ward had perfected the confident, no-nonsense walk of an East End woman—a woman without a true protector, someone who must be on guard at all times. She pushed her way through the dim station, firmly smacking the hand of a sailor who ventured too close. Because she moved so quickly, Archer tamped down the urge to smite the young fool, and followed her up the stairs onto the crowded sidewalk.

Off to the side, colorfully dressed Mountebanks called to the newly disembarked, offering peep shows and slight-of-hand entertainments. An old man played a crank organ while his monkey, adorned in a cap and vest, danced with a tin cup in hand. Omnibuses, hackneys and wagons scuttled past in both directions.

Elena proceeded down Whitechapel. At first he assumed her destination to be the hospital, but almost immediately she turned north onto Commercial Street. A quarter mile later, Christ Church towered above them, but unfortunately she didn't climb the steps to the church—she went to the pub just across the street.

Archer's mood went decidedly dark. What respectable reason would his lovely ward have for patronizing a Spitalfields public house midday on a Sunday?

The sour-stale stench struck Elena full in the face as she pushed inside the Ten Bells Pub. She paused, allowing her eyes a moment to adjust to the dim light. The windows on each side of the door did little to illuminate the dreary interior, or the faces of the customers. A long bar spanning the back wall was serviced by two barmaids against a backdrop of walls tiled in green, red and dingy yellow. A number of tables and chairs cluttered the room and were populated by a grim, midday crowd.

For a moment she feared she'd have to continue on to the Horn of Plenty or the Brittania, but thankfully, though she didn't see Lizzy or Catherine, she found the familiar face of one who might be able to tell her what she wished to know.

"Mrs. Scott?" She sidled between the tables. "Hello—do you remember me from the hospital?"

Mrs. Scott had five sturdy sons ranging in age from eight to eighteen who worked at any job they could find, be that laying brick, peddling newspapers or blacking boots. In Elena's brief time at the hospital, she'd met all but one of them for various injuries, but rarely sickness.

"Oh-ay . . . 'at you, Nurse Whitney? Come 'ave a seat. Yes, come."

With the heel of her shoe, Mrs. Scott shoved out an empty chair. She sat with a younger woman, neatly dressed in a black, long-sleeved dress and a black felt cap. On the table before them sat stout, earthenware mugs and two half-eaten meat pies, wrapped in greasy newspaper.

"Good morning to you both." Elena sat down and placed her bag securely on her lap.

Mrs. Scott grinned. "Say, 'ave you met Mary? No? This is Mary Kelly, a good friend of mine from Miller's Court. The two of you sort of look like each other, ay?"

"Hello Mary." Elena smiled and nodded at the

girl, who was strikingly pretty, with blond hair and mischievous blue eyes. "So good to make your acquaintance. Mrs. Scott, how is Jimmy's hand?"

"So much improved, thanks to you and 'at fine Dr. 'arcourt. I been tellin' anyone who'll listen, too, what fine attention we got at the 'ospital."

"Pint for you, miss?" called one of the barmaids.

Elena nodded, then to Mrs. Scott, said, "I'm so glad Jimmy's recovering. Say, I stopped by to see if I could find one of my patients. Might you know Lizzy Harper, or her friend Catherine Eddowes?"

Mrs. Scott nodded. "Oh, ay. I know Kate all right. It's still a bit early for 'er to be out and about." The woman leaned toward Elena and chuckled. "Not that I'm one to judge, but when I saw 'er last night, she could barely put one 'eel in front of the other. In the end the coppers 'auled her off to Bishopsgate."

The barmaid slid a mug in front of her, and Elena provided the necessary coin for payment.

"Really? That bad off?" Elena tried to conceal her disappointment. So Catherine hadn't used the money to safely board for the night. Instead she'd been out drinking and getting herself arrested.

Mrs. Scott chuckled jovially, rocking back to her chair. "Old girl's probably still sleepin' it off in 'er cell."

At least, though, if Mrs. Eddowes spent the night in a jail cell she was safe. What about young Lizzy?

"Be right back," said Mary, pulling a small, leather purse from her waistband. "Got to settle part of me arrears with Geneva, else they won't let me in the door tonight."

She set off in the direction of the bar.

Elena asked Mrs. Scott, "Was Lizzy with Catherine when you saw her last night?"

"Lizzy . . ." The woman squinted in thought. "Lizzy with the curly red hair? Young thing, lives with one of them strappin' navvies over off Fashion?"

"That's her." Elena lifted her mug and took a sip. She had not acquired a taste for stout, especially not as a midday beverage, but kept a grimace from her face.

"Not last night, but if we're talkin' about the same girl, p'raps I saw 'er just this morning on the back of a cart, 'eaded toward Aldgate. Lots of folks going that way this morning. Say, you *did* 'ear the news, didn't you?"

"I did."

The woman shook her head, her expression a mix of revulsion and fear. "Word on the street is that those women were butchered, Nurse Whitney. Butchered like animals."

"Have you heard the names of the victims?"

"We're all waitin to 'ear who they are, miss, and find out whether they are kith or kin. Either way, everyone's certain they'll be next, once night falls again. It's a sorry thing, livin' on these streets."

"I know, it's terrible. Worse than terrible." Elena frowned. "And so you think Lizzy went toward Aldgate?"

"I 'ear they're 'avin a public meeting down there, and one up in Victoria Park, 'oping to organize and get the police to do something more than what they been doin' "

"I see." Elena, crossing one leg of the other, nodded, while listening intently.

"Those in charge don't care about us over in this part of the city. Not unless we all band t'gether and make some noise. I'll be 'eaded 'at way meself after I finish me breakfast."

"Perhaps I'll see you there, then." Elena stood.

"Oh, say—" Mrs. Scott glanced pointedly at Elena's mug, still filled to the brim. "Do ye mind?"

"Not at all."

She turned, and at the same moment, a large wall of a man stood up from the table beside hers, blocking her exit.

"*Mor*ning, lovely." He had high, pronounced cheekbones, a dark mustache and black eyes, and stood almost a head taller than she. His words were heavily accented—Eastern European, she believed, from her experience at the hospital. "Saw you walk by. Was *ho*ping to *in*troduce myself."

Elena met his gaze directly. "I'm sorry, I'm on my way out."

"I shall make it worth your while."

Mrs. Scott interjected, "She's not your sort, Ludwig. Let 'er pass."

He didn't budge.

"Truly sir. I've somewhere else to be."

She sidestepped him, only to have his hand grip her forearm and yank her toward him.

"Oh, say here!" bellowed Mrs. Scott, pushing herself up from her table. "Get your hands off her."

The men at his table guffawed loudly.

Elena froze and stared down to where he gripped her. She wasn't naive about the East End, or what could happen on its streets, day or night. She fully realized what chances she took in coming here.

"Please remove your hand from my arm."

"Don't you speak so clean and *fancy*?" he sneered, having lost all pretense of politeness. "Sorry, *princess*. Not until you share a pint with me and my friends."

Mary, who had been leaning against the bar,

turned and bravely wedged herself between them.
"Let her go, Ludwig."

His fist swung high—

Mary's arms went up to defend herself.

"No!" Elena shouted.

"*Severin Antoniovich,*" a man's voice interjected in
a quietly commanding voice. The pub went silent.

Elena glanced aside—

Lord Black sat in a chair just a few feet from them,
his dark hair a midnight cascade over his shoulders,
and his icy gaze fixed on her assailant.

Chapter Eight

Exclamations and curses rose up around the room. Shock reverberated through Elena. How could Lord Black, sitting just there, have gone unnoticed until now?

The smallest, most provocative of smiles turned his lips. Never breaking gaze with the man, he leaned forward in his chair and slowly stood to his full, impressive height. Waning light gleamed off the rich fabric that fashioned the lapel of his coat. The pub seemed like a dingy coal bin in comparison to his dark splendor.

"I believe you'd like to remove your hand from the lady," he murmured, staring intently into the man's eyes. "Wouldn't you, Severin?"

Ludwig or Severin, or whatever the man's name was, gave an anguished shout and released her. He staggered backward, his eyes wide and unfocused, and gripped his hand as if in excruciating pain, only to be shoved by Mary in the opposite direction.

Archer retrieved his hat from the table and took Elena's elbow. With no change of expression, he escorted her toward the door. As they passed through, into the midday light, Mrs. Scott and Mary scuttled out behind them—Mrs. Scott, with a sloshing pint clutched in one hand, and her unfinished meat pie in the other.

"Thank you, sir," Mary called, grinning.

"Be seein' you soon, Nurse Whitney," hollered Mrs. Scott.

Elena watched both women hurry across the street to disappear into the crowd on the far sidewalk.

Left alone with her guardian, she braced herself, for certainly he would demand an explanation. She had been so careful leaving Black House. How had he followed her all this way without her knowing?

But he didn't say a word. Nor did he release her elbow. His quiet intensity, as they progressed down the crowded street, sent a dark thrill of anticipation through her. She feared his fury, but in some mor-bidly torturous way she craved any audience with him.

Seeking to gauge the gravity of her situation, she glanced up beneath the deep brim of his hat.

"How long were you there before all that ugli-ness began?"

He met her inquiring gaze with a level one. "Long enough to realize you've done this sort of thing be-fore. And don't tell me you think you could have handled that yourself. I don't want to hear it."

She hated to admit how relieved she'd been, seeing him inside the Ten Bells, but why pretend otherwise?

"I am glad you were there."

"I'm not glad *you* were there," he responded darkly.

"I know," she admitted. "And I understand why, really I do. But it was important for me to find some-one today. How did you know where I'd gone?"

"Leeson saw you leave Black House, dressed like that. He is in a panic that you went out unaccompa-nied. Do you know how dangerous the city is today?"

She nodded. "I shall have to thank Mr. Leeson for his kind concern."

Lord Black guided her around a buckled slab of sidewalk and in doing so, moved his hand from her elbow to the small of her back. He walked close to her, so close at times his trousers brushed against her skirts. Lord help her, he excited her with his presence, even if he was angry.

Pedestrians thronged alongside them, and in the opposite direction. Most of them, *especially* the ladies, stole a second glance at the handsome gentleman with the exotic long hair and elegant clothing. A few even turned in a half circle to gawk as he moved past.

One thing Elena had learned in her time working at the hospital was that the East End was an uncommon place and there were uncommon sights to be seen everywhere within it, at all hours of the day or night. In some inexplicable way, he fit in perfectly here.

She said, "Back there, at the Ten Bells, the ladies called that man Ludwig. You called him something else."

"I overheard something one of his friends said," he responded vaguely, looking ahead over the crowd. "I simply took the chance I could get his attention with it."

"That was remarkable, the way you looked at him and he—"

"Who is it you are here today trying to find?"

"A girl, Lizzy Harper."

"She is someone you are very close to?"

"Not really," Elena confessed. "Actually, I met her only yesterday at the hospital. She was one of my patients. I don't know why, but somehow I felt very connected to her. You know how it is with some people."

"I suppose I don't," he answered coolly.

Despite his attractiveness, it was easy to see why he wouldn't. While "hauteur" was no accurate description—for he was not arrogant in his mannerisms or speech—he emanated inaccessibility, as if every emotion and impulse were kept behind an impenetrable wall. Elena could not help but wonder what he would be like if that wall were destroyed.

She said, "I'm worried about her, and the friend she was supposed to stay with last night. I know it's foolish. But when I heard there were two more murders . . ."

He didn't answer, but his jaw tensed visibly.

Across the street, a row of narrow tables had been set out on the sidewalk. Solemnly dressed women pressed handbills into the hands of passersby. Beside them was propped a large sign bearing the words WHITECHAPEL VIGILANCE COMMITTEE.

They shouted out into the crowd, "Ladies! All of you ladies, yes, you there, and you. Please come and sign the petition. A petition that will be presented to our most gracious lady, Queen Victoria. Let us demand the closure of all wicked houses of sin and impurity in our city!"

"Do you wish to sign the petition?" Lord Black asked in a cordial tone.

"Thank you, but no."

His dark brow lifted. "Why not?"

"It's not wickedness that drives these women to the street; it is desperation and poverty. I'll sign any petition that proposes some solution to those problems. Oh, dear. Look at all these people."

They had arrived at the juncture with Whitechapel

Road. Though before, the sidewalks had been crowded, now there was barely room to walk. Hundreds, if not thousands of people jammed the street, to such an extent that the thoroughfare appeared to be a bobbing sea of heads and hats, flowing toward Aldgate.

She said, "They're trying to get a look at the places where those women were killed."

"So it appears," he answered, frowning.

Street vendors, normally uncommon in this part of the neighborhood, had followed the crowd and set up their carts off to the side. They sold steaming coffee, tea and a variety of cakes, fruits and nuts.

Lord Black scowled like the devil at a passel of children and a barking dog who circled around them.

"Perhaps the best thing we can do if you've any hope whatsoever of finding your girl, Lizzy, is to stay in one spot. Perhaps we could sit over there on that bit of half wall. At least for a time. I've an appointment this afternoon."

Inwardly Elena was stunned. She'd assumed he was taking her to the train station so he could escort her directly home. Instead, he was staying with her to watch for Lizzy. Perhaps Lord Black wasn't the devil.

"She's on a crutch, so I think she'd stay to the outer edge of the crowd, so yes, let's do that." Elena smiled her gratefulness. She touched her hand against his forearm. "Just a moment, if you will."

She darted away into the crowd, pressing through the shabbiest of citizens, toward one of the vendors.

For a moment Archer lost her, but he quickly spotted the crimson bird on her hat. Keeping his sites on her, he made his way to the wall and seated himself on the edge of its mortar. There was just enough space for the two of them, for a host of others lined the wall as well, watching the spectacle in the street.

Her smile upon returning sent his stomach muscles into clenching. In her gloved hand, she held out a small paper envelope. "I wanted some sweets. I bought some for you too."

They were cachous, identical to the ones he'd seen clenched in the hands of a dead woman the night before.

"What's wrong?" Her brows furrowed. "Oh, dear, you dislike peppermint."

He met her gaze directly. "I don't like how things ended between us this morning."

She looked away, flushing, and placed one of the cachous between her lips. "Neither do I."

He confessed, "I only want the best for you."

"I know," she answered, perching herself upon the wall beside him, closer than would be proper on the other side of town. He wasn't at all sorry. "But obviously we've different ideas of what that should be."

"I . . . admire your ambition and your selflessness in wishing to help others who cannot help themselves," Archer ceded, forcing the words, which were true, but not very easy to say, from his lips.

Her lovely features showed surprise, and pleasure. "You do?"

Being ancient as time itself, he didn't subscribe to so-called contemporary ideas about Elena's sex. He had known many scholarly and powerful women. Olympias. Cleopatra. Boudaccia. Women were capable of the same greatnesses as men. Of course, he couldn't tell her that. Such forthrightness would not serve his current purposes—namely, to keep her safe, happy and alive for the next six or seven decades, even if he were not present to witness what he vowed would be a contented and happy life for her. He had not humiliated himself, intervening to give her a second chance, only for her to get herself killed just a few blocks away from the squalid street where he'd first found her. He wanted better things for her than Whitechapel, and the burden of its hopelessly lost inhabitants.

He added, "At the same time I am responsible for your future."

Her face fell, in obvious recollection of their morning discussion and his announcement that he wished her to marry.

With a sigh she tugged at the cuff of her glove, and he glimpsed the very outermost border of her serpent tattoo.

She said in a soft voice, "We still have had no real opportunity to talk and become acquainted with each other. Tell me, how did your responsibility for my well-being come about? How did you know my father?"

"I knew him . . . only in passing."

In *passing*, yes. Depending on how one defined the word, he was either a bloody liar or telling the absolute truth.

Disappointment showed plainly on her face. "You weren't friends, then?"

"Just acquaintances, really."

Her brow furrowed beneath the brim of her hat. "If you weren't a friend or relative, why did he choose you as my guardian?"

"Because, Miss Whitney, there was no one else."

Her eyes glazed with sudden tears. God, he was a bastard through and through.

"You met him in your travels, then?"

He nodded. Again, the truth depended on one's definition of "travels."

"Had you and I met before?"

"No."

Her voice went husky. "Was my father truly so alone?"

Archer pulled a handkerchief from his chest pocket. When he handed it to her, she grasped both the handkerchief and his hand with both of hers.

"Not at all," he assured her. "He had your mother, and then you, and of course all the people of the villages he served. He enjoyed the deepest satisfaction throughout his life."

What a wonderful picture he had just painted— so simple, yet perfect. He suddenly realized he was astoundingly envious of the counterfeit Dr. Phillip Whitney he had created.

"You know I still don't have any of my memories from before."

"I'm very sorry for that."

He *was* sorry. He had admittedly brought a certain amount of misery upon her. But considering the alternative, he wouldn't change a thing.

"What if the memories never come back?" Her voice reflected a faint desperation. "Life is so short, Lord Black. Can't you see? It's important that my new memories be ones of importance. I'd like to be someone my mother and father would have been proud of."

"You already are."

She shook her head in apparent frustration, as if he did not understand. "Did my father, by chance, leave me any sort of inheritance?"

His smile faded. He had feared she would ask him that. He could see her mind working, trying to figure out some way to be independent of his governance. He pulled his hand free, leaving the handkerchief in hers.

"Yes, of course, but no more than a widow's pension. Certainly not enough to support you through three years of medical school, and five years of hospital practice. Your father was devoted to you, Elena, but just as devoted to his cause. One doesn't become rich running a free hospital in Africa."

The light flickered out in her eyes, and he hated himself for being the one to extinguish it. But he refused to set her free, alone, into this world. Not yet.

"You're right, of course," she said quietly.

"I'm sorry."

"It's not your fault."

"Nurse Whitney!" shouted a female voice. "Nurse Whitney! Over here."

Elena searched for the source of the voice, admittedly relieved by the interruption. Yes, Lord Black had given her the answers she sought, but they weren't exactly what she'd hoped to hear.

The crowd split just long enough for her to see a young woman waving a gloved hand and leaning on a single crutch.

"Lizzy!"

Relief overwhelmed her, and she jumped off the ledge and set off across the street, pausing only to beckon to Archer that he should follow as well. He did so, his gaze dark and somehow possessive—something that confused her, given the serious guardian-ward discussion they'd had only moments before.

As she drew nearer, Lizzy called out, "Hullo, you. What a surprise. You live over 'ere?"

"No, but I followed the crowd."

She wouldn't let the girl know how worried she'd been about her. Really, they didn't know each other all that well, and Elena didn't want to make her uncomfortable. "And you, Lizzy. Weren't you staying with Mrs. Eddowes over on Shoe Lane? Don't tell me you came all this way on crutches."

Lizzy chuckled. "One of me mates let me ride along on the back of 'is cart, but I haven't seen 'im in a good while. Not sure how I'll get back."

"How's your leg?"

"Better than y'sterday, I'll tell y' that." The girl glanced at Lord Black, who loomed above them a few paces to the side. She leaned closer. "Who's 'at gent you're with?"

"Just someone I know," Elena acknowledged quietly.

"Now I know why you ain't with the good doctor. I'd take the devil over a saint any day meself. O' course, that's what got me into most of me life's predicaments." She grinned.

Elena's cheeks burned, and she prayed his lordship hadn't overheard.

She quickly changed the subject. "Did Mrs. Eddowes find a place for the two of you to stay last night?"

Lizzy nodded. "Oh miss, she got me in a real nice place. Real nice place indeed, and they're holding me bed for tonight as well."

"And what of Mrs. Eddowes?" Elena decided not to mention what Mrs. Scott had told her about Catherine being drunk and getting arrested.

"I haven't seen 'er since last night." Lizzy's grin faded. "She told me it was too early for a wandering soul like 'er to be locked up inside. They lock them doors at eight o'clock sharp, y' see, to keep the riffraff out, and they don't unlock 'em again until eight the next morning."

"A reasonable policy, I think."

The girl nodded, and as she did so, her red curls bobbed. "Yes, indeed. I slept right sound, I did, without a worry in the world. Kate told me she'd meet up with her old man and stay the night with 'im."

Lizzy smiled again, but an edge of wistfulness mellowed her brightness. She was certainly a brave soul, and still very much on her own. Elena feared it was only a matter of time before she was forced to seek the protection of any man who would have her.

Lizzy put a hand on Elena's arm. "She told me what you done for us miss, the way you gave 'er the coins and insisted I stay in a safe place. Thank you ever so much."

Lord Black's lips quirked downward in disapproval.

Elena didn't care. She'd done the right thing, at least in this instance. "You're very welcome, Lizzy."

"I was sure I'd see 'er 'ere." Her eyes scanned the crowd. "She's usually wherever the party is, 'at one."

"I'm sure she'll show up," Elena reassured her, hoping the same.

"I suppose that since you're 'ere, you 'eard about those women who were murdered last night?"

"I did. I was hoping that beast had been swallowed up by a big black hole."

The set of Archer's jaw grew rigid. She wondered what could have turned his mood so downward. He flicked open his coat and tugged his timepiece from his vest. "Miss Whitney, I regret to interrupt."

"Yes, your lor—" Elena caught herself. It wouldn't do to reveal his aristocratic status to Lizzy, or anyone else on the street, She cleared her throat. "Sir?"

"As I told you before, I've an afternoon appointment."

"Do go on, then." She waved him off with a gloved hand. "Don't worry about me. I'll find myself home."

His dark eyes flashed. "I wouldn't think of it."

Elena knew she shouldn't protest. He'd been amazingly patient with her, more than she'd ever expected. She had found Lizzy, and felt certain Mrs. Eddowes was safe as well. There was no other reason for her to remain, and the crowd did grow quite out of hand.

Elena opened her bag. "Lizzy, I want to give you—"

Lizzy held up a hand and leaned on her crutch. "No, miss. You already done enough for me."

"How will you get back to the boardinghouse?"

"I've got around all this time without your charity, Nurse Whitney," she answered softly. "And I imagine I will this day as well."

Down the street the speeches had begun, one man taking a turn after the other, calling for the resignation of various public officials who were apparently held by many to blame for the lack of arrest.

Archer took a few steps toward the less populated end of the street and waited for her. He unexpectedly took her breath away, standing so tall and darkly handsome, his hair, and his knee-length coat rippling in the breeze.

"Very well, Lizzy," Elena said reluctantly. "Please try to stay off your leg, and do come by the infirmary if your pain worsens."

"I will, Nurse Whitney. Be safe yourself." Lizzy waved, before turning to hobble down the sidewalk.

Elena joined Lord Black, and they walked toward a row of hansoms for hire. "I hate to leave her."

"You can't save them all."

"I'd be happy with just one."

Archer surveyed the hansoms and appeared to choose the one that appeared most reputable. He walked forward and spoke with the driver. Helping Elena up into the cab, he shut the door behind her.

She leaned out the open window. "You're not coming?"

"I've got my appointment."

"He could drop you there. I could wait for you."

"Not this time. I will see you later this evening at Black House."

He signaled to the driver, and the carriage clattered into motion.

Elena sat back in the seat and pondered her mysterious guardian. Where was he going? What business did he attend to? She still felt as if she knew nothing about him.

She sank lower into the seat, clasping her bag against her chest. He was so handsome, he made her heart hurt. Why couldn't he be the one for her, her heart secretly pined? For the first time, she wondered if he was a spy. Yes, a spy in the service of Her Majesty herself.

Really, if medicine didn't work out for her, she ought to become an authoress of romantic novels. Sometimes she came up with the most entertaining notions.

Twilight fell as Archer stepped down from the hansom. He gave the driver a crown and, before striding across the train yard, instructed him to wait. His boots crunched against the gravel.

Two black, unmarked locomotive engines and four passenger cars sat on the third, and most distant, track, their windows covered by dark curtains. Seven guards, dressed in nondescript suits and all exceedingly well muscled and armed, stood at various vantage points. One of them held a leash, at the end of which wandered a small Skye terrier.

As Archer approached, one of the guards stepped down from the rear platform.

"Your name, sir?" he asked.

"Black."

The man glanced toward the train. A curtain moved, and a hand motioned from within.

He gave Archer a curt nod. "Do go on, your lordship."

Archer grasped the handrail and climbed the metal stairs. The railcar door opened from inside, and another steely-eyed Foot Guard welcomed him.

"Your lordship."

Archer stepped into a fully furnished saloon, its rich crimson walls illuminated by a number of table lamps. Gargantuan arrangements of primroses and violets covered several side tables, scenting the air. Two more Foot Guards stood at the opposite end of the car.

The woman he had come to see sat upon a small couch, her round face a pensive portrait above the froth of lace at her throat. A walking cane leaned against the cushions beside her.

"Your Majesty." Archer approached, extending his upturned hand.

"Black." The queen placed hers over his palm, and he bent to kiss her fingers. While her eyes revealed only the slightest glimmer of fascination, he felt the rush of excitement race through her.

With a wave of her hand, the Foot Guards vacated the room.

"Please, please sit. Thank you for returning to London in such haste."

"I am honored to be of service." He seated himself into a gold-brocade-covered chair. "I had not expected your summons, knowing you were at Balmoral. Will you go on to Buckingham from here?"

"No, dear immortal. Bertie sees to all the necessary London appearances. I came only to see you, and indeed, shall return this very night." She chuckled faintly. "If you desire to see me again, you shall come to Scotland."

"Perhaps one day."

Victoria nodded, her dry smile an indication she realized he would never present himself for holiday at her beloved castle in the Highlands.

She said, "Once again—thank you for answering my summons. It's not that we do not appreciate the enthusiasm of the younger Guard, but we believe our situation deserves attention from the highest levels of your organization." Her lips pressed into a thin line. "Be frank with me, Black, as we have always been with each other, and tell me what sort of monster walks amongst my subjects?"

Archer chose his words carefully. Though the Amaranthines enjoyed a beneficial relationship with the Crown, and had since William the Conquerer, only so much could be revealed.

He answered, "I can tell you only that this particular soul has been marked for Reclamation. That, in and of itself, testifies to the excess of evil within him."

"But this"—Her Majesty's lips turned downward in distaste—"Jack the Ripper, as he has chosen to call himself, is different, is he not?"

"He proves a challenge."

Her brow went up. "Even for you?"

"Some souls take more time and skill to Reclaim than others. The more deteriorated they are, the less defined trace they leave behind for us to follow. It does not help matters that he has chosen London, a crowded city of millions, for his hunting grounds. The density of population, and the resultant complexities of poverty and pollution, only add dimension to the challenge."

"What motivates him to kill these women in particular? Each one has been a lost soul. A prostitute."

"Make no mistake. The Ripper's intended victims are not only these four women, but an entire city, and indeed, the world. The killer feels no remorse for the savagery he inflicts, and revels in the attention he receives, though vanity does not inspire his killings. He is, quite simply, a vampire of emotion—he feeds off the fear his killings produce. If allowed to continue unchecked, he will grow infinitely stronger from it."

"Which elevates him to a level of concern for your organization."

"Indeed."

The queen worked a bracelet on her wrist, one that concealed a small portrait of her beloved husband, Prince Albert, who had died almost thirty years before, and for whom she had never ceased to grieve.

"Are the efforts of our authorities meaningless?"

"Not at all. Deteriorated souls aren't perfect in their madness. They make blunders, and are sometimes captured and Reclaimed because of them. It is imperative the Home Office continue their investigations, especially in this case where the villain seems so intent on taunting them. He likes to give clues. We cannot discount their importance."

"Please know that any resource will be made available to you. You have only to ask. The prime minister is with me on this."

"I prefer, as ever, to work alone."

Her hands balled into fists against her skirt. "I hate feeling helpless. I hate that this beast terrorizes the streets of my kingdom. Do whatever you must to Reclaim him, Lord Black, and send the bastard to hell."

"I am certain I want that even more badly than you, Your Majesty."

"Very well, then. I suppose I must release you and allow you to do what you do best. I must admit I feel reassured for having seen you."

Archer stood. "I will inform you of any developments."

He bowed, as if to make his leave.

"Wait. Please," the queen called softly, biting into her bottom lip with uncharacteristic anxiety. She lifted both hands and beckoned him forward. He went to her. After she fumbled in the cushion of the chair, he felt the press of parchment against his palm.

"Please, Lord Black. Take it."

He looked down on her in compassion. Though an eternity of time had passed, he remembered the raw wound of grief, and the pain of carrying on through time alone.

In a low voice he said, "You know I cannot play courier. My authority extends only to those corrupt mortal souls who threaten the existence of the Amaranthine race. All others are beyond my domain."

"Can you tell me nothing of him?"

"Only that he is at peace, and wishes the same for you."

She nodded, tears heavy against her lashes. She blinked them away. "I wish for nothing but to be with him again."

He squeezed her hands. "When it is time."

He left her then. His last image of the queen was of her clasping a handwritten message of undying love against her breast, in that moment, not the world's most powerful monarch, but a grieving widow.

Chapter Nine

"Miss Whitney, have you seen the countess today?" Mary Alice asked as she arranged a small stack of clean towels beside the basin.

"No, I haven't." Elena looked away from the skirt she'd worn to the East End that afternoon. She'd hung the garment behind the door on a wood hanger and had just finished sponging its hem clean. "I know she left the house last night, but after that I've not been aware of her comings and goings. Why do you ask?"

Honestly, she'd tried to forget the countess and their odd exchange the night before. She still wasn't sure of the woman's relationship with his lordship, and wondered if she'd ever know. Despite the time she'd spent with Lord Black that afternoon, she didn't feel as if she knew him any better than before. Everything and everyone associated with him remained hidden behind a wall of impenetrable mystery.

The more she thought about it, her silly idea that he was an agent for the Crown wasn't all that ridiculous. She went to the basin and poured water to wash her hands.

Mary Alice supplied a fresh towel. "Well, miss, this morning she returned from wherever she'd been all night. She stormed up the stairs and ordered a pot of 'strong Turkish tea' be brought immediately to her room."

"But no books?"

"Pardon, miss? Books?" Mary Alice's frown revealed her confusion.

"Oh . . . nothing."

"So I hurried to bring her tea, only to find she'd thrown every piece of linen out of her room. The bed sheets, the towels, everything, out her door and into a pile in the hall."

"Did she say why?"

"Oh, yes. She was very forthcoming," Mary Alice responded with the mildest edge of sarcasm. "She told me—no, more like shouted—that she'd be using only *high quality linens* on account of her skin being so delicate."

Elena chuckled, glancing pointedly at the towel in her hand. "What kind of linens have we been using?"

"Linens woven out of rubbish, apparently. So right away, the housekeeper, wanting to please his lordship's guest, sends out to Harrods for the highest quality *everything*, and two hours later, once it's all been delivered, I go up to make over her chamber."

"And?"

Mary Alice's cheeks flushed. "When I knock at the door she *shouts* for me to go away."

Elena shrugged. "The countess *does* seem to be a woman of extreme passions and temperament. Still, perhaps we should give her the benefit of the doubt. Did she shout in an angry sort of way, or could she have been overwrought?"

"Can't say I know the difference, not with her anyway. I've gone to her room three more times and knocked, to no response. I don't wish to pester her. Neither do I wish to be held to blame for her delicate

NIGHT FALLS DARKLY 141

skin being torn to shreds by bare ticking." Her brow furrowed. "What do you suppose she's doing in there?"

Elena thought back to the night before. "You know, now that I think on it, she didn't feel well last night. Something to do with her digestion, I believe."

"Perhaps that's it, then," Mary Alice said doubtfully.

"Do you have the towels with you?"

"On my cart, in the hall."

"Give them to me. I'll take them in to her."

"Really, miss?" the girl asked. "I'd be ever so relieved. I must confide I'm a bit intimidated by the countess. Not only that, but I've a new maid to show about, just hired today. I left her downstairs changing into her uniform, and she's likely waiting on me now."

"Then do go on. I'll call on the countess."

Elena followed Mary Alice to the hall and took possession of the towels; there they diverged in opposite directions, Mary Alice toward the service stairs and Elena toward the countess's room, situated at the far end of the house, just across from Mrs. Hazelgreaves's. She passed beneath the skylight, already darkened with the coming night.

At the countess's room, she rapped on the door.

"Lady Pavlenco?" she called, but received no answer. Perhaps the countess had left Black House again, this time without anyone noticing.

With a turn of the bronze knob, she entered the countess's room and paused. The draperies had been pulled, and the room was dark as a cave. She allowed her eyes a few moments to adjust. A few coals glowed faintly on the grate, but they had long ago burned to mostly ash.

She heard a sound, a sigh or a brush of fabric, and

a few words mumbled in the countess's voice. Words she didn't understand. Perhaps Selene was feverish? She made her way toward the bed—and tripped over something. A large basket, woven from thick reeds. There were several scattered about, along with their lids.

A low moan came from the direction of the four-postered bed. Suddenly, it occurred to Elena that perhaps she had misinterpreted things, and that the countess might not be alone.

She knew full well the passionate relations that took place between a man and a woman—not first-hand of course, but one could not go uneducated long while working with the boldly speaking female patients of the Whitechapel infirmary.

An image of the countess and Lord Black, naked and entwined on the bed, blazed unbidden into her mind. The depth of pain she experienced just imagining such a thing stunned her.

Now that the image was in her mind, she felt compelled to make it disappear.

"Your ladyship?" Elena called in a clear voice, believing it only fair to announce herself before embarrassing anyone. No one answered.

Elena went to the end of the bed. It took a moment for her eyes to adjust to the even darker shadows formed by the heavy bed curtains, drawn along the sides. Yet when they did, she blinked, not believing what mere vision revealed. Indeed, the countess was not alone.

Something dark *slithered* toward the end of the bed. Toward *her.*

Elena yelped and tossed the towels.

"Who's there?" the countess demanded, her voice blurred by sleep.

"Snakes," Elena gasped, veering backward until her back slammed into the wall beside the mantel. "There are *snakes* in your bed."

"Miss Whitney?" The countess pushed herself up from the hazy darkness, seemingly unconcerned that no less than a score of serpents slid over and about her legs, waist and arms. Other than the snakes, there were only pale gleaming skin and dark hair. The countess did indeed sleep nude.

"What are you doing in my room?" she muttered crossly.

Elena grasped up the iron poker from beside the fire grate.

"I . . . er, assumed that since you had come to my room last night and we had such a lovely conversation, we were on sociable terms."

A serpent wriggled out of Selene's hair and flopped onto her bare shoulder, before falling onto her pillow and coiling away.

"You mean . . . as *friends*?" Selene asked with suspicion.

"Of course. As friends."

The countess gathered up a large, exotic-looking square of cloth from the bed, and after carefully transferring several of her slithering companions to the mattress, wrapped herself toga-style.

She stood and approached Elena through the darkness. "I must seem rather eccentric to you."

"Well, yes. The snakes . . ." Elena laughed nervously, keeping one eye on the bed. The whole scene was so surreal. "Very uncommon."

"I adore them."

"I'm afraid I don't."

A serpent undulated across the floor toward them, barely visible against the carpet. Elena skipped aside, clasping the poker against herself. Obviously the snakes were pets. She didn't think it would go over very well if she were to smite one to bits.

"I didn't always." Selene bent down to scoop up the creature. "Asps used to terrify me, but I learned long ago to embrace that which frightens me most. It's made me stronger." She smiled. "Besides they are a symbol of royalty."

"Oh, yes?"

"Here, touch Xerxes along his back with your finger."

The countess held Xerxes out for her. His narrow little body sagged between her hands. Elena didn't really want to touch him, but neither did she wish to appear the ninny. And curse her impulsivity, if she hadn't gone and gotten that tattoo on her wrist! It made no sense that she would bear the permanent image of a serpent on her skin, yet refuse the challenge to touch one.

Gingerly she ran her fingertip over the smooth obsidian scales. "What a surprise. He's cool and dry. I'd imagined him to be slimy. Is he . . . poisonous?"

"Deadly." Selene smiled, revealing her straight white teeth.

Elena froze.

"Just don't make any sudden movements, or start *screaming* or anything ridiculous like that and you'll be fine." She shrugged. "And if he does bite you, from all that I've been told, it's not such a bad way to go."

Elena swallowed hard. "I feel very reassured."

"Here, let me put him around your neck."

Before Elena could decline, Selene had brought Xerxes around her shoulders. She quickly lifted her hair so he would not become entangled.

"There," announced the countess, sounding pleased.

"He's . . . he's not so bad." Elena stared down, out of the corner of her eye. Xerxes's narrow forked tongue darted out to touch her chin.

"Oh, look, he's given you a kiss. He *likes* you," Selene cooed. A broad smile lit her face. In the next moment, the smile disappeared and her eyes flashed. "Now give him back."

Moments later, Elena escaped into the hallway and pulled the door soundly shut behind her.

She glanced between the pointed tips of her shoes to be sure nothing slithered out from beneath the door. Seeing nothing, she sagged against the wall in relief.

Lord, she had never met anyone as bizarre as the countess! She had finally extricated herself by saying she could not keep Mrs. Hazelgreaves waiting for supper, which was hardly a lie. Her elderly companion grew rather terse when she'd gone too long between afternoon tea and her evening meal. Crossing the carpeted hall, she knocked and waited, but received no answer. An outlandish image flashed through her mind, that of a naked Mrs. Hazelgreaves smiling and writhing languidly on a bed of snakes. Lord, but she wasn't ready for another revelation of that sort! Likely Mrs. Hazelgreaves had already summoned the footmen to carry her down.

Elena hurried down the stairs, imagining she saw snakes everywhere from the corner of her eye, dangling from the chandeliers and encircling the banisters. How would she ever sleep tonight? Should she tell anyone?

Just as she was about to enter the dining room she heard female voices. Mary Alice and a companion housemaid made their way down the hall—a housemaid whose curly red hair peeked out from beneath her white cap, and who limped over a crutch.

"Lizzy!" she exclaimed, astounded and shocked.

Lizzy grinned, lurching forward. "I didn't want to say anythin'. I wasn't sure if you lived 'ere. And, look! You do."

Mary Alice hurried along after her, frowning suspiciously. "The two of you know each other?"

Elena grasped the girl's hand in greeting. Lizzy fairly quivered with excitement.

"What are you doing here, Lizzy?"

"That man who was wi' you this afternoon—his *lordship* I am told—came back to find me after you'd gone. 'E told me the position was mine if I wanted it. Blimey! If I wanted it?" She pressed a hand against her flushed cheek. "Next thing I know 'e put me in a carriage and sent me off. I can't believe me good fortune."

Lizzy was off the streets! Of course, she was only one of thousands who deserved better, but the relief Elena felt was immeasurable. And she couldn't quiet the voice inside her head that shouted in absolute delight that his lordship had brought Lizzy to Black House to please *her*.

She asked the women, "Are you aware, has his lordship returned from the East Side?"

Mary Alice shook her head. "No, miss, not that I've seen or heard."

" 'Is lordship," Lizzy sighed dreamily. "I shall be f'rever indebted to 'im. If only Kate Eddowes could see me now."

Mary Alice glanced over her shoulder. "We'd best be about our business before Mr. Jarvis finds us here rubbing shoulders with Miss Whitney." She eyed Lizzy with queenly hauteur. "It's not allowed, you know."

Lizzy's head bobbed. "Right."

"I'm very happy for you, Lizzy."

"Thank y', Nurse Whitney."

As they moved past, Mary Alice leaned in and muttered, "She's a bit street-rough. We'll have to work on her speech and manners."

"Thank you for welcoming Lizzy to the staff, Mary Alice. I'll just go in now and see if Mrs. Hazelgreaves has come down for supper."

Mary Alice shook her head. "I forgot to tell you, she won't be. She's a bit beneath the weather."

Elena remembered how they'd parted that morning in Lord Black's study. She had rather shocked her elderly companion with her announcement about medical school. "Are you certain she's not . . ."

"Not what, miss?"

Elena winced. "Avoiding me. I may have upset her earlier today."

"Why, just this afternoon she told me what a delight you are. And she couldn't stop going on about his lordship being the perfect gentleman. She had only pleasant things to say." She cocked her head. "Rather unlike herself, now that I think back on it."

"Perhaps I should go up to check on her."

"I've already put her to bed with one of her tonics. I'm certain she'd welcome a visit in the morning."

"All right," Elena reluctantly agreed. Of late she'd heard far too much mention of Mrs. Hazelgreaves's "tonics." She'd address the situation with Dr. Harcourt when she returned to the hospital tomorrow morning. "I suppose I'll take my meal in my room, then, and catch up on my reading."

"Very well. Miss Harper and I will inform the kitchen. Oh, and were you able to speak with the countess?"

"Yes." *Snakes!* "Ah—I gave her the towels, and as

for the rest, such as the bed linens, I would leave them outside her door, and allow her to replace them at her leisure."

Elena returned to the stairs, and grasped up her skirt to ascend, feeling as if she could float right up. She had just received the most wonderful and unexpected gift, and she was so excited, she'd *almost* forgotten about the countess and her snakes.

She recalled Lord Black's expression that afternoon as her hansom had rolled away. He had appeared so stern, so guarded.

To think that in the next moment he had pressed back into the crowd to find Lizzy.

How could she ever thank him?

Hours later, Leeson pulled the weighty draperies along their brass rail, blocking out the fathomless night sky.

"My lord, I've left your daily correspondence on your dressing table."

He crossed the room, and with a few jabs of the poker quickly roused the fire.

Archer emerged from his dressing closet, tying a pair of flannel trousers at his waist. "Anything interesting?"

"Not that I recall. Just the last of the ledger statements. And scads of calling cards and letters of introduction from people who wish to make your acquaintance. Mr. Jasper asked if you will be at home to accept callers one afternoon soon."

Archer frowned. What an awful idea. If not for Elena, no one but his barristers and bankers would even know he was in residence.

"I suppose we must do that eventually." Archer needed to visit with Mrs. Hazelgreaves. Many of the world's rarest jewels were displayed in private and highly exclusive venues. Perhaps Elena, and he, for that matter, could indeed be spared the discomfort of a large formal event, and they could entertain potential suitors on a smaller scale.

Lord Black's secretary circled the room, retrieving whatever articles of clothing his immortal employer had strewn off as he'd passed through on his way to the bath. "Will you return to the city tonight?"

"Yes." Archer sifted through the stack. "Before midnight."

His gaze snagged upon something.

"Leeson, do you remember this one?" He lifted an envelope.

As a matter of course, Leeson opened all his correspondence—everything but those missives that bore the triangular seal of the Primordials. This envelope, smaller than those in the remainder of the pile, had gone unopened.

Leeson's eye squinted. "No sir. Odd, that one must have got by me."

Archer stared at his name, written in a heavy, dark script above Black House's address, yet there were no other markings. Something jabbed at his memory— something vicious and ugly. Taking up his letter opener from the desk, Archer slit the envelope along its upper crease.

Jack's vile scent spilled out like a plague. With a curse, Archer reflexively crushed the envelope in his hand.

"What is it, your lordship?" Leeson considered him with concern from the far side of the room, over the pile of garments in his arms.

Archer wanted to shout. To curse. But alone. In a hushed tone, he answered, "It is nothing. You may go."

"Very good, sir. I'll just take these downstairs,

then, for the laundress to tend to. Are you hungry? Would you like something sent up from the kitchen?"

"Not tonight."

Archer waited until his secretary pulled the door closed before spreading the envelope flat on the wooden surface of his desk.

He had received a letter from his bloody target.

Jack the Ripper had Transcended. But this was unparalleled. He had never received a direct communication from any of the souls he hunted, even those who crossed over into that dangerous, supernatural state. The rules of the game had changed and become infinitely more dangerous. But when did it happen? How strong had Jack become?

With a growl he opened the letter.

> *Black.*
>
> *Welcome to London. Did you enjoy the two lovely presents I left for you?*
>
> *Your ward is a lovely girl. I have heard she prepares for an occupation in medicine? I could teach her a thing or two about human anatomy, as I have recently become an expert on the subject . . . haha! Perhaps I shall call upon her and offer a lesson when I return from my brief journey?*
>
> *Until then.*

Elena started up from the pillows, breaking free of the unsettling dream. She'd been running along a dark, fog-laden street. She had been frightened. Terrified. Suddenly, all the lampposts had transformed from metal and glass into black trees with blazing limbs. Someone had been pursuing her—someone whose heavy footsteps matched the rapid beat of her heart.

Thankfully something had awakened her. The close of a door? Voices?

From her place on the window seat she peered toward the mantel clock. Eleven o'clock. She lowered the text she'd been reading from where it lay on her lap, to the cushion beside her and went to her door.

Opening it, she caught a glimpse of Mr. Leeson, his arms piled with clothing, going in the direction of the servants' staircase. Just down the hall from her room, light gleamed from beneath the door of his lordship's private apartment.

She exhaled, a bit nervous now.

She'd purposefully tried to stay awake until his lordship returned. She had to thank him for giving Lizzy the housemaid position. She might not have the opportunity to speak with him in the morning before departing for her shift at the hospital.

She ensured that the buttons on her dressing gown were all properly fastened, and ran her fingers lightly through her hair.

A moment later, she knocked on his door.

"Come in," he shouted tersely.

She froze, having fully anticipated he would come to the door, where she could briefly offer her thanks and make a quick retreat to her room.

In the next second, the door flew inward. "Leeson—"

Elena stepped back.

His lordship towered above her, his broad shoulders preventing any view of the room beyond. He wore no shirt—only a pair of loosely tied trousers, low across his sculpted hips. Obviously he had just bathed. His hair was damp, and she could smell the soap on his skin.

"No, not Leeson," she answered breathlessly. "It's only me."

"Hello . . . only you." He didn't appear very pleased to see her. His gaze was intense, and the set of his jaw rigid.

"I—I wished to speak with you about something."

"Good. I wish to speak with you as well."

Before she could respond, he turned from her. Dry of mouth, she watched him go, taking in the sight of his well-turned shoulders and his corded back. His hair clung to his skin, a rich, damp curtain. Had she ever seen anything so beautiful? She'd seen statues and artwork, but Lord Black was vibrant and alive, and his leonine grace profoundly distracting.

She followed, but only so far as to stand beneath the threshold of the door. "I know it's late, and I don't wish to intrude. But I had to thank you."

Standing at his shaving table, he glanced over his shoulder. "For bringing your girl, Lizzy, to Black House."

"Yes."

Firelight illuminated his chamber. Massive black furniture, elegantly done in pale Asian silks, dominated the room. She couldn't bring herself to look directly at the bed. Instead she sought out his reflection in the gilt-edged mirror.

His eyes flashed darkly. "If you knew me better, you wouldn't thank me."

Her smile faded. "Don't ruin the wonderful thing you did with words."

He dragged a loose linen shirt—very un-English in style—onto his shoulders, but didn't bother to fasten the buttons. "I want you to do something for me now."

Elena steeled herself. Certainly he would remind her she must find a husband as soon as possible. He rummaged in a drawer, eventually producing a comb and a glinting pair of silver scissors with long, pointed blades.

"Would you cut my hair? I could wait for Leeson to do the honors, but since you're already here . . ."

Elena exhaled in relief that the expected words had not come from his lips. Until his request sank in.

"Cut your hair?" she frowned, horrified. "Why would you ask me to do that?"

"Because I wish it."

"But you're hair is—"

Remarkable.

Divine.

"What?" he demanded impatiently.

"I just don't want you to cut it."

"It will grow back. It always does." They stared at each other until he spoke again. "I take your lack of response as a refusal."

His eyes were hard, yes, and his manners lacking, but something simmered beneath his surface, something intense and bordering along desperate, that convinced her she must stay.

"You're wrong," she answered softly.

The briefest flash of surprise showed in his eyes.

"Come inside, then." The ferocity of his expression eased, but only by a fraction. "I won't bite."

Wrong again, Elena countered silently. She was already soundly bitten.

He disappeared into the shadows of his dressing closet and brought out a stool. Sitting, he hooked one bare heel against a rung, then offered her the scissors and comb.

"I suppose cutting your hair is the least I can do in exchange for your sparing Lizzy a life on the streets." She took possession of the tools. "Let's hope I don't make you look like a fool. I'm not sure if I've ever cut anyone's hair before."

"It's just hair." He straightened his shoulders and waited. "Go on, Delilah. Cut."

The memory struck her like a blow, and the room spun. She swayed and felt his hands at her waist—felt him pull her close.

Chapter Ten

"I used to cut my father's hair," Elena whispered. She kept her eyes clasped shut, afraid the beautiful, long-awaited memory would vanish as quickly as it had come. "On a chair beside the window, where the morning light was its brightest."

In her mind's eye she saw her father, and he smiled at her with the intense power of love in his gaze. She smiled too. Tears gathered against her lashes.

"Are you all right?" Archer asked, his hands moving to her back. His hands were large, and capable, and she liked the way they held her.

"I'm afraid to open my eyes."

"Then don't. Not yet, if you don't want to," he said softly, his lips against her cheek.

Elena returned to awareness—and realized she all but embraced him. She'd dropped her arms about his shoulders, and her breasts were firmly pressed against his solid, mostly bare chest. The heat of his skin burned through the fabric of her dressing gown.

Her eyes flew open. "I'm so sorry."

She drew her arms in, carefully turning the scissors so as not to—

Blood stained his sleeve, just above his elbow.

"Oh, my God. I've cut you."

Dropping the scissors and comb to a nearby tray, she grasped his shoulder. His muscles rippled beneath the linen as he again caught her at the waist, bringing her back to look into his eyes.

"No, you haven't."

"There is *blood*," she insisted, mortified. "I must examine you. You might need stitches."

"For God's sake." He tore his shirt open and dragged it down over his shoulder to reveal his upper arm. He grasped her hand and forced it against the unmarred skin.

"Oh." She snatched her hand away, feeling scalded. Wonderfully, deliciously scalded.

Lord Black's lips went hard. In silence, he yanked the shirt to his shoulders. His fingers went to the buttons.

Until Elena pressed a halting hand over his.

Archer's gaze veered up to find sensual hunger burning in Elena's dual-colored eyes.

Desire flared within him as well, sparked moments before by the press of her lush body against his. Hell, if he was honest, he'd wanted her from the moment he'd opened the door.

What had he been thinking, inviting her into his room? Obviously he had judged himself to be so consumed by Jack's letter that he would not be tempted.

Instead, like the ancient warrior he was, on the eve of a great battle, he felt the overwhelming urge to make love. And no one but Elena, with her expressive eyes and soft, beautiful mouth, would do.

"Good news!" she blurted suddenly and brightly.

"Good . . . news?" he growled, feeling as if he'd been forced to seize the reins of twenty out-of-control horses.

"If this new memory serves me well, I am a very proficient barber." She reclaimed the scissors and comb. "Are you certain you won't change your mind?"

Darling girl, she thought this was about cutting his hair. She didn't realize how close she stood to the edge of a dangerous precipice. Didn't realize he wanted to grasp her by the shoulders, press her to the carpet and tear her respectable, sprigged-muslin dressing gown off her body and indulge in every imaginable sensual pleasure. If she did realize, she feigned her innocence well.

"Proceed."

"How short?" she asked blithely.

He waved a finger near his ear. "Here."

She frowned and pressed her fingertip lower, against the skin of his neck, setting him afire all over again. "Why not here?"

"Here," he specified tersely, at a level even with his jaw.

She snipped. The first strands fell to the floor in a heavy whisper. He sat rigid, steeling himself against every touch. Eventually, after a torturous eternity, she made the last cut. Her breast brushed his shoulder. He hissed.

She froze. "Did I cut you again?"

"Not with the scissors."

Tellingly, she did not ask what he meant.

Better to say what he had to say and send her back to her room. "Miss Whitney."

"Yes?"

"As I said before, I must ask something of you."

"And to think I believed once I cut your hair, my debt would be settled." Solemnly, she clasped the scissors between her hands. "What is it that you want?"

"I would request that you delay your return to the

hospital. In fact, I have already sent a note to that Dr. Harcourt—"

Her expression transformed from tense expectation to one of furious disbelief, as if with those few words he had betrayed her unforgivably.

"You *can't be serious*. You would use Lizzy against me in a way such as this? After this afternoon I thought—I thought—oh, bother with what I thought."

She slammed the scissors against the table and whirled toward the door.

"Elena!" he thundered.

"Leave me alone," she gasped, thrusting a hand behind, as if that, alone, could ward him away.

Just as she gripped the doorknob he caught her and spun her around to face him. He grasped her face, trying to make her look at him, but she backed away, pressing herself against the wall as if she wished to disappear into the wood. Tears glistened against her lower lashes, threatening to spill, but still, her eyes flashed in defiance.

"You're going to take it all away from me, aren't you? Just because you can."

"No. I'm not, I swear it. Just a few days, Elena. Until this killer has been captured. You've read the newspapers. There are a number of suspects. It's only a matter of time."

Her lower lip trembled, until she bit it.

"I want you to be safe." Archer stared at her mouth, entranced. He brushed his thumb along the flushed slope of her cheek. She exhaled and shuddered. Ever so slightly, she turned her face to accept his caress. A thousand warnings tolled through his mind but fell silent beneath the roar of his desire.

Everything happened too quickly for him to stop. One moment they stared at each other, and the next, he pressed his mouth against hers. They became a tangle of arms and clothing. She seized him closer, moaning softly into his mouth. He had never tasted anything so innocent, or so sensual. He held her, melded to her, so fiercely her back hissed up the paneled wall. The toes of her slippers jutted against his trousers. God, the press of her hands on his shoulders, and her uncorseted breasts against his chest—not to mention her sweetly open mouth—sent his mind into a spiral.

Just as suddenly, realization of what he had just done tore through him in an icy tide of shame.

Slowly, regretfully, he turned his face from hers, pressing his cheek against hers, and carefully lowered her to the floor. She sagged, alluringly dazed, against the wall, her lips pink and swollen, and her hair a pale, tousled mass.

"You've got to go," he uttered low.

She met his gaze unwaveringly, and whispered, "What if I don't want to?"

He wrenched open the door, grasped her by the elbow and pushed her through.

"Lord Black—"

He shut the door in her face.

Impulsively, Elena reached for the knob, only to hear the metallic turn of the lock.

"Go," he commanded through the thick wood, his voice hoarse, and sounding so tortured her heart ached. "And lock your door against me."

Elena did as he commanded. She escaped to her room, her cheeks burning and her heart overflowing with too many emotions to name. God forgive her, she wanted to stay, to discover the full measure of his desire, and hers, regardless of good sense or consequence. She yearned to know him, emotionally and physically, to discover the tragedy hidden within his dark eyes.

She stared at the doorknob—and at the key that lay beside a small lamp on the nearby table. She backed away from the door until the skirt of her dressing gown met the edge of the bed.

A short time later she heard the sound of his door open and close. She went to hers to listen, her heart beating like a drum, but the echo of his footsteps quickly faded.

Within moments, there arose the clatter of a carriage coming round from the mews.

"You've cut your hair," Leeson observed with a scowl of realization. "You only do that when—"

"Look at this."

The two immortals stood in his lordship's study. Archer handed him the letter. Leeson opened the folded page and, by the light of the fire, scanned the contents.

"Bloody hell," he exclaimed, looking up. "This has never happened before."

Archer offered no response. What could he say?

"How did the letter get inside the house? Even if it came through with the morning post, I should have sensed something. God, it reeks like a dead horse."

"He's learned to cloak himself, at least in some ways."

"Even so!"

"Perhaps he is something worse than Transcended."

"Worse?" Leeson's eye widened with alarm. "What do you mean worse? What is worse than a Transcended soul?"

"I don't know," Archer mused darkly. "Not yet. But I'm going to find out. I want you to be vigilant with Black House and protect its perimeter. Watch the servants. It may be he's seduced someone into doing his work."

"Damn, bloody soul."

Archer pulled his coat over his shoulders. "Stay close to Miss Whitney at all times, do you understand?"

"Yes, sir."

"The killer may try to hurt her—" Archer clenched his eyes shut, for "hurt" didn't begin to describe what the Ripper did to women. The image of the dead prostitutes kept surging into his mind, but with Elena's face transposed upon them. "He might try to hurt her to get to me. Don't let that happen."

"I won't." Mustache twitching, Leeson flicked aside the angled lapels of his jacket to reveal twin daggers, artfully secured against his brocade vest. The daggers' blades, forged of Amaranthine silver, gleamed with a surreal light. Soul slayers. "I might not be a Guard, but I can be a damn nasty secretary when need be."

Archer nodded and headed toward the door. His instincts told him to stay with Elena, to go into shadow and guard her through the night. But his eternal purpose was not to protect a mortal woman— a young woman whose earthly existence would end in a blink of eternity—but to maintain the balance of the world's mortal population, so as to protect the endangered realm of the Amaranthines.

Leeson called after him, "What of the Ripper's claim that he has left the city?"

Archer paused. "Today, while in the East End, with my powers returned to their full strength, I found not the faintest trace of him. There were faded strands, days old, which I will investigate tonight. He may have gone underground, into the subterranean tunnels beneath the city. Or he may have gone to Paris, or even New York. Another city of London's size and complexity. He would prefer them. Advise

Charon to be ready, for we may depart at a moment's notice."

There were no working streetlamps on Thrawl Street, Spitalfields's most notoriously dangerous avenue. Archer moved along the refuse-cluttered sidewalk.

"Matches for sale," a little girl rasped as Archer moved past.

A solitary soul, she leaned against a brick wall in a too-large dress. A tray of matches hung from a strap around her neck. Thinking of Elena, Archer dropped a few coins amongst the small rectangular boxes, and continued on.

Normally there would still be people out and about, gossiping on stoops, fighting and bartering, but tonight those who could afford shelter had taken it. The rest had migrated on foot to the parks and public areas of West London, hoping to escape the next murderous slash of the Ripper's blade.

Not Archer. Fury made him ruthless. With the delivery of the letter to Black House, he could not help but feel as if the Ripper had invaded his very sanctuary, left the doors swinging open in the wind and gleefully splashed the blood of his victims across the walls . . . and Elena.

Archer had destruction on his mind. He craved a reason to turn, to feel the raging burn beneath his skin.

Midway down the street, he halted outside a building—one in an endless row of rat-infested lodging houses owned by rich men who lived on finer streets, and who left the day-to-day unpleasantness of their business to ruthless house deputies. Most were five stories high with windows over the street. Weak penny-candle light glowed from within a few, but most were dark. Foul-smelling refuse clotted the alleyways and gutters.

He peered up, and removed his top hat. Just above, an indolent wind coaxed dingy canvas curtains out of an open window. In the next moment, he rapped his gloved knuckles on a ramshackle, street-level door that appeared to have been kicked in on numerous previous occasions.

Muttered curses sounded from within. A pallid young man with hollow eyes answered. He wore only an undershirt and sagging trousers.

"Yer too late. We're full up." The house deputy gave a wicked, empty laugh, revealing tobacco-stained teeth. "My gain, nobody wants to get ripped on the streets tonight."

Archer halted the door's closure with his hand.

The man snarled, "Say! I just told you—"

He looked into Archer's eyes. Instantly, all the challenge abandoned him, and he paled a shade lighter.

"I don't need a room," Archer said. "But I'd like to look at one. In particular, the one on the third floor, just above us."

The man's Adam's apple bobbed erratically. "Sorry. No. That room's rented."

"Then I'd like to speak with the tenant."

The deputy snapped anxiously, "I said rented, bloke, not occupied. 'E's not 'ere, but he keeps the room regular."

"What is his name?"

"Can't see why I should tell you." His gaze moved over Archer, assessing. "You ain't Scotland Yard— yer coat's too fine. Wot you doin' in this part of the city at this time o' night? You need a girl 'at bad? I can get y' a girl if 'ats what you want."

"*His name.*" Archer tossed a coin.

The man snatched the crown, midarc.

He breathed erratically and glanced over his shoulder, into the darkness of the room behind him. His eyes gleamed with conflicting sparks of fear and avarice. Avarice clearly won out.

In a hushed tone he said, "I don't know 'is name, and I've only seen 'im once. 'E pays twice the normal rate through the pay-box in the wall, and 'e comes and goes as 'e pleases."

"I'll have a look inside."

"F'get it." His informant shook his head vehemently. " 'E's me best tenant. Pays on time, an' don't make no trouble."

Archer could, of course, transform into shadow and simply ascend the wall, but sometimes mortals— especially frightened ones—provided the most excellent information. This mortal seemed terrified on two fronts.

Archer tossed a second coin. Again, the grimy hand snapped.

"This way, then. Hurry now."

Archer ducked beneath the threshold and, after securing the door, followed the house deputy into the black oblivion of a narrow, creaking staircase. An old man slept on a pallet at the first-floor landing, a rat perched at his feet. They stepped over him to continue up the next flight of stairs.

On the third floor the deputy announced, " 'Ere we are."

He pulled a ring of keys from his belt loop, and with a metallic rattle, thrust one into the dented knob. As the door creaked inward, Archer clamped a hand upon the deputy's shoulder, and held him in place as he moved past.

"I won't be long."

"Now see 'ere—!"

Archer shut the door—but not before coaxing an image from the man's memory. It wasn't hard to do, as the memory of the unnamed tenant hovered in the forefront of his mind. Again, as Archer had seen in the prostitute Kate's memory, all he saw were eyes. Cold, blank eyes.

Hands wrenched and turned at the knob, but the lock Archer mentally put in place defied any key or violence. Standing in darkness, he surveyed the narrow room. A cool, damp wind gusted through an open window, carrying the fetid stench of the street. All around him stood teetering stacks of newspapers, some almost as high as his shoulders. He touched the nearest ones, and found them damp through and through, as if the windows had been left open for days, through the recent rains.

A shoddy desk occupied the space beneath the window. Its surface gleamed with moisture, as did the slightly buckled wood floor. A narrow bed spanned the adjacent wall, its wool blanket tucked neatly in place.

Wretched sobs penetrated from the floor above, and in the room next door a man cursed with rage. There was so much misery here—thin walls, misery and madness. Never before had he experienced such an intense concentration of human deterioration.

This was why the Ripper had disappeared so effectively last night after the murders of Liz Stride and Kate Kelly. Most assuredly the Ripper had chosen this place because he fed off such suffering, and in doing so, he had found a near-perfect hiding place from the Shadow Guards who hunted him—at least in the first hours, while Archer's powers grew attuned to his target's elusive trace and the emotional tangle of the city.

Here, the Ripper's trace would have been soundly

buffered by rows upon rows, and floors upon floors of tenants, and the complex emotional turmoil they exuded.

He went to the desk. Atop it was a pair of rusted scissors, devoid of residue. If they had been used by Jack, he had worn gloves. Archer pulled the handle of the solitary drawer, but the wood had swollen tight against its frame. He easily wrenched it open and found the space packed tight with newspaper. More precisely, newspaper headlines, each carefully cut.

He lifted a few. They dealt with the murders of Mary Ann "Polly" Nichols and Annie Chapman. The investigations. Suspects. False arrests. He sifted deeper, and paused.

There were headlines about natural disasters: China's Yellow River Flood in 1887; North America's Great White Hurricane in March. There were also headlines about other crimes, solved and unsolved, all over the world—names and locales familiar to Archer. No, he hadn't hunted each of the souls himself, but other Shadow Guards had.

He uttered an oath.

He reached the bottom, only to find what seemed like a thousand bits of snipped newspaper, headlines cut down to the individual letter. They covered and almost concealed a leather-bound journal. Here again, there was dampness, as if rainwater from the open windows had trickled in to gather at the bottom.

He brushed away the sodden fragments as best he could, and laid the journal on the desk. The pages were warped and swollen, and the green, leather cover bleeding and stained. Opening the book along the center, Archer pried apart two random pages.

There were words, mostly illegible because of the

damp, and a few cartoonish drawings. He squinted, trying to make them out.

Separating another pair of pages, his immortal blood went cold.

There, he saw a drawing of a man and beside it, the words "Alexander" and "shadow." On another page was drawn what appeared to be a—

Volcano.

Ancient memories hurtled out of the dark vault of his mind. Unease rippled beneath his skin. He closed the journal and slipped it into his coat pocket. He shoved the drawer closed, and stared out over the dark street, trying to make sense of everything he'd seen.

A sudden gust swept through the room. Something rustled behind him. He felt as if a jagged fingernail had been dragged down his spine. He turned.

On the wall above the door, in large black letters formed of hundreds and hundreds of newspaper fragments, was the word:

TANTALUS

Elena awoke uncomfortably early Monday morning. She lay in bed for a long while, staring at her nurse's uniform, carefully cleaned, pressed and hanging on the brass rung where she'd placed it the night before.

Before her visit to Lord Black's chamber.

She rolled her face into her pillow and groaned.

She spent the next hour on her window seat, fully dressed and staring at the pages of *Gray's Anatomy* before she admitted to herself she hadn't read a single word. One image kept replaying itself in her mind— that of Lord Black's stricken expression as he pushed her into the hall and shut the door in her face.

But it was childish to sit here, hiding in her room. She was a grown woman, and she had done nothing wrong in responding to the passion of a man whom she found soul-searingly attractive—even if he was her guardian. She didn't expect anything from him. She didn't want marriage or promises.

Usually by now her door would have received its morning knock from Mary Alice telling her Mrs. Hazelgreaves had gone down for breakfast. This morning there had been no such knock, but then again no one had been privy to the discussion between her and his lordship the night before in which he'd insisted she avoid Whitechapel and the London Hospital for the next few days.

Putting her book away, she left her room.

"Miss Whitney!"

Elena gasped, startled. Mr. Leeson hurried toward her out of the shadows. Had he been sitting in the chair at the far end of the hallway?

"Good morning, dear," he said graciously. "Going down for breakfast? I'll escort you there."

"Thank you, Mr. Leeson." She hadn't gotten to know Mr. Leeson since his arrival with Lord Black. His eye patch and swirling mustache gave him a rather flamboyant appearance, but he seemed to be a very pleasant sort.

At the central staircase, Mary Alice and Lizzy polished the banister.

"Good morning, ladies, Can you tell me whether Mrs. Hazelgreaves has gone down to breakfast?"

Mary Alice paused, rag in hand. "I checked on her earlier, miss, and while there doesn't seem to be anything wrong with her that I can see, she didn't want my help with dressing. She told me she still doesn't feel up to her normal snuff."

Elena placed a halting hand on Mr. Leeson's sleeve.

"Mr. Leeson, I'll be down in a moment. I'd like to visit Mrs. Hazelgreaves."

"Very well." He smiled, his one eye crinkling at the corner.

Elena went on toward Mrs. Hazelgreaves's room, and thankfully, saw no snakes slithering along the edges of the hallway. She prayed Xerxes and his companions were each coiled up happy and tight in their little baskets inside the countess's apartments.

She knocked and heard a faint reply from within. Mrs. Hazelgreaves reclined on a rose-hued sofa, her slippered feet on a striped pink and white pillow.

"Good morning, Mrs. Hazelgreaves. Mary Alice tells me you are not feeling well. I could not help but notice you did not come down for supper last night, or breakfast this morning."

Mrs. Hazelgreaves smiled blandly. "I'm fine, dear. I'm fine."

Mrs. Hazelgreaves didn't look fine. While she wore an elegant dressing robe, its buttons had been fastened all out of order. Her always-perfect hair was decidedly askew. Gray curls sprang out in all directions. One in particular bobbed over her left eye. She tried to peer around the curl, but with each turn of her head, the coil interfered, blocking her view.

"I do believe, however, that I shall need spectacles," she groused. "To think, after all these years of managing without."

"How many tonics have you had today?" Elena had never been sure what the tonics contained, but the lady's behavior had her suspicious.

The older woman's shoulders drew in sharply, and she scowled defensively. "No more than my usual."

"Are you certain?" Elena searched the tabletops and dared even to pull up the long bed skirt, but found no flasks or bottles hidden anywhere.

Mrs. Hazelgreaves didn't look offended by Elena rummaging about. Instead, she softened like melted butter. "Really, I'm just tired."

She rolled on the chaise, away from Elena, to look out the window.

A little bird perched on the outer sill, peering in.

She yawned delicately and touched her fingertips against her mouth. "Could you come back tomorrow dear? I'm certain I'll feel more like talking then."

"Wouldn't you like to come down for breakfast? Perhaps just some toasted bread and cocoa?"

Mrs. Hazelgreaves grimaced. "That sounds absolutely horrid." She turned her face away, into the palm of her hand. "I suppose I'm just not hungry."

She wondered if Lord Black had anything to do with Mrs. Hazelgreaves's sudden malaise. "Have you spoken to his lordship since yesterday?"

"Ah, his lordship," Mrs. Hazelgreaves sighed, rolling again to her other side to face Elena. She attempted to smile around the dastardly curl. "Delightful man. So handsome. So rich. Might you consider a match with him?"

Elena blinked. "Pardon me, what did you say?"

"Lord Black. He'd make someone a divine husband. Why not you?"

Elena remembered the door slamming in her face. She could practically hear its echo in her mind. "I don't get the feeling his lordship is looking for a wife."

"Nonsense," chuckled Mrs. Hazelgreaves. "The most difficult catches are the most satisfying."

Elena sat with Mrs. Hazelgreaves a while longer. While her companion did not appear to be in any real mental or physical distress, she would send Harcourt a note asking him to make a call. She needed to speak with the doctor anyway to assure him of her plans to return to her work at the hospital as soon as possible.

When the lady started to doze, Elena tucked a blanket around her and slipped out the door.

"Miss Whitney!"

Elena jumped. Mr. Leeson swept toward her from the end of the hall.

He said, "I got a bit distracted myself. Come now, dear." He took her hand and placed it on his arm. "Let's go down for breakfast."

•

Chapter Eleven

Buttoning the front of his frock coat, Archer hurried down the front steps of Black House. His visit had been limited to a quick meal, a bath and a change of clothes. He had not so much as taken the time to review correspondence, business or otherwise, as Leeson had assured him there had been no more letters from the Ripper.

Ducking beneath the black canvas calash top of the Victoria, Archer seated himself on the leather bench. He had spent the past four days in the city, observing the police investigation, and evaluating the spate of letters received by various entities throughout the city, all claiming to be from the Ripper, though few proved to be authentic. When not at Scotland Yard, Archer had immersed himself into the many subterranean tunnels beneath the streets and the Thames, searching for any trace of his elusive soul. He had found exactly that. The Ripper's trace—a faded trace that led everywhere, and nowhere.

Everything—from the killer's ability to move beneath Archer's awareness, and his continual taunts to the police—pointed to the likelihood this soul was not merely Transcended, but Transcended to some extreme level never before experienced by the Shadow Guard.

Tantalus.

Everything he'd discovered in the Thrawl Street boarding room put a different slant upon things. Perhaps the Ripper's advanced level of Transcension was not due to any fault on anyone's part, including his or Mark's. Perhaps the Ripper really was unique.

God curse him, but his blood quickened at this new and unparalleled challenge. For one who had existed from the earliest of times, new didn't come around often enough. As a result, the dark thrill of danger had become something he craved, but rarely ever experienced. If it weren't for the Ripper's drawing Elena into the game, he'd actually be able to enjoy it.

Out of the corner of his eye, someone raced down the stairs: Elena, fully dressed with a hat and bag for an outing. His stomach muscles tightened. He had not seen her since that night in his apartments, and with only a glance, he was reminded of everything that made her irresistible to him.

"Wait," she shouted to the footman, who had approached to close the door.

She scampered up, a brief *ping* ringing out with each strike of her shoes against the metal stairs. She swept her skirts inside, gracefully tucking them about her legs, and seated herself beside him.

Leeson raced out of the manse, appearing traumatized. Being that Archer had chosen to take the Victoria today, there was no space left for another passenger.

"What are you doing?" he asked coolly.

"I'm going with you." Her black bonnet, richly trimmed with pleats upon pleats of shining ribbon, artfully concealed everything about her face except her unsmiling lips.

"You don't even know where I'm going."

Spying Elena in the carriage, Leeson's arms fell to his sides. He appeared infinitely relieved.

"I'm afraid I forced it out of your man, Leeson, there. The British Museum. Wonderful! I've never been." Her words, spoken in her rich, low voice, carried a mildly sardonic edge.

Her beautiful orange-blossom scent filled the air around him, making him want to press his lips against the small, bare space of skin above her high collar. Her skirts were pressed tight against the length of his leg, and he could not help but imagine everything beneath. He really needed to get her out of the carriage, and out of his reach.

He managed to hold his distancing tone. "I'm going to the museum on business, not for pleasure."

She crisscrossed her hands over her bag. "I don't expect you to escort me through the exhibits. You may go your way, and I'll go mine. I'm simply grateful for the ride."

The carriage sagged slightly as the driver took to his perch.

"And grateful," she muttered, "to get away from my dear shadow, Mr. Leeson, if only for a few hours. Is it my imagination, or has he been appointed my new companion until Mrs. Hazelgreaves returns to good health?"

Rather than provide an answer, Archer raised his gloved hand and waved Leeson off.

"How is our dear Mrs. Hazelgreaves?"

"Dr. Harcourt visited on Wednesday and diagnosed her with melancholy."

"Melancholy?" he repeated doubtfully.

"She's just . . . melancholy. He believes she'll come

out of it in a few days' time. We've got a nurse to sit with her. If she doesn't improve, he intends to telegraph her son."

With a tap of the driver's long cane-whip, the two black horses in silver harnesses jerked the Victoria into motion.

They sat in rigid silence until the vehicle slowed in the congested, midmorning traffic. He sensed her agitation growing with each passing moment. She shifted in her seat, and one of her gloved hands fidgeted with the lacquered bamboo handle of her bag.

"I won't have you avoiding me," she announced suddenly.

"Why would I be avoiding you?" He had known they must have this talk, and he supposed he was glad to get it underway.

"You know why."

She spoke quietly, even though the clatter and tumult of vehicles around them ensured not even the driver would overhear a syllable of their conversation. Still, she refused to lift her chin. He grew weary of speaking to her bonnet.

"You are referring, I believe, to all that kissing between us the other night in my chamber."

Ah, that did get him a full, head-on view of her face.

"Yes," she said, sounding slightly strangled.

Her cheeks burned as red as roses, and despite the four days exile from her, he wanted nothing more than to seize her in his arms and resume where they had left off. Here, on the carriage bench, in the midst of London traffic.

"For your information, I haven't been avoiding you. My interests have required the entirety of my attention in the city. It was more convenient for me to lodge there."

"Oh, yes?" Again, the sardonic edge. "For four days? Did you sleep on your banker's couch?"

"No, I didn't."

He hadn't slept at all. Fortunately, he needed very little rest in comparison to mortals. In his mind, beds were more for sex than for sleeping.

A silent half hour later, their carriage clattered off Great Russell Street, drawing in front of the Grecian-columned façade of the museum. After assisting Elena down from the carriage, Archer pulled her reluctant hand inside the V of his elbow.

"You say you've never visited the museum?" They walked beneath the colonnade.

"The grounds were too extensive for Mrs. Hazelgreaves to walk, so we always went to smaller exhibits."

They entered through the grand doors. Off to the side was a large desk serviced by library employees.

"What would you like to see first?"

"Really, your lordship." She pulled free of him, her expression bland. "I shall do very well on my own. I've my watch here, in my bag. Just tell me when, and I'll meet you here."

Elena was as transparent as a pane of glass. He had hurt her, kissing her, then forcing her from his room. He couldn't do anything to repair that hurt. To do so would mean drawing her closer, only to hurt her all over again. Still, he could be her guardian and do the proper things a guardian would do. He was disciplined enough for that. Wasn't he?

"Would you like to see the Reading Room?" he asked.

Her chin lifted an inch higher. "I have heard much about it."

"Come along, then."

"Don't we need a ticket?" She gestured toward the

desk, specifically at the short queue of people beneath a sign designated READING ROOM. She hurried
over and purchased a copy of the guide. Returning,
she thumbed through the opening pages. "I remember reading somewhere that one must first apply to
the principal librarian."

"Not if you are with me."

That was all it took—a crooked, clearly forced grin
on his part and Elena's resolve shattered. She had
not thought it possible, but he was handsomer with
his shorter hair, with nothing to distract from his
stark male features.

She took his offered arm, and they left the crowded
entrance hall and passed into what, according to her
guide map was the Room of Inscriptions. There on
display were several busts, and an impressive pilas-
ter of the Temple of Athene. Against the opposite
wall were a number of narrow columnar stone tablets
bearing Greek and Roman inscriptions.

"This way." Archer rested his hand against the
small of her back as he led her toward a pair of large
glass doors. A dour-faced young man wearing a
tunic and the badge of a library employee stood beside them.

"Sir, do you have a ticket?" he inquired wearily,
as if he had been standing in the same spot, asking
the same question for days on end.

Lord Black discreetly identified himself.

The young man's expression transformed into one
Elena could only interpret as awe. The youth practically tripped over his feet in an attempt to hold the
door for them. Archer escorted her through, into a
narrow corridor, at the end of which, Elena gasped
in surprise and admiration.

Towering rectangular cases circled the expansive

room, each filled to the top with texts. Above those was a row of soaring arched windows—but it was the ivory and gilt dome, spread above them at a height of at least a hundred feet, that stole her breath. At its center gleamed a spectacular medallion of faceted glass.

"It's more beautiful than I imagined," she marveled, slowly turning in a complete circle to admire everything.

"Lord Black," a man's voice called from the direction of the research tables. Archer took hold of Elena's elbow and came to stand very close beside her, almost as if he thought he must protect her. A well-dressed gentleman with a mustache rushed toward them, spectacles perched high on his forehead.

"Your lordship, what a delight to see you here. Do you remember me? It's been some time, but we met two years ago on the train in—"

"Belgium, yes." Archer nodded, a bit rigidly, as if the man were some sort of intruder. How odd that such a physically beautiful man would be so cool to the concepts of sociability. Certainly, he had his reasons. "Miss Whitney, I would like to introduce you to Mr. Stoker. Sir, are you still the manager at the—ah—"

"The Lyceum," Stoker supplied, nodding. "Yes, indeed. Miss Whitney, it is a pleasure."

Elena tilted her head graciously. "Thank you, sir. The Lyceum, you say? My companion and I attended a performance of *Dr. Jekyll and Mr. Hyde* in August. Mr. Irving was absolutely maniacal in his portrayal of the character. We enjoyed the evening very much."

Elena could not help but notice the way Mr. Stoker stared at Archer, as if her guardian were something to be marveled at.

Archer asked stiffly, as if the merest bit of polite talk required his every concentrated effort, "What brings you to the library today, Mr. Stoker?"

The gentleman waved a self-deprecating hand. "I dabble at writing stories. Would love if I could make a living at it one day. Today I am researching the particulars of Wallachian folklore."

Archer scowled. "Vampires, Mr. Stoker?"

"Actually, yes." The gentleman's smile broadened beneath his mustache.

"Vile creatures."

"Which suits my purposes perfectly." Mr. Stoker chuckled. "Who knows if my idea will ever come to fruition? Miss Whitney, I told my wife, after meeting his lordship, that I should one day like to write a character based upon him."

"Really?" she smiled at Archer, whose scowl only deepened.

Mr. Stoker carried on. "Not a vampire, of course, but someone dashing and heroic. Ah, I see we are receiving looks of chastisement from the main desk. But please, your lordship, I insist. You and Miss Whitney must come to the Lyceum one evening as my guests."

They thanked him and with a final glance over his shoulder, Mr. Stoker returned to his volume-strewn desk.

Archer appeared relieved they had been left alone again. "I'm sure one of the librarians would be pleased to assist us in locating a section on whatever you might be interested in. Perhaps medical history?"

Elena glanced at her little map. "Actually, I think I'd like to see a few of the antiquities collections. Perhaps the Egyptian, or the Graeco-Roman, if you don't mind."

Moments later, they stood in one of the museum's myriad exhibit rooms, the Elgin Room.

"The Parthenon," Elena breathed, awestruck. "Dating to 454 B.C. It defies all rationale that something so ancient could be here, in modern-day London, for us to admire." Elena tilted her head, analyzing the huge frieze. "What do you suppose that is?"

Archer barely glanced at the display. "It's a depiction of the birth of Pallas Athene from the head of Zeus."

She peered up at him. "I remember something of mythology, but am largely unfamiliar with these characters. Who is that on the chariot, rising up out of the ocean?"

He moved closer, to stand just beside her, so close she felt his heat along her back. She closed her eyes against temptation, aching to lean against him. What would he do if she did?

"That is Helios, the Sun, in his chariot. Do you see? The frieze follows the progression of day to night, ending over there, with Selene, the Moon, racing beneath the horizon in her chariot."

"Selene." She repeated the name and forced herself to move a few steps away. She gripped her guidebook with both hands. "Are you and she lovers?"

Archer coughed, appearing mildly alarmed.

"Pardon me?" He glowered, appearing to grow in height.

"It's all right. We are both adults." She glanced about the room. "And there's no one to overhear. Selene, the Countess Pavlenco. Are you and she lovers?"

"No." His silver eyes darkened to pewter.

"But were you, at one time?"

He hesitated a long, quiet moment. Finally, he answered, "A very long time ago."

She felt a sudden rush of impatience. Why did he speak in such elusive terms? "Both of you are still young. How long ago can long ago be?"

He smiled tightly. "It seems like a thousand years."

Just then, several visitors entered the room.

Elena lowered her voice. "You're aware of the snakes, then."

He blinked. Hard. Twice. Lord Black looked as if he wanted to strangle her. In many ways, she wished to strangle him too. She couldn't even put a finger on half the reasons why—she only knew part of her hated him for bringing her so close to some mysterious paradise that night in his room, only to slam the door in her face.

He gritted, "Yes, I am aware of them."

"Then how did the two of you manage to—"

"*Miss Whitney.*"

Elena closed her lips. Somehow it gratified her to make him squirm. She proceeded on her own, into the next room, deciding he could follow if he wished. When he found her again, she peered at a black-handled vase or krater displayed upon a narrow pedestal.

"Isn't it beautiful?" she marveled, acting as if nothing had happened moments before.

"I suppose."

She bent, scrutinizing the scene painted on its side. "It's the abduction of Persephone. I've always loved that story." She pointed with a gloved finger. "There she is, reaching for her mother to save her from Hades. I never understood why she had to stay with that cretin, if even only for a third of the year."

She straightened and saw that his face had gone hard as granite. "Lord Black, aren't you interested in history?"

"Of course I am," he muttered darkly.

"Then why won't you so much as look at the vase?"

"Because what you're looking at is a myth. A story Not history."

"But isn't it interesting to wonder whether the myths had their origins in reality?"

"A reality so convoluted by time, no ounce of truth remains? Really, what is the point?"

He brushed past her, as if to move to the next exhibit.

Heat burned Elena's cheeks. "If you're not enjoying yourself, you can go on without me and do whatever it was you had originally intended."

She knew she sounded like a petulant child, but somehow Lord Black had a way of jabbing at her emotions and making her behave in ways she'd never act otherwise.

Suddenly he pulled her against him, so fiercely that her breasts crushed into his chest.

"I don't want to go on without you."

Her heartbeat raced. Everything she'd been feeling— the irritation and impatience—went into a complete reversal at his touch. He gazed down at her with sensual, almost intimidating intensity. She still heard the voices of the museum visitors in the next room.

Lord Black kept his voice low and discreet. "I want to kiss you. To drag you off like the cretin you just vilified and ravish you behind that partition."

There was an earnest, raw, tone to his voice that thrilled her to the core. Gone was his emotionless façade. Her guidebook fell to the floor, forgotten, as she grasped his forearms and instinctively leaned into him, boldly matching her hips against his. The stiffening length of his arousal seared through the multiple layers of her undergarments and clothing.

She required no explanation to realize this as proof of his desire for her.

She gasped as he seized her by the waist, his thumbs curling possessively against her stomach.

He murmured, "Do you see why I have stayed away?"

"So, you were avoiding me," she accused softly.

"What is the alternative?"

She peered up from beneath the curve of her bonnet. "Kissing me again."

"I can't stop at kisses."

Approaching footsteps sounded against the carpet. He firmly set her from him and bent to retrieve her guidebook.

A male voice effused, "Lord Black. What a pleasure. What a pleasure indeed."

A man in a neat, dark suit hurried toward them. "As you can see, word travels fast within the museum, especially when our greatest benefactor chooses to visit."

Elena, still heavily affected by the intense moment that had just passed, barely registered the man's greeting. Greatest benefactor? What was this?

"Please allow me to introduce myself." He bowed sharply. "I am Edward Matthews, an assistant director here at the museum. Mr. Bond, our principal librarian, would certainly have welcomed you personally if he were not at this moment in Cyprus doing what paleographers do best."

With a heated glance into her eyes, Archer introduced Elena as his ward. Elena almost laughed.

Mr. Matthews clasped his hands behind his back, beaming at her. "Any guest of his lordship's is a welcome guest of the museum. Being that we have never before met, Lord Black, may I personally recognize that your contributions to the museum, both in artifacts and benevolent funds, have been profoundly significant, as were your father's, and your grandfather's before you."

So Lord Black was, indeed, an antiquary. How thrilling! This was also the first she'd heard mention of Archer's family. This pleased her, for Elena had started to wonder if he were not human, like the mythical Athene, who had sprouted from Zeus's head.

"I'd be more than pleased to offer my personal services as guide to the both of you today. Miss Whitney, has Lord Black shown you the Nereids?"

Archer said, "Actually, I would very much appreciate your escorting Miss Whitney through the remainder of the exhibits. I had come today to view one of the texts held in the museum's private archive."

Elena stared at Archer, altogether displeased at being foisted off on a member of the staff, especially after the moment they had just shared.

Mr. Matthews nodded agreeably. "I would be pleased to take Miss Whitney about. You're in possession of the necessary keys, of course?"

"I am."

Archer handed Elena her guidebook. "I'll rejoin you shortly."

Elena didn't answer him. No, she wasn't happy about his leaving her, but she yearned to learn more about Lord Black . . . and Mr. Matthews did seem very forthcoming.

Archer strode through the Elgin Room, unnerved by how easily his hard-fought reserve crumbled after a mere hour in Elena's company. Fortunate for both of them Mr. Matthews had arrived. Elena's obvious willingness to enter into an illicit liaison did nothing to settle his passions. He could not help but imagine what it would be like to be naked and thrusting, fully ensheathed inside the beautiful young woman who was his ward.

He might be immortal, but he was still, above all, a man.

By necessity he forced his overly aroused mind to the matter of the Ripper, and his original purpose for coming to the museum.

Just beyond the Elgin Room lay a smaller chamber containing the colossal Lion of Knidus, crouching ten feet in length and six feet high, carved entirely of Pentelic marble. Long ago, and from the vantage point of a Greek sailing vessel, he had seen the lion high upon a cliff looking out over the sea. Then, its eyes had glittered green with emeralds. He could not help but feel regret the majestic creature no longer held vigil there.

He entered its shadow, going to a nondescript door cut into the wall just behind. He fished a pair of brass keys from his coat pocket.

Once inside, he descended a long, dark staircase, toward a faint light visible at the bottom. There he entered a large but narrow room. Two copyists looked up, their faces illuminated by the lamps on their desks. So intent were they upon their work they only briefly greeted him as he passed through.

The walls were fully lined with sturdy wooden shelves, and upon them, hundreds of ancient clay sleeves. Each, if opened, would contain a scroll, perhaps two. All had been spared from the destruction of the Royal Library of Alexandria, thousands of years before.

He knew because he had spared them. Over the centuries, he had moved the collection from one location to the next. Transferring them to the Inner Realm had never been an option, as the clay and papyrus would never survive the fiery crossing. Eventually he had no other choice but to deposit them with the museum for preservation. Many had already fallen to pieces, ravaged by time and climate. Over the past hundred years, museum assistants had worked to piece together the fragmented remains, and copyists recorded their priceless contents. However, the rarer text he sought would be found behind yet another portal.

At the far end of the chamber, Archer came to that door and used the second key to gain entrance. He carefully secured the lock behind him. The room was much smaller than the first, but also lined with scrolls, each detailing a history long ago mythologized by mortals—that of the Amaranthine race.

A large wooden structure traversed the center of the room and would contain the text he sought. Archer dropped the keys into his pocket. He carefully lifted the lid from the first boxed section. Inside were rows and rows of tablets, the oldest items in the collection. They were of different sizes and hues, but most were formed of reddish-colored clay. A thin catalogue lay on top, written in his own hand, providing a precise listing of each.

He found the numerical identifier for the tablet he sought and searched the clay edges for a match.

"You say Lord Black won't allow his name to be listed amongst the other benefactors of the museum. Why, if his contributions have been so great?"

Elena walked alongside her attentive guide, Mr. Matthews, bending from time to time to read the small metal-rimmed placards explaining the significance of the artifacts they passed. As she had hoped, he had been very gracious about answering all her questions, and not just those about the exhibits.

"Believe me, if he would, his name would be emblazoned on one of the collections, likely even a wing of the museum," Mr. Matthews gushed. "I am told it was the same with his father, and his grandfather before him. They rejected any accolades or public recognition for their contributions."

"How uncommon."

Mr. Matthews glowed with obvious admiration for the subjects of their conversation. "I cannot even express to you, Miss Whitney, how our collections have benefited because of his generosity, and the generosity of his forebears over the past century. How fortunate you are to be associated with such a gentleman."

Yes, how fortunate. Remembering the intensity of his gaze just before Mr. Matthews interrupted them, Elena could not help but glow as well.

Upon hearing the knock, Archer crossed the narrow room and opened the door.

One of the copyists stood there, wearing a curious expression. "You've visitors, your lordship. They say you are expecting them."

The Countess Pavlenco and Lord Alexander stood just behind him.

"Yes, thank you."

The copyist backed way, granting the other two access to the narrow portal. Once they were inside, Archer again locked the door.

"You've cut your hair." Selene stared at Archer, her expression stricken.

"Please, sit down. Here at the table."

Mark refused the invitation. Instead he stood rigid

and guarded, in the shadowed corner of the room. Archer moved closer and stared into the younger Guard's eyes.

"You were correct in your assessment of this soul, Mark. The Ripper had Transcended."

Relief transformed Mark's features. He thrust his fingers through his golden hair. "God, you believe me. I thought no one would. It all happened so fast. Too fast, Archer. I don't understand Jack's rapid Transcension."

"I believe I do. The answer is here, in this vault."

Chapter Twelve

Selene lowered herself onto a stool. "Go on."

"Do either of you remember anything about the Tantalytes?"

Mark also lowered himself to a seat at the table. He frowned, and after a moment of silence, nodded.

"They were before our time, of course, but yes, I remember reading something about them during my scholarly training at Alexandria. I can't claim to recall the particulars, but weren't they a reclusive sect who lived in a remote region of the Haemus Mons, and worshiped Tantalus?"

Archer nodded, "Yes."

"Tantalus. Nasty fellow. Cannibalism. Human sacrifices." Selene shuddered, unpinning her flamboyant, ostrich-plumed hat, and setting it beside her on the table. "His name alone gives me the chills, and I don't chill easily."

Archer seated himself across from her. "So were his followers. The Tantalyte priests called themselves *brotoi*, sons of Tantalus, and saw themselves as his servants. They sought to raise Tantalus and his dark minions from the eternal punishment of Tartarus, with the intention they would rule the earth at his side."

Selene gazed at Archer, her eyes aflame with reverent admiration. "But they never succeeded because you Reclaimed the whole lot of them, and cast them into Tartarus to join those they sought to raise."

Mark rolled his eyes and scowled. He leaned back from the table. "This all happened before 8000 B.C. What does this have to do with Jack?"

"It appears our boy Jack is a Tantalyte."

Selene stood, scowling in thought, and walked along the wall of scrolls. She drew a path along the dusty ledge with her fingertip. "How can that be, when their history has been hidden away under lock and key in this secret collection for centuries?"

Archer reached into his coat pocket and withdrew the Ripper's letter, and the journal. He pushed it across the center of the table, toward Mark. Selene quickly returned to her brother's side and took up the letter. After scouring the contents, she lifted the parchment and drew her nose across the crease.

"Please don't eat that," Archer said.

She made a face and passed it back to him. "Who would want to? It's rancid."

Mark swore over the journal. "He's drawn pictures of me. He knows my name."

Selene looked over his arm. "What about this picture. Is that what I think it is?"

Mark asked, "A volcano?"

Archer pointed to the center of the page, where a vertical row of letters had been drawn, one beneath the other. "Look here. It's difficult to read because of the damage, but it spells Krakatoa."

Selene frowned. "Ah, yes, the one that erupted so fiercely in Indonesia five years ago. Thousands upon thousands were killed. Remember how the resulting ocean waves struck even here, against the shores of England?"

Archer stood up from the table. "It's exactly those

waves I'm concerned about. Not the actual ocean waves, but the reverberations that continue to this day. I believe there's a pattern to them, and that they were sent up by Tantalus to awaken a sleeping army, of which Jack is only the first."

Again, impatience tensed Mark's features. "Why have you called us here, Archer?"

"Simple." He took the journal into his own hands and flipped a few pages back. "Do you see these numbers?"

Mark squinted. "Barely. The water has damaged them so badly, most are unreadable."

"What else do you notice about them? The ones you can read?"

A slow smile of realization spread across Mark's lips. "They are written in ancient Akkadian."

Selene grinned and thumped her brother on the shoulder. "I told you that would come in handy one day."

"I don't even think Jack really understands them. He's simply recording what he sees inside his mind. But I believe once they are translated, we will be able to align them with a number of events that have taken place since the eruption of Krakatoa. Natural disasters. Pandemics. And various incidents of violence and murder, including those that have happened here in London in recent months."

Mark's eyes burned with fervent excitement. "Most importantly, we'll be able to predict when he'll return."

"Precisely."

Mark shoved himself up from the table, his jaw tight and his eyes flashing fiercely. "Hell, why didn't I pick up on this?"

"Give me some credit. I've been around since the earliest of times. I've seen a lot."

"So, I am to act as your translator? And then what? Do you expect Selene and me to stand back while you claim the glory?"

Archer argued, "It's not about glory, Mark. It's about finishing the Reclamation. It's about protecting the Inner Realm."

"That's not enough," Mark concluded in a low voice. "The Ripper was my assignment. What of my record? What of my repute?"

"I have communicated my sworn testimony to the Primordials, detailing Jack's uncommon deterioration and your blamelessness in the occurrence of his Transcension."

"Excellent," breathed Selene, grasping her brother's shoulder in celebration. "Back together!"

Archer shook his head. "Do not misunderstand. We cooperate on this Reclamation only."

Selene frowned in disappointment.

Mark crossed his arms over his chest. "Whatever. Let's get things under way."

"I agree," his twin added sharply."

Archer interjected, "You've your own Reclamation to pursue, Selene."

"Yes, I do." She scowled. "And have you heard the latest? A headless torso, deposited at Whitehall on the very grounds of the New Scotland Yard. Can you believe his audacity? But I assure you, I'll manage both hunts to successful completion. I refuse to be excluded from this thing with Jack. We're making history here, gentlemen."

"Good." Archer rested both hands against the table. "Unfortunately, any translation will take longer than I'd hoped."

"Why is that?"

"The original tablet we need is missing."

"Missing? How can that be?" Selene went to the

open box, and after scrutinizing the catalogue, came to the same conclusion as Archer. "Who would have the keys to gain entrance to this room?"

Mark glowered. "And who would have managed to steal something so cumbersome from the grounds of the museum, unnoticed?"

They all stared at one another silently.

"That's right," Archer said. "Either Jack's been here, or he convinced someone on the staff to steal the tablet for him."

Mark searched the walls. "The tablet would have been copied by a scribe, centuries later, at the library at Alexandria. Many of the scrolls are here. Is it possible the copy might be here on these walls?"

"I've already found it." Archer went to the shelf and selected a sleeve. "Here's our problem."

Prying off the seal, he tilted the sleeve to the table. Two ivory scroll rods and a thousand disintegrated bits of papyrus slid out.

"Bloody hell," muttered Mark.

"Exactly."

Bloody hell, because Mr. Matthews was about to walk through the door.

There came the sound of muted voices and a key rattling inside the lock. The door swung inward.

"Your lordship?" Mr. Matthews pushed in, his eyes wide and searching. After a moment, he raised a lantern high. "Anyone?"

Elena appeared beside him, squinting toward the table. "Why are you all sitting here in the dark?"

Archer gritted his teeth. Reclaimers required no light to see, so there had been no need for a lantern.

"Ah!" Selene leapt up, and quickly grabbed an unlit lamp from the peg on the wall. "Our flame flickered out when the two of you walked in. There must be a draft. Fortunately for us you have brought another, and we shall not have the bother of relighting this one."

Mr. Matthews appeared uncertain. "I hope it's all right that I showed Miss Whitney down."

"Of course." Archer went to stand beside Elena.

Her gaze, however, had settled on Mark, who had pushed himself up from his chair as well, and now stood smiling at her.

Archer threw Mark a warning glance, while saying, "Mr. Matthews, one question before you leave us. Who, besides me, has copies of the keys for this interior room?"

"The principal librarian himself. In his absence, of course, the privilege of their custody has fallen to me. One of our language scholars, Mr. Limpett, also has a copy."

He had already scoured Mr. Matthews for any trace of abnormal deterioration and found nothing of concern. Archer's eyes narrowed. "Is Mr. Limpett available for me to speak with this afternoon?"

"Mr. Limpett has been on holiday for the past week. I can certainly relay a message to him for you."

"No message."

"Very well. Miss Whitney, it was truly a pleasure."

"Thank you for your kind attention, Mr. Matthews."

"Your lordship, is there anything further I can do to make your visit all it should be?"

"I've everything I need here."

Everything but an original tablet, and Mr. Limpett.

Mr. Matthews quietly pulled the door shut behind him.

Mark strode forward. "Miss Whitney, I've not had the pleasure. I am Marcus Helios, Lord Alexander. The Countess Pavlenco is my sister."

Elena smiled, looking back and forth between the two tall, slender immortals. "Don't tell me you are twins."

"Indeed we are."

"Helios and Selene." She gasped. "I have just come from the Egyptian Saloon, and suppose the two of you were named after Alexander Helios and Cleopatra Selene, Queen Cleopatra's twins with Mark Antony."

Selene drew closer. Her eyes held a provocative gleam. "Our mother was, indeed, fanatical about all things Egyptian."

Elena's brows went up in question. "And you are both associates of Lord Black? The three of you are involved in the acquisition and preservation of antiquities?"

Mark rolled his eyes and muttered, "Hell, I suppose that's it."

When they left the museum, evening shadows claimed the streets. A thin haze hovered about, wisping around Elena's skirts as they waited for the driver to bring the Victoria around from the stables. The other two had already left in a hansom, the fragmented scroll concealed in its sleeve and wrapped in packaging paper under Mark's arm.

Soon, Lord Black's spotless carriage clattered to a stop before them. Just as Archer assisted Elena up, the gas lamps lining the avenue blazed to life.

Elena shivered as he seated himself beside her.

"You're cold."

"A little," she confessed, rubbing her gloved hands together.

He sensed the tension within her and knew, like him, she revisited their passionate embrace in the exhibit room.

"Then sit closer to me."

With a shy smile she nestled closer against him.

The carriage traveled down the avenue and rolled to a stop behind a number of other vehicles, all waiting to proceed through the intersection. Shouts of impatience came from all around.

Lord Black's coachman called to another wagon driver whose vehicle clattered past. "What's the problem up there?"

"Everyone's trying to get home for the evening, and there's no officer to direct the traffic. They've all been called to Whitechapel for extra patrols."

The driver nodded and tipped his hat in thanks.

"Sirrah! Sirrah! And milady!"

Elena glanced out the side of the vehicle, to find a man in a red velvet top hat calling to them, and anyone else in hearing distance.

"No need to go to Tussaud's, not when we've got the best wax on two legs right here. Jack the Ripper an' 'is ladies. Come see their awful faces for yerselves."

Behind him, a curtain had been set up, formed of heavy, gray canvas. The material furled up at the corner, to snap in the wind, offering her a teasing glimpse of a woman's garment dressed onto a rigid, humanlike shape.

A sign on the breast said EDDOWES.

The wind lulled, and the canvas fell straight, blocking her view.

She jerked up to twist the door handle.

"Elena?" Archer called.

She jumped down to the street, and grasping up her skirts, rushed over the curb and across the walk.

The man in the hat pivoted as she ran by. "Say, miss. Y' got to pay first."

She brushed past the canvas, and gasped.

There, in the shadows stood a woman made of wax, with horrid, false brown hair, her face sculpted into a garish expression of terror. Wrapped round her neck was a kerchief, splattered with fake blood. Pinned to her apron was a crudely painted wooden sign: KATE KELLY, and below that, CATHERINE EDDOWES. Just beside her loomed another figure, this one tall and costumed in a shabby cloak and a top hat. His sign read JACK THE RIPPER.

She heard heavy footfalls. Boots running on the walk behind her. Archer's voice.

"Elena? What is it?"

She whispered, "Doesn't look anything like her."

And slumped against him.

Elena lay on her bed, propped up on two stacked pillows, her eyes and nose red from crying.

"Really, I'm fine. Just shocked. I did not know her well. It's just very disconcerting to realize someone you have spent any amount of time with has subsequently died a horrible death at the hands of a monster such as Jack the Ripper."

Archer faced her on the edge of the bed, his leg bent at the knee. He hated that this news made her feel so wretched. He looked down at the newspapers. "That day you were looking for Lizzy and another woman. The other woman was Catherine Eddowes?"

"Yes," she sniffled, and pushed herself up. Her hair, fallen free of its chignon, fell over her shoulders. "And so when I originally read in the newspapers that the name of the second victim was Kate Kelly, I thought nothing of it besides what a horrible, horrible thing to happen to that poor woman. But apparently she lived with a fellow by the name of Kelly, and considered herself married to him. She used both names. Many women from that part of the city do."

"I'm sorry, Elena."

He really was sorry. And unsettled, realizing she'd come into direct contact with one of the Ripper's victims—the very same one he had spoken to, and who had been left as a "gift" for him by the murderer. That day at the Ten Bells, he'd heard the names Catherine and Kate bandied about, but hell, it seemed half the city's female population boasted those names. He'd had no reason to believe the two women were one and the same.

Was there any significance?

"How am I going to break the news to Lizzy? I don't believe she's heard. She considered Catherine to be a sort of mother figure."

"We'll do it in the morning, together if you like."

He saw the appreciation in her eyes, awash in a new surge of tears, but she shook her head. "Actually, I think it would be better if you weren't there. She's quite in awe of you, you know. Perhaps too much so for such a private moment."

"Whatever you wish."

She clasped his hand, and with a tilt of her head, whispered, "Thank you."

"For what?"

"For not pushing me away."

Her words stole his breath, more than her tears.

"Elena—"

"I know you can't stay. I don't even want to know why. It's all right." She smiled bravely, her eyes wide and hiding nothing. "I have my own plans, my own dreams, and I will be fine without you. In fact, my admission to the medical college will arrive within days. Perhaps it will be I who must say my good-byes first. Whatever happens, I'm glad to have had this time with you."

Slowly, he pulled her against his chest, bewildered at how she seemed to belong in his arms. No matter how he tried to keep her at a distance, he couldn't. His mind absolutely balked at the whole idea of good-byes, although he knew that time would come, and soon.

He remembered the woman she mourned in vivid detail, torn, bleeding and far worse than dead on the filthy London sidewalk. Elena's talk of medical school made his blood go cold, because he knew her ambitions would return her to the East End, and all the madness and death to be found there. Elena's spirit thrived on optimism—but he knew those she sought to save would eventually swallow her whole and destroy the young woman he had come to care so deeply for.

He wouldn't allow that to happen.

Eventually, her breathing slowed, and he knew she slept. He eased her to the pillow, and darkened into shadow. He twined himself about her, leaving only when dawn pinked the sky.

Six days later, Archer moved in shadow along the spacious corridor of the as-of-yet unopened Savoy Hotel. Though scaffolding still covered the outer walls of the structure, and on the lower floors workmen hurried to paint trim and install artwork, here there were only silence and polished luxury. Without announcing himself, he slipped beneath the door of room 712.

"Fancy," he said, taking shape to stride across the lush pile carpet.

Mark sat in a chair beside the window, pondering a sketchbook, pencil in hand.

"Greetings." Selene looked up from where she

bent over a mahogany table, her long hair draped over one shoulder. At the sight of him, color arose in her cheeks. "How was France?"

"Jack wasn't there. Nor was he in Belfast or Dublin. I suspect he's still here, in London, watching and waiting."

Selene worked over a large piece of canvas. Atop it lay the reassembled scroll. She employed narrow silver tongs to place a miniscule fragment. "I am almost finished here."

Archer perused the luxurious furnishings, the richly detailed mantel piece and Japanese wall hangings. Selene's fur-trimmed coat lay draped over the high back of a wing chair. "Almost like your own miniature mansion. But how can you suffer being surrounded so closely on all sides by this many people?"

Outside on the busy street, and even here to some extent, he'd experienced a sensation similar in some ways to that of the Thrawl Street boardinghouse—except here the thoughts, rather than reflecting misery and madness, centered almost exclusively upon a whole different type of insanity: Bond Street and shopping.

"How did you manage to get these accomodations? Before the hotel has even opened to the public?"

Selene answered for her twin. "Mark is one of the Savoy's major investors."

Archer glanced down at Mark, who frowned over a page. "Why don't you get yourself a house? It's not as if you can't afford one."

Mark answered quietly, "I prefer my rooms here."

Archer moved to stand beside the window, covered in white and red–striped blinds. "Actually, the intrusion is not so bad over here."

"It's the placement of the granite columns and the steel joists. Apparently they used very little wood in the construction."

Archer flicked aside the blinds and peered out. In the distance, Cleopatra's Needle speared up from the dense fog layering Victoria Banks.

"A pleasant view," he said quietly, understanding Mark's choice of lodgings a bit better now.

"Mark always was a mummy's boy," Selene cooed. She chuckled at her own jest, and repeated, "Mummy's boy."

Mark threw her a disgusted look.

Archer intervened. "What of you, Mark?"

"While I waited for Selene to refurbish the scroll, I tracked down Mr. Limpett's daughter at his home in Manchester."

"But no Mr. Limpett?"

Mark shook his head. "And no Jack. I'm in agreement with you. I think he's still here in the city."

"What did the daughter say about Mr. Limpett?"

"She told me he returned from London a week ago, but disappeared, and she hasn't seen him since."

"And her thoughts reflect the truth of this?"

Mark nodded. "She's no idea of where he's gone, but I could easily perceive she's suspicious of her father."

"In what way?"

"She fears he's dealing in stolen artifacts."

"Interesting."

"There's no telling where the tablet is now. We'll have to find it after this business with Jack is settled."

"What have you translated thus far?"

Mark responded, "Nearly all of it. I'll try to be brief, but why don't you sit?" He indicated the matching chair beside him.

As Archer seated himself, Mark flipped a few pages back in the sketchbook. "The scroll opens with several prophesies, namely cataclysmic events—the foremost being the eruption of volcanoes—and they explain this theory of waves you identified at the museum."

Archer nodded, waiting to hear more.

"The waves would of course initially take the physical form of earth tremors, aftershocks and tsunamis. But they tell their followers to remain receptive to unseen ripples in the atmosphere, which would continue for decades, perhaps even a century after the event. They predicted a volcano, at some unspecified point in the future, would be a beacon from which Tantalus would shout his call to arms, in the form of a dark energy that awakens those who have the hidden ability to turn *brotoi*."

Archer removed his hat, and his gloves, and set them on the marble-topped table beside the chair. "Tell us more about these *brotoi*. What is their evolution?"

"The tendency to become *brotoi* already lies within a certain population of mortals—and from all I've read in the scroll, they are the same mortals who are prone to Transcension, those who suffer excessive moral and mental deterioration."

Archer rubbed the bridge of his nose, pondering all Mark revealed. "At least there is that—we are concerned with the same fraction of population as before, only as I understand things, the *brotoi* will eventually unite their efforts, whereas Transcended souls remain solitary in their deviant pursuits."

Mark nodded. "That's right. Once awakened, they'll become stronger during each ripple. The events will not only be a source of power, but of communication and instruction from the depths of Tartarus."

At the table Selene stood, stretching like a lithe, dark cat. "I'm finished here. You can record the last of these sequences, Mark."

Both Reclaimers left their seats for the table.

Selene took up the two ivory scroll rods, and twisting her hair atop her head, used them to pin the weighty mass in place. She dropped into the chair Archer had just vacated. She idly selected three of the decorative books from the side table and scrutinized the words typed in gold upon their spines, like a connoisseur selecting wine. "The thing I don't understand is if Krakatoa erupted in 1883, why has it taken until 1888 for this first soul to emerge as a *brotoi*?"

Having settled on her choice, she ripped a long narrow strip, and twirled it about her finger. Tilting her head back, she dropped the paper between her lips.

"Because he only now understands the messages," Archer answered solemnly. "It's like any other language. One must be immersed for a certain period of time before the pattern makes sense. It's like a code, unlocking the potential of evil within."

Mark nodded. "From what I've read, the Ripper could very well be the Messenger referred to in the prophesies, and the purpose of his deeds here in London is to rouse an army of sleepers, or unperfected *brotoi* around the world. The end plan is, of course, for this vicious army to multiply and inhabit the earth . . . and of course, overtake the Inner Realm."

"Hmmm," mused Selene. "I wonder if my Thames murderer is a *brotoi*. He or she has been unusually difficult to trace."

Archer met her gaze. "At this point, anything is possible."

Mark laid the sketchbook on the table beside the scroll. Glancing back and forth between one and the other, he wrote out a string of numbers below the ones he'd already recorded.

Finally, Mark straightened. "It's as you believed, Black." He handed the sketchbook to Archer and pointed to what he'd written. "Look at the first few lines and compare them against one another. A little tinkering with their numerical code and you can see the pattern of the waves. They extend outward from Krakatoa and strike various points on the globe at specific times. When you compare that pattern with a calendar of the last five years, the dates correspond to everything you detailed before. Disasters. Outbreaks of disease. And murders. Lots of very nasty murders."

Archer studied the characters on the scroll, comparing their number to the ones recorded by Mark. "Based on this particular pattern—the one encompassing London's latitudinal and longitudinal location, I would expect the Ripper to strike again on the tenth of November."

Mark nodded. "That's the date I arrive at as well."

Archer met Mark's hard stare. "Excellent work."

Mark appeared to take not the slightest pleasure in the commendation. "One more thing, Black. If this Messenger *brotoi* is as strong as the scroll prophesies . . ." Mark's voice trailed off.

"What?" Selene demanded.

"I've read the scroll again and again. This is a nasty fellow. He's only growing stronger with time."

"Say it." Archer crossed his arms over his chest.

"The only way to ensure the defeat of a *brotoi* would be to fight him on his own level. One of us would have to Transcend."

Chapter Thirteen

"We're not going to do that," Archer stated firmly. "Once a Guard Transcends, there is no way back. He would risk—"

"Or she would risk," Selene interjected, eyes flashing.

With a nod of acknowledgment, Archer continued. "He or she would risk eternal madness, and be forever cast out, not only from the ranks of the Shadow Guard, but the Inner Realm as well."

Selene added, "And invite their own assassination. You can be certain the Primordials wouldn't suffer the existence of a Shadow Guard–turned-*brotoi* on the loose."

Archer shook his head. "Again, that's not going to happen. Perhaps if there were only one of us forced to do battle with this soul alone, but there're three. Together we can defeat him."

"Together?" Selene repeated quietly, straightening in the chair. The heavy blue silk of her gown hissed against the brocade. "Do you mean that, Archer?"

Archer lifted his chin, unsmiling. "It is the only way to ensure Jack's defeat."

Mark growled, "What if that isn't good enough for me?"

"Don't," warned Selene.

"What if I want to hear it from your lips that you understand the reasons for what I did, Black?"

Archer leveled a dangerous look at Mark. "I am here now, willing to go into this Reclamation on equal footing with the two of you. Can we move forward rather than backward?"

"Mark." Selene pushed herself to her feet, imploring.

Her gaze veered from one immortal to the other. "Tell him yes. Tell him we will work together on this."

Mark stared coolly into the center of the room, at no one. His starched collar contrasted pale against his throat. "Let's do it, then. Let's prepare ourselves for the battle to come."

Archer claimed his gloves and hat from the table. "I'll inform the Primordials of our intended strategy. When they learn of all this, they may wish, as a precaution, to temporarily close the portals. If you've any communications to be sent into the Inner Realm, I would make your dispatches sooner rather than later."

Selene pursued him to the door. "What will you do in the meantime?"

He barely heard her, for already he had darkened to shadow.

Lizzy nodded over the tops of the roses. "Yes, miss. I'm certain they are for you. Mr. Jarvis read the florist's card 'isself." Lizzy winced. "I mean *him*self."

Obviously Mary Alice had been at work attempting to polish Lizzy's speech.

Elena stood up from her escritoire, where she'd spent much of the morning organizing pages of notes. She'd welcomed the diversion. The knowledge that Lord Black was expected to return today from his weeklong foray into France kept her constantly distracted.

She'd already filled two boxes with the books she must return to Dr. Harcourt. After her acceptance to the college arrived, it would only be a matter of time before she left Black House for a student boarding-house closer to the campus. She wouldn't have room to store them there.

Had Lord Black sent the flowers? Pleasure spiraled through her at the possibility. She accepted the vase, which contained a vivid scarlet display of at least two dozen fat, red buds, their petals as rich as velvet.

"They are beautiful."

Lizzy cleared her throat, and with a purposeful tilt of her head said, "Miss Whitney, I wanted to thank y' again for takin' me to Catherine's funeral, and making sure I got those few days off to gather me thoughts. *My* thoughts, that is."

"There are no thanks necessary. I know she was your friend. It's important you remember the Catherine you knew, and not what she has become in the newspapers."

Catherine had died such a horrible, violent death. The macabre details, fully described in the newspapers, had served to memorialize her as a garish caricature of a woman, more akin to the wax figure Elena had seen on the street than a human being.

Lizzy clasped her hands in front of her apron. "You've been more than kind to me, miss, and I can't say I know what I've done to deserve it."

"Everyone deserves kindness, Lizzy. Everyone but monsters like Jack the Ripper. He'll get his comeuppance in the end, for what he's done to these women. I've no doubt of that."

After Lizzy had gone, Elena settled the vase on her

desk. She didn't need to bend her nose to the blooms. Their aroma filled the air around her. She coaxed the tiny envelope free. There was only her name, MISS WHITNEY, typed in black ink on the card. Again a knock sounded on her door.

When she opened it, her heart stopped. Archer stood there, silver-eyed and handsome.

"Hello," she said.

"Elena." He tilted his head. Warm pleasure swept through her, hearing the intimate pronouncement of her name, spoken by a voice she'd come to crave.

A dark swath of hair swept down to brush his cheek. He looked swarthy and mysterious. A fissure of excitement speared through her center.

"How was France?"

"Inconsequential," he said. "I know you've been confined to Black House all these days, at my selfish request. I've got the afternoon free of appointments. I wondered if you might wish to go for a ride."

Her heart leapt. "Yes, I would."

The roses. If he'd sent them, wouldn't he have mentioned doing so? Perhaps he was waiting for her to say something. She bit her lip, half delirious that he stood there staring at her with such intensity. Perhaps it was more exciting to leave some things unsaid. "Would you like to come in and wait while I gather my things?"

"No," he answered, laughing and raising an elegant hand. His lips turned up at the edges, in a faintly wicked smile. "I'd better not. I'll wait for you downstairs."

He backed several steps away and pivoted toward his room, she supposed to collect his coat and hat. She could not help but glance down at his buttocks, which even beneath the concealment of his fine woolen trousers were perfectly shaped and muscular.

Her heart beat an erratic tempo. She hurried to her wardrobe.

When she arrived downstairs he was already waiting, his top hat and gloves in hand. His frock coat, expertly cut to display the masculine burl of his shoulders, fell in an elegant descent to his knees. The footman stood back as Lord Black, rather than the servant, held the door for her. She passed him by, moving into the bracing chill of the afternoon. At the bottom of the steps, he assisted her up into a carriage—one that required no servant to drive. Going round, he climbed up to take his seat beside her, and accepted the reins and whip from the stableman.

He glanced over his shoulder toward a finely dressed servant, who waited on horseback at a discreet distance behind them.

"Leeson has informed me that in lieu of our perpetually melancholy Mrs. Hazelgreaves, we must take a groom for propriety's sake."

Elena grinned, and agreed in a hushed, conspiratorial voice, "We don't wish to be tomorrow's scandal."

They drove between the high iron gates onto the street. Archer caught her gaze, but only fleetingly. "Where would you like to go? This is your afternoon, you know."

"Really? Mine? What is the occasion?"

Archer stared over the tops of the horses' heads, to the street beyond. "In your room the other evening, you brought up the subject of good-bye."

"You'll be gone soon."

"Yes."

She had known he would go all along, and had been sincere in her bedchamber when she told him she expected nothing from him. They both had dreams and obligations that took them in different directions. Still, that did not mean they could not share an afternoon of memories.

She smiled to soothe the sting of her heart. "Then let's make the very most of my afternoon. Since it is I who will make the decisions on where we are to go, don't you think I ought to drive?"

Without the slightest question, Archer handed over the reins. "Certainly, if you wish."

"Consider yourself at my mercy, your lordship. If you were hoping for a gentle ride in Hyde Park, you shouldn't have handed over the reins to me."

Only a brief ten minutes or so later she turned the horses and carriage onto Jermyn Street. They passed a number of five-storied buildings crowded with shops and offices. She continued east until the shop fronts took on a bit shabbier appearance.

She drew the carriage to the curb. "In one of the city guides I read of a shop I'd like to visit, and I believe it's just over there."

She tied the reins, and the groom sidled alongside to mind the vehicle. Archer climbed down and caught Elena by the waist to bring her beside him on the sidewalk. In the shop window were advertisement placards for a host of items. Tea. Medicinal powders. And near the door there was a sign: TATTOO.

"Tell me again why we are here?" The dark slash of Archer's brow drew up in suspicion.

"I read about the gentleman who owns this shop. He sells all sorts of things from around the world and claims to be descended from Omai, the Polynesian native Captain Cook brought back from the Marquesas." She shrugged. "Who knows if that's true."

"And he's a tattooist."

"Yes."

"Why am I starting to feel as if I am somehow in danger?"

"I've already got one." Elena smiled, angelic and devilish all at once.

He'd seen the serpent before, but of course she didn't know. Darkly playful, he grasped her wrist and boldly pried down the fitted kid leather of her glove. When he saw it again, wrapped around her pale, delicate wrist, a fiery impulse arose within him to press his mouth to the marked flesh.

"This is what Mrs. Hazelgreaves was so over-wrought about?"

"I am not as scandalous as she'd like to believe. Small, discreet tattoos are considered very chic in even the most exclusive of female circles."

"Tell me why are we here."

A blush spread high across her cheeks. He still held her wrist. It was almost as if they held hands on the busy street, while everyone moved around them.

"I couldn't help but notice on the first night I met you in your study, and then again that night in your room . . ."

Now he felt as if *he* were blushing. When was the last time that had occurred? "Notice what?"

"You don't have one."

"There's a reason for that. The damn things last forever."

She tilted her head. "What's wrong with forever?"

She could not know how deeply her words cut him. He would not say or even think the word "love" for it was too impossible to consider in the context of his solitary existence, but he had developed the most dangerous and consuming of passions for his beautiful young ward. It was torturous to know each moment brought them closer to good-bye. He blinked away the morose thought.

"You're testing me."

Her dual-colored eyes dazzled him with their candid mischief. "More like daring you."

"You don't think I'll do it?"

"No, I don't," she goaded lightly. "I think you're a prude, Lord Black."

She was an ethereal thing of beauty in a world painted in shades of gray. The street, the buildings and the sky—everything seemed dreary in comparison. She had been so destroyed at learning of Catherine Eddowes's murder, he wanted to keep her smiling.

He wanted her to remember their time together like this.

Elena watched as he backed toward the door, a smile slowly spreading across his handsome lips. "Coming?"

He turned on the heel of his gleaming, pointed boot and pushed through the door, holding it until she followed him inside. The shop was shadowy and crammed to the ceiling with all manner of goods, such as candles corded into twelve-count bundles, and bulk foodstuffs. The haze and scent of incense hovered on the air.

A hulking man with a shining, bald pate and twinkling eyes sat in the far corner, surrounded shoulder-high by crates of all sizes. The tattooed head of a green and red dragon peered around his neck. At least four cats perched around him, each a different size and color.

He called congenially, "Hello? May I help you?"

Archer glanced toward Elena, and back to the storekeeper.

"I'm a man in search of a tattoo."

Moments later, Archer sat beside an enormous lamp, a huge ginger cat curling round his trouser ankle. On the wall behind him were tacked various regimental insignias, likely guides for the inking of British officers and soldiers. The tattooist emerged from a dark curtain at the back of the store. He had donned a pristine white tunic, and brought with him a bundle of bamboo-handled tools and a small pot of ink.

"What sort of design would you like? A dragon? A ship?" He chuckled. "A woman?"

"Miss Whitney, I think you should have the honor of deciding."

"Really?" Elena hovered several feet away, shocked Archer had even agreed. "Don't tease, because I won't decline."

"Tell the gentleman what mark I shall have on my skin." He grimaced. *"Forever."*

"One like mine, I think." She pushed down the cuff of her glove and showed the man her wrist. "Only wrapped around his upper arm."

She indicated the space between her shoulder and elbow. "What do you say, Lord Black?"

Archer tilted his head, admittedly pleased she wished to share this thing between them at such an intimate level. He knew even without the ink and the needles he'd been forever marked.

"Proceed, sir."

"I'll just wait over here," Elena said, going to the far side of the room, where shelves created a haphazard screen of privacy. There she meandered, stopping to consider a row of stoneware pots filled with various tobaccos. She lifted a glass lid and inhaled the woodsy, chocolate-sweet scent.

Glancing between the tins of tea and bottles of vinegar, she glimpsed Archer unbuttoning his shirt. Fixated, she watched as he parted the linen as far as the buttons would allow and shrugged the one sleeve off, leaving half of his chest and his arm entirely bare.

He looked up, catching her. Everything in her went scalding hot, but she did not look away. Heat smoldered in his gray eyes, evidence of the unspoken attraction that continued to flare between them. Overwhelmed by her intensity of feelings, Elena turned back to peruse the goods.

An hour later, Archer was tattooed, bandaged and clothed. Elena petted the cats while Archer paid the shopkeeper.

As they emerged onto the busy sidewalk, Elena experienced sudden desperation. She didn't want the afternoon to end, not with their good-bye so near on the horizon. Somehow she knew when he was gone, he would be gone forever.

"Where shall we go now?" she mused aloud.

"I'm afraid to ask."

She feigned offense. "You said this was my day. Not my"— she glanced at her watch—"hour and a half."

"What is it you wish to do next?"

"Well, since you've asked . . ." She grinned.

"Tell me."

"I've always wanted to smoke a hookah."

Archer towered above her, broad shouldered and dark. He shook his head slightly, and pressed his lips together, but his eyes smiled. "And I suppose your guidebook has told you where we might go to smoke one?"

"No." She glanced around at the pedestrians moving past. "This time you'll have to ask someone."

Elena coughed behind her fist. "I do believe my curiosity has been satisfied as far as hookahs are concerned."

She passed the tube and mouthpiece to Archer.
They half reclined atop a mountain of shining, multi-
colored pillows, their coats and hats strewn across a
small table in the corner. The walls of the semiprivate
room had been painted a vivid turquoise.

Archer grinned. "That's it? Three puffs and you're
finished?"

On a low, richly inlaid table beside them, the cylin-
drical hookah pipe rested on a gilt, lotus flower base,
and bubbled like a purring cat.

"Pardon me? That's three"—she coughed again—
"three and a half puffs."

He expertly looped the tube onto its hook.

Archer could recall no occasion where he'd driven
to and fro, and passed such an extended amount of
idle time for the simple sake of enjoying someone
else's company, but lounging beside Elena in this
steamy, smoky place sent a tight curl of pleasure
through his lower stomach and groin. Her hair had
loosened from its pins, and glowed in mussed, shining curls around her face. Her fitted, high-necked
bodice skimmed over her firmly corseted breasts and
narrow waist. The contrast of propriety and sensual-
ity teased to life every masculine impulse within him.

Unaware, Elena observed, "This is quite the gathering place for the dilettante crowd, is it not?" She
crossed her legs at the ankles.

"Hmmm. Yes?" Archer closed his eyes, savoring
the rustle of her stockings, one thigh brushed against
another.

"I believe we passed Mr. Wilde and Mr. Dodgson
sitting together at a table on our way in."

Their male attendant, adorned in a long white
tunic and linen pants, returned to place before them
two small glasses, full of amber liquid.

"Yes, indeed," he confirmed in a confidential tone.

"Whistler the artist is also a regular, as is his young associate, Mr. Sickert, but to my understanding, they are on holiday in France."

The attendant disappeared once again. Elena sat up from her splendorous throne of cushions. She took up the glass from the table and sipped the drink—only to cough in earnest.

"What *is* that?" she asked, her eyes watering.

Archer took the glass from her hand and returned it to the table. "Anise-infused brandy."

"It's very good. I do want to finish that." She fanned her face and again lay against the pillows, this time closer to him—so close he suffered a distinct stiffening in his trousers. He shifted, not wishing to alarm his oblivious companion. To his consternation she unfastened the top three buttons of her bodice. Beneath, she wore a white muslin blouse, just sheer enough that the lacy edge of her chemise and the lush swell of her breasts were apparent.

"Much better," she sighed, meeting his gaze.

"I'm glad," he responded tightly.

So as not to kiss her, Archer talked. "I have gotten a tattoo, and we've smoked a hookah. What else, Elena? What else would make this a . . . perfect day?"

"I've had two wishes already. Am I so lucky as to be granted three? Hmmm," she mused, smiling. "If you could arrange for us to attend a dissection, I'd be in heaven."

Archer blinked.

"An autopsy?" He reached for his brandy and tossed the entire glassful down. "Sometimes you say the most unexpected things."

She laughed, pressing her hand to his arm. "I didn't really expect you to *comply*, but you've been so cooperative—and you are such a man of *influence*—I thought I might as well ask. It's very difficult for women pursuing the study of medicine to view an honest to goodness autopsy—particularly of a male specimen. We must rely largely on illustrations, wax models and lectures. Can you believe I could possibly make my way through medical school without ever observing the true particulars of male anatomy? It's a shame our governing bodies find women's sensibilities too delicate for such a reality."

He didn't respond, wishing to avoid the whole subject of her medical inclinations.

He stared down into his empty glass. "In the absence of an autopsy, have you any other wishes?"

Her eyes went smoky, and she swallowed as if gathering courage. In a quiet voice she said, "Forced to confess my deepest, most secret wish, it would be that you'd kiss me again."

He set the glass on the tabletop. "You know I can't."

"Don't you want to kiss me?"

God, her eyes, her voice, her mouth. She tortured him.

"I won't tell anyone." A small, teasing smile lit upon her lips. "Just like I won't tell anyone about your wicked tattoo, or that solitary puff you took on the hookah."

Impulsively he grasped her by one shoulder. Her eyes widened. He pressed her back into the pillows. The firm construction of her bodice lay evident between them, but even so, he felt the full crush of her breasts beneath.

Looking up, she was all shadowy seduction and pink lips. A vivid backdrop of blue silk spread all around. He caressed the underside of her jaw, marveling at how she made any other woman in his past fade to nothingness in his memory. He bent his face to hers.

She quickly turned hers aside, grinning. "I've changed my mind. I don't want you to kiss me now."

"Wicked girl," he whispered.

But that was her whole allure. She wasn't wicked. She was just Elena.

"I'm not a girl, Archer."

He dragged his thumb against her lower lip. Her pupils grew huge and dark.

His mouth pressed over hers, tasting the sweetness of the tobacco and spiced brandy.

Voices continued their conversations outside their door. His hand slid beneath her bodice to spread against her stomach. Even through the layers of her blouse, chemise and corset, he felt her warmth, and the gentle flex of her stomach beneath. Elena sighed. Her hand slipped round to the nape of his neck. Innocently, with the tentativeness of one just learning passion, she met the impassioned thrust of his tongue.

The blood rushed into his ears, and other more dangerous parts of his body. He felt deliciously out of control, and in so public a place. He let out a husky growl, and rolled off her to fall back against the pillows.

"That's it," he muttered. "This has to stop. We can't spend any more time alone together."

When she did not move or speak, he turned his face to her, and found her still reclined against the pillows, her hair mussed and her cheeks pink. She grinned, a bit dazedly.

"And to think I asked for the autopsy first."

Mary Alice followed Elena into her bedchamber.

Elena unpinned her hat. "If there's time, I'd like to have a bath before supper."

She wanted to wash the hookah smoke out of her

hair and look especially nice for the evening to come, because it would be spent with Archer—likely in the company of Mr. Leeson, if Mrs. Hazelgreaves did not come down. She only admired Archer more for his determination to ensure things did not go too far between them.

She paused, seeing the roses. She'd completely forgotten to ask whether he had sent them.

"There's correspondence for you on your desk, Miss Whitney, and a number of cards of visitors who called while you were out."

Elena dropped her coat to the bed and went to see. Her pulse jumped as she spied an official-looking letter atop the calling cards, its printed return address the London College of Medicine for Women. She snatched up the envelope, smiling.

Her acceptance. The perfect end to an absolutely perfect day.

Soon, Archer would be gone. Without medical school to look forward to, she'd be left with nothing.

She slid her finger beneath the flap and unfolded the letter. The parchment bore the official letterhead of the college. She scanned the words.

She blinked, not believing.

She reread every word to be sure she had not misunderstood.

She hadn't. The letter she held in her hand was not an acceptance, but a rejection.

Chapter Fourteen

Tears stung her eyes. Confused, and blindly seeking Archer's comfort, she veered out of her room, the letter clasped in her hand, and quickly arrived at his apartment. She knocked. When he did not answer, she rushed down the central staircase, and onward to his study.

"Lord Black."

He sat at his desk. Beside him stood Mr. Leeson, his arm cradling a stack of documents.

"Yes?" Archer looked up.

Leeson stepped back.

"I don't understand this," she gasped, rushing toward him, stricken. "I don't understand this at all."

"What is it?" His face expressed immediate concern.

"I received this letter."

Alarm flashed over his features, and he lunged up. Rushing around the massive rectangle of the desk, he snatched the letter from her hand. His gaze raked over the contents.

"Do you see?" She worked to keep her voice calm, though inside she was frantic. "It's a letter rejecting my application to medical school. I don't understand. I easily passed the required examinations. My references were impeccable."

He did not say anything—he did not even meet her gaze. Before her eyes his concern transformed into something else, something hard and dark. Distance rose up between them like an icy northern wasteland.

"You don't seem surprised."

Finally, he looked up, his cool gaze, his tense jaw confessing everything.

She thought back to that night in his room, his insistence that she not return to the hospital. She recalled how he usually listened in silence when she discussed her plans. She had interpreted his silence as approval.

"You had something to do with this letter?"

Leeson clasped his documents against his chest, his expression one of pity.

"You used your influence to have me rejected from the college? Why? Why would you do that?"

Archer spoke in a low, yet resolute, voice. "Because, Elena, I will not have you destroyed by your noble, yet naively optimistic dreams."

She recoiled, angry, hot tears welling against her lashes. She had not realized the full involvement of her heart with Archer until this moment. She backed several steps away from him, to grasp the curved back of a chair.

He continued. "I have not invested so greatly in your life, and in your future, for you to waste yourself on prostitutes and orphans, and a multitude of people for whom there is no hope."

"Waste myself?"

"If it's not Jack the Ripper, it will be some other criminal or vagrant who hurts you, or disease, or—" He bit down on his words, clearly tortured by what he had done, but firmly resolute. "Don't you understand?"

"Yes . . ." She blinked away her tears, never believing until this moment betrayal could cut one so deeply. "I understand that you said you admired my ambition and my desire to serve others—and that despite everything that has taken place between us, you didn't mean those words at all."

She rushed from the room.

Archer moved to go after her, but felt a hand seize his arm.

" 'Everything that has taken place' between you, my lord?" Leeson repeated softly.

Archer bristled, wanting to capture her, to hold her, to make her understand.

"You test dangerous waters," Leeson whispered. "Better to let her go."

"Miss Whitney, dear?"

Elena looked toward her door from where she perched on her window seat. She hadn't heard anyone knock, but there stood Mrs. Hazelgreaves. Odd, but her companion wore a green tea dress, not her customary pink. The bothersome gray curl had been secured at the center of her forehead with an enameled butterfly hairpin.

Elena smiled faintly. "You are out and about. You must feel better. I'm so glad."

She really was glad, but found it difficult to summon much enthusiasm about anything since the confrontation in his lordship's study three days before. Since then, she'd kept mostly to her room, trying to decide where her life must go from here.

Elena made another observation.

"Your cane. You don't need to use one anymore?"

"My recent rest has done wonders for me." She smiled blithely. "We've got visitors in just an hour. Are you ready?"

Elena stared out her window. Yes, visitors. Despite all that had passed between them, Lord Black was again determined she snare a husband, or so Mr. Leeson had gently explained as if it were the most normal solution in the world for her future. They were to accept callers that afternoon. She hadn't yet decided whether she would appear.

"He cares for you, darling, I know he does."

Elena turned her head back in surprise. "Why would you say something like that?"

The old woman pulled the door closed behind her. "I may have been confined to my room, but I hear what goes on in this house."

Elena's heart stopped. "What, exactly, have you heard?"

"That's not important, dear. What matters now is that we've got to come up with a way to *punish* Lord Black. That's right, darling girl, we must show him the error of his ways." Mrs. Hazelgreaves chuckled gleefully.

Elena stared at Mrs. Hazelgreaves in disbelief. At the same time, she'd grown accustomed to the bizarre and unexpected over the previous weeks.

"First things first." She eyed Elena up and down. "You aren't planning on wearing that frock, are you?"

Archer glanced at his watch. Where the devil was Elena? He had never been adept at polite conversation, and had not anticipated he would be left alone, for some twenty minutes, with the ridiculous expectation he be gracious and charming.

He smiled tightly, over the square table covered in white linen and tea equipage, at a marquess and two earls, each in the company of a dowager mother or sister. He had personally chosen them based on an intensive investigation into their finances and reputations. Certainly Elena could find someone she could abide amongst them, despite one being astoundingly corpulent, and the other two approaching Selene and Mark in age.

They all sat rigidly on the chairs and on the sofas, their gloves and hats resting properly upon their knees. They reeked of old money, old houses and old sensibilities.

All returned his tight smile—and stared at him as if he were the devil.

His selection had not included an obvious choice: Dr. Harcourt. Admittedly, after that night at the ball, he had developed a childish envy of the handsome doctor.

Soft footsteps sounded upon the marble outside the salon door, and suddenly Mrs. Hazelgreaves and Elena stood in the doorway, Elena more beautiful than he had ever seen her.

Her hair had been swept upward into a polished, sophisticated style, one that only enhanced the brilliance of her eyes and the shape of her delicate nose. She'd rejected the white standard of a society debutante, and instead wore aubergine silk, artfully cut to display her lush, womanly attributes to perfection. Society's celebrated darlings had nothing on his beautiful ward.

Despite Elena's claim of disinterest in society, she didn't appear the slightest bit uncomfortable delving into the room of strangers. Indeed, with the first smile, her warmth radiated throughout, and the mood immediately transformed from tense and somber to lively and gay. Each of the gentlemen leapt up from their seats, two colliding at the shoulders in their attempt to assist her to her chair. Mrs. Hazelgreaves fluttered off to the distant corner of the room.

Once Elena was seated, the gentlemen returned to their seats. Archer sighed with relief, thankful to have everyone's attention drawn away from him. At the same time, his heart remained weighted like a great clod of lignite in his chest, knowing one, if not all of these gentlemen would be vying for the right to court his Elena.

For the briefest moment he envied their mortality and wondered how it would be to live their life, instead of being charged with the eternal responsibility of culling the vilest and most deteriorated of souls from humanity.

"Tea, your lordship?" Elena leaned toward him, her breasts delectable in their silken cradle. She balanced a dainty teacup and saucer in her hands.

He accepted the cup, feeling huge and bullish. Really, the whole tea ritual was ridiculous.

Lord Rathcliffe openly ogled Elena's breasts. Archer scowled, mentally crossing him off the list.

Lord Levinger leaned forward in his chair. "I understand you've spent some time volunteering at the charity hospital in Whitechapel."

Elena smiled sweetly. "I'm actually employed there as a probationary nurse."

Rathcliffe's matronly sister nodded and glanced about with obvious nervousness. "I'm sure your time there is very rewarding."

"You must tell us all about it," someone else encouraged.

Elena crossed her hands on her lap. "Oh, I don't wish to bore you."

Lord Nevil, who stood near the mantel, gushed, "I'm certain any story you tell will be nothing short of fascinating."

"Very well," Elena conceded graciously. "One afternoon a gentleman came in with his foot so swollen we could hardly get his boot off to see what was wrong. And then once we did, do you know what we discovered?"

"Tell us, Miss Whitney."

"*Maggots.*" She smiled as innocently as if she were talking about rainbows and butterflies. Only now did Archer suspect the depth of the rebellion within her. "Yes, it's true. A boot—and a leg—full of maggots."

Heat blazed up Archer's neck, into his face.

"Oh, dear," a dowager-countess-someone-or-other exclaimed, sounding ill. "Look at the . . . at the time. We promised Lady Eggerton we would stop by this afternoon as well."

With that, Elena stood. Though she said nothing to Archer, her level stare brazenly confessed all. He had never imagined Elena capable of such outright defiance. She politely stood near the door and thanked everyone as they passed through, for calling. When everyone had gone, she bustled out of the room.

"Elena," he thundered, going after her, but she lifted her skirts and escaped up the stairs.

He would have followed her, but he heard the sound of a woman's muffled laughter in the room behind him. Pivoting around, he returned to the salon to find Mrs. Hazelgreaves watching their visitors' hasty escape from her perch beside the bay window. Now that everyone else was gone, and he focused his attention on her, he realized the frozen, rather plastic quality of her features.

"*You,*" Archer growled, advancing on her.

Mrs. Hazelgreaves pushed herself up from her chair. "Your lordship. I am so mortified things did not go as we had planned."

"Oh, I believe they went *exactly* as you planned," Archer accused threateningly.

"What are you saying?"

Archer shoved his palms hard against her narrow shoulders, sending the old woman flying over a low table, and back into her seat with such force the chair tipped backward on two legs.

"Ooooh! Oh!" Her arms flailed for a moment, until she went over in a profusion of frilly-lace underskirts.

Two bare, very *hairy*, very *masculine* legs jutted straight into the air, ending in black trouser stockings and large, leather ankle boots.

Archer planted his foot against the edge of the seat, and shoved downward hard enough to bring the chair upright again. Mark stared back at him, the old woman's green gown hanging in loose tatters around his muscular shoulders.

"Damn it," he shouted, clearly furious to have had his ruse discovered.

Archer hissed, "I thought we had an agreement."

"Hang me at Tyburn, why don't you?"

"I would. But you'd only come back. That's the sorry thing about immortals."

Mark shoved himself up from the chair and stalked in a wide circle around his superior Guard, the destroyed silk dragging along behind. "You know who bore me, Black. You know my history. It's against my nature to abide by any agreement when I'm not the one who will come out on top."

One of the kitchen maids bustled in with an empty silver tray.

"Oh," she gasped, her eyes as wide as wagon wheels at the sight of Mark standing like a half-naked god in the remains of the shredded gown.

Archer met her on the carpet.

"Let me take that." He reached for the tray.

Too shocked to do anything otherwise, she handed

it over. He touched her hands, his eyes flashing metallic black. The girl's face went blank. Like a sleepwalker, she exited the room.

Archer lowered the tray to a table and returned his fiery gaze to Mark. "But why this? Why did you take on the appearance of Mrs. Hazelgreaves?"

"I've improved, haven't I?" Mark grinned rakishly. "You sat in this room a whole half hour with me and didn't realize."

"Why?" Archer thundered.

The muscles along Mark's shoulder rippled with tension. "Because it's obvious you care for the girl."

"I've a responsibility to her, yes."

"It's more than that, Black. You're utterly distracted by her. A *mortal*." He laughed derisively. "I thought that if I could thwart your efforts to marry her off, she'd keep your attentions elsewhere."

Archer gritted his teeth in impatience. "While you Reclaimed Jack."

"That's right."

"Alone?" Archer laughed acidly. "Do you plan on Transcending to do it?"

"Maybe I made that part up. Perhaps when I translated the scroll, I—"

"I can read Akkadian, Mark."

Mark glared at Archer, disbelieving.

Archer rattled off verbatim a few lines from the prophecies. As Guards had the ability to do, with one glance he'd recorded the entire document in his mind and had mentally scrutinized every character at a later time.

"You were testing me?"

Archer nodded curtly. "Guess what? You failed. I had to know if I could trust you. And just like before, Mark, it's obvious I can't."

"You can't hold this grudge forever. What happened in Paris must be relegated to the past."

Archer clenched his eyes shut. Paris. Paris had been a bloody farce. "This is no petty grudge. You and Selene lied."

"Lied. What a nasty interpretation."

"You used lies and subterfuge to intercept correspondence about that soul."

Mark crossed his corded arms over the tautly stretched green silk of his bodice. "You were occupied with a bigger hunt. Time was of the essence—"

"Sealed correspondence, from the Primordials, intended for me. And you used the information therein to Reclaim the target. My target."

"One bloody soul off your perfect record, Archer, and you would punish us forever for it."

"My displeasure has nothing to do with that soul, or with my record. It's called trust, Mark."

"No, it's called ambition," Mark growled. "You're not the only Amaranthine who's got it. Yes, you were our mentor after our recruitment by the Primordial Council. Yes, you taught us to Reclaim, but did you think we'd remain under your thumb forever? It was time for the both of us to break free."

"Do you think I wanted the both of you constantly dragging on my coattails? It is the Primordials—not I—who determine your independence, or lack thereof. You knew the rules, Mark, and you broke them, all for a bit of glory. Look what it got you. A blown assignment, the distrust of your peers and the displeasure of the Council. Selene, at least, attempts to make her amends. But you—you continue with your reckless arrogance."

Mark's jaw clenched into a rigid line. His eyes flamed with defiance, but he offered no further response.

Archer required none. He was finished with this conflict.

He demanded, "Where in the hell is the real Mrs. Hazelgreaves? You haven't killed her, have you?"

"She's fine," Mark seethed. "She's in one of the unused bedrooms, resting until I return."

"How long has she been there? Have you been impersonating her all this time? Since the onset of her *melancholy*?"

"Of course not. Only this afternoon. She's been ever so malleable, and from a matchmaker's standpoint has become your greatest champion. Still, I couldn't have her meddling too deeply in Miss Whitney's affairs, or there'd be no room for all that delicious impropriety between the two of you." He chuckled. "I'd hoped she could preside over tea, but she'd tippled one too many of my special tonics this morning and wasn't at all able to receive guests."

"Special tonics?" Archer glowered.

"Melancholy. Such an inaccurate diagnosis."

"You've had her high as a hot air balloon on black lotus flowers for the past two weeks, haven't you?"

Mark's eyes narrowed. "She's never been happier."

Elena descended from the hackney with her hastily packed valise in hand. She entered through the rear entrance of the hospital. Down the hall she found Nurse James at her desk.

The woman looked up from beneath her white cap. "Nurse Whitney, I wasn't sure we'd be seeing you again."

"I hear you are a bit shorthanded."

"That we are."

"I'll just sign in at the dormitory, and I'll be back to see where I am needed."

A quarter hour later, Elena returned in uniform to

the sick ward. The fastest way to forget Lord Black and her feelings for him was to move forward with her life. Alone. She didn't know how she was going to go to medical school with no inheritance from her father, and no support from her guardian, but she would find a way.

"Nurse James, who is the next patient to be seen?"

"Actually, could you return Mr. Stephenson to his room?" Nurse James nodded toward a man who sat in a wooden chair against the wall. He wore pajamas and a bowler hat. "A policeman found him outside a few moments ago, crawling down from the common room window. That's the third time this week."

"What's wrong with him?" Elena studied him. His shoulders were slumped, and he stared at the open palms of his hands.

"Nervous exhaustion, the doctors say. He's consumed by these Ripper murders, always writing letters to the newspapers and the authorities, laying out his theories. Anyhow, he's harmless as a mouse. Could you take him up to the Currie Ward?"

"Certainly." She patted the man gently on the shoulder. "Mr. Stephenson, I am Nurse Whitney. I'm going to see you to your room."

Elena escorted Mr. Stephenson up the stairs to his room. After tucking him in for a rest, she pulled the door to a crack behind her.

"Nurse Whitney."

Elena turned to see who called her. Dr. Harcourt exited one of the neighboring rooms. With him were three gentlemen who wore official-looking badges. He nodded to them, and they moved past Elena to descend the stairs.

Harcourt shook his head. Lines of frustration creased his brow. "Detectives. They're interviewing everyone, thinking the Ripper might be someone with surgical or medical knowledge. They've even made inquiries as to Mr. Merrick."

Elena protested, "Mr. Merrick can't hold his head up straight, let alone attack a woman on the streets."

"After interviewing him themselves, I think they understand better now."

"Do you think it might be possible the killer is associated with the hospital?"

Harcourt shrugged. "I've no idea. I'd hate to think someone I worked alongside was capable of something so vicious. But enough talk of that morbid subject. I am so pleased to see you. You've come back to work, then?"

"Yes. And I hope I still have the hospital's approval to take residence in the nurses' dormitory? I've already moved my things in."

His brows went up. "Certainly. We can use all the nursing expertise we can get. We received three more resignations over the previous days, each insisting they will not return until the Ripper is captured."

"I'm sorry to hear that. And I'm sorry I haven't been here for the past two weeks."

"It's not your fault. I completely understand Lord Black's feelings on the matter. In fact, I can't believe he's changed his mind."

"I don't know if he has. I didn't consult him before returning."

Dr. Harcourt's smile faded. "Elena . . ."

"Really, I'm sure he's delighted I'm gone. I don't think he ever really wanted the responsibility of a ward. It's obvious he doesn't know what to do with me, other than marry me off." She smiled faintly.

"His name carries power, Elena. If he's displeased by your return to the hospital, he could cause trouble. Perhaps you should return to Black House until things are settled."

"He won't cause trouble. In fact, I doubt he's even noticed my absence."

A petulant statement on Elena's part. She could not deny looking around each corner, secretly hoping Archer would be there to beg her forgiveness and tell her everything would work out just as she'd planned. And then, of course, there could be more kissing.

When had she become such a ridiculous woman?

Leaving Harcourt, Elena returned downstairs and spent the rest of the afternoon and evening immersed in the injuries and maladies of the district. The intensity of the work soothed her frayed nerves and made her remember exactly why she loved medicine, and serving the less privileged of the city. She'd just dropped off a bundle of dirty linens at the laundry when Nurse James approached.

"We're glad to have you back, Nurse Whitney, but don't exhaust yourself. Remember—we'll need you again tomorrow, bright and early. Go have a bite to eat before the dining hall closes, and turn in for the night."

Only then did Elena realize the intense ache of her back and legs, from being on her feet for hours on end.

She nodded, "Thank you, Nurse James. I'll see you in the morning, then."

She didn't feel at all like eating. A vague curiosity had prodded at her for the past several hours, one that wouldn't be silent until she eased her mind. The detectives had come here looking for suspects, but what about victims? She delved down the corridor to the reception rooms, which had already been closed for the night. Only the light from the hallway lamps illuminated inward.

Elena went to the porter's desk and lit his lantern

before seating herself in his chair. Five leather-bound registry books occupied a shelf beneath the desk, each with a span of dates written on the spine—all but the last. She selected that volume and flipped backward through the pages, until she came to the previous July and August, leading up to August 31, when the Ripper's first known victim, Mary Ann Nichols, had been murdered. Drawing her index finger down the columns, she proceeded through each of the pages, scanning the names, all written in the porter's fine script.

Rose Smith, 16 George Street.
Jane Ransom, 107 High Street.

After an hour of scouring months and months of entries, she stood and stretched, exhausted but relieved. While she'd spotted a few variations on names that might match the Ripper's victims, there was no obvious pattern or concentration of incidence. She supposed one could not forget women from the street had a habit of changing names to suit their purposes. She closed the registry book and stared out into the darkened room, only to be startled by a face staring back at her.

"Mr. Stephenson! What are you doing here?"

He groused, "I couldn't sleep with all those wagons clattering past my window, and there are lunatics in the common room, so I came here for some quiet."

"It's very late. I'm sure the street traffic has settled down. Let's get you back to your room."

Elena helped him up by the arm and led him on a familiar path to his room.

"Home again," he announced morosely as they passed through the narrow threshold.

"You've been a patient here at the hospital since July?" Elena asked.

"Yes. I do like it here." With gentle guidance, she lowered him to sit at the edge of his narrow bed, then removed his slippers. He lay down on his side. "I used to be a surgeon, you know. I studied medicine in Paris."

"Did you now? You'll have to share your experiences with me some time. But for now, I'd like you to get some sleep."

"Thank you, Nurse."

"You're very welcome."

Elena turned down his lamp and pulled the door closed behind her. Exhausted, she made the brief trek to her room in the dormitory, wanting nothing more than to sleep for a few hours before she'd have to return to the floor.

The next two days passed quickly, a rapid succession of patients, illnesses and emergencies—and stolen snatches of sleep on her narrow dormitory bed. One benefit of being so tired was that she didn't have the energy to think about Archer, and his betrayal, which still stung her deeply. She welcomed the oblivion, going so far as to cover an extra shift for a nurse chum who had had fallen ill. On that third night, as she fumbled through the darkness into her tiny room well after midnight, she smelled something—something out of place.

Roses?

At last she found the packet of matches on the bedside table, and after three failed attempts, struck a flame against the candle's slender wick.

Indeed—on her bed lay a bundle of roses. Red, like the ones she'd received at Black House. A dozen this time, wrapped in fine black tissue, and tied with a black bow. Black. Black like Lord Black?

Beside the flowers was a card.

Her hand shook as she lifted it. All the hurt came back, but alongside that, the memory of his lips on hers. She still didn't understand what had happened between them. Was she such a fool to think he had understood her?

She ached for him to explain away his betrayal, to make her believe he'd done it because of some misguided depth of feeling.

Finally, able to bear the curiosity no more, she tore open the card. Ah, she realized with crushing disappointment, it was a note from Lady Kerrigan inviting her to dinner next Wednesday evening, November 7. A sudden thought occurred to her—one that caused her to sink down on her narrow mattress.

What if Lord Black had finished his business in London?

What if he intended to leave without saying good-bye?

Chapter Fifteen

"My dear Miss Whitney, are you certain you won't stay the night?" Lady Kerrigan asked from the door of the small, first-floor dressing room where Elena had freshened up after arriving from the hospital.

She'd worn her uniform on the hackney ride to Mayfair and changed only after arriving, not wishing to draw the attention to the fact she'd received a dinner invitation to Dr. Harcourt's home, which might make things awkward with some of the other nurses.

Elena set her valise on the table. "Thank you, my lady, but I've accepted an early shift at the hospital, and I'd rather sleep as late as possible at the dormitory than suffer a predawn ride to Whitechapel."

Lady Kerrigan nodded sympathetically. "Yes, I can see why you would."

"By the way, thank you also for the beautiful roses that accompanied your invitation."

Her ladyship's brow furrowed quizzically. "Roses?"

"Yes, the roses delivered with the card. At least I assumed they arrived with the card. . . ." Embarrassment heated Elena's cheeks.

A knowing smile curved the elder woman's lips. "It seems you've an admirer."

The flowers could have come from anyone. Perhaps Harcourt? He knew she was going through a difficult time. But she had seen him numerous times at the hospital, and he had indicated nothing.

Elena's heartbeat quickened. Her throat grew uncomfortably tight.

Archer?

Doubtfully. More and more, she believed he must have departed London. If he were still in the city, wouldn't he have at least made inquiries as to her well-being?

Regardless, if whoever sent the roses wished to be appropriately acknowledged, they should identify themselves with a card. It was impolite to have twice put her in the position of guessing who had sent them.

Elena and her hostess quit the room to make their way toward the grand gallery, where her ladyship's birthday ball had taken place nearly five weeks before. That night seemed like forever ago. Elena could not help but marvel over how much her life had changed since then.

Charles stood up from an elegant chaise. Tall and handsome, he greeted them with his customary enthusiasm.

"My lady." He bent to kiss his mother on the cheek. "And Miss Whitney, what a pleasure it is to have you here this evening."

He kissed the tops of her fingers, and tucked her hand through his elbow. Offering the same to his mother, he escorted them up the ivory and gilt staircase to the formal dining room. They passed beneath the doorway, which was lavishly framed in gilt flourishes.

Elena froze. There, amongst the other invited guests stood a tall, powerfully built gentleman in impeccable evening dress. He conversed with Lord Kerrigan—but his lips stopped moving the moment their eyes met.

The floor seemed to fall out from beneath her. Lord Black had not left London. Elena had been in residence at the hospital for a full week, and though he had been in the city all along, he had not made contact with her once.

"What is it?" Charles asked her in a low voice.

She had unknowingly seized his arm. Wordlessly, she shook her head.

Cursed protocol, she should have anticipated his attendance. A young, unmarried lady would not be invited to dinner, without her family member or guardian receiving an invitation as well. Her heart thundered as he cut toward them, his gaze inscrutable. All eyes followed him, curious and admiring.

"Lady Kerrigan. Miss Whitney." With one sweep of his glance she felt naked, as if her gown had been stripped from her. She could only pray her straight shoulders and false, serene smile hid the depth of his effect on her.

"Your lordship." Elena acknowledged him with a tense nod.

"Miss Whitney," trilled a familiar voice.

Mrs. Hazelgreaves pushed through the small crowd on the arm of a middle-aged gentleman. Introductions were quickly made. Mrs. Hazelgreave's son, Theodore, acted as her escort, and quickly snared Archer into conversation, drawing him off to the side.

"Mrs. Hazelgreaves," Elena said. "You look positively . . . radiant."

It was true. A vibrant pink flush complemented

the elderly woman's cheeks. Barely leaning upon her cane, she appeared more hale and hearty than Elena had ever seen her. Even her hair seemed to gleam a brighter shade of silver.

Harcourt nodded. "It seems that a few weeks of quality rest was all Mrs. Hazelgreaves needed. She has fully recovered."

Mrs. Hazelgreaves added, "I can't explain why, but I feel completely invigorated—so invigorated, Teddy and his dear wife have agreed to take me to Paris until December."

"How wonderful for you," exclaimed Lady Kerrigan.

"We depart immediately. In the morning actually. He's breaking the news to his lordship now." The elder woman's smile wavered. "After all, it's not as if I'm needed here, is it, my dear Miss Whitney?"

Her pointed gaze settled on Elena.

"No, Mrs. Hazelgreaves," Elena agreed softly, not realizing until now how fond she'd grown of her companion. "I'm afraid not. I shall be residing elsewhere from now on. But I thank you for all your wonderful companionship these past two years."

Mrs. Hazelgreaves tilted her head and studied Elena carefully. "And I you, dear. I am certain, though, that we shall enjoy each other's company again."

"I would look forward to that."

"Then we won't say good-bye." She reached a delicate, veined hand to clasp Elena's, and leaned forward to press a kiss on her cheek. "Until then."

Elena allowed Charles to draw her off in the opposite direction to be introduced to Lord Lister, an esteemed scientist-surgeon and member of the council of the Royal College of Surgeons, a gentleman she would have been thrilled to meet if not for the distraction of Archer's presence. Just knowing he was near after so many days of being apart from him raised the tension within her to an excruciating level.

Thankfully, the same protocol that had brought her guardian to the event precluded her from being seated next to him. A quarter hour later, and having not eaten a bite, she chanced a glance at the far end of the table to find his gaze on her. He didn't look away at being caught.

She, on the other hand, looked down at her plate.

The conversation rambled on around her.

"I think the Ripper is gone. Probably dead. The burden of what he did to those women too much for him. I propose he's committed suicide." The gentleman turned suddenly in his chair toward Lady Kerrigan. "My apologies for speaking so crudely in front of the ladies."

Her ladyship tipped her head. "Nonetheless, I hope what you suppose is true. I pray the villain is at this moment floating with all the other rubbish at the bottom of the Thames."

Lady Kerrigan's cheeks went pink with the fervency of her statement. Chuckles went up from around the circumference of the table.

After an excruciatingly extended rotation of culinary courses, the meal finally came to an end. As was customary, the gentlemen drifted in the direction of the library, where they would enjoy their cigars and spirits. The ladies set off toward the salon.

"Miss Whitney?" Lady Kerrigan stood at the center of the grand corridor. "Aren't you coming?"

"I'm afraid I don't feel well," Elena said. "Please don't worry about me. I think I'm just tired. I'm going to return to the dormitory."

After reassuring her ladyship, at least a thousand more times, that there was no cause for undue concern,

Elena scurried down the stairs, and then the hall, like a child fearful of being caught sneaking about after bed-time. She would just get her bag, and be on her way. She could not take that chance that she and Archer would find themselves standing beneath the porte cochere at the same moment, waiting for their conveyances.

It wasn't Archer she was frightened of; it was her-self. By blocking her entrance to medical school, he had destroyed her dreams, left her with nothing. He had soundly communicated to her how little respect he had for her.

So *why* did she want nothing more than to be in his arms again?

"Elena."

She nearly screamed—but realized almost instantly the voice belonged to Dr. Harcourt. Reluctant, and rigid of stance, she turned and found him standing some distance behind her, appearing winded, as if he'd pursued her all the way from the dining room.

"Yes, Doctor?"

"Might I speak with you for a moment?"

No. She needed to keep running. She smiled. "Of course."

"Here." He held out a hand, indicating. "The Blue Drawing Room will do."

Elena returned to where he stood, and passed through the indicated portal, her head pounding.

Harcourt drew the large wooden doors almost closed but did not shut them completely.

"Elena."

"Yes?"

"Would you like to sit?"

"No, I'm fine standing, thank you." As soon as the doctor said whatever he had to say, she intended to proceed with her escape.

Did she imagine things, or were his cheeks flushed,

and his posture tense? She couldn't recall him ever looking nervous. One thing she liked about Harcourt was he seemed so completely at ease and confident in his own skin. Something was wrong.

"What is it, Doctor?"

"Charles," he insisted firmly, reaching to touch her hand.

"Charles."

Suddenly the realization struck her.

"He's spoken to you, hasn't he? He wants you to force me to leave my position at the hospital and return to Black House."

"I assume you refer to Lord Black. No, he hasn't."

For a moment, Elena felt a dash of irrational disappointment. "That's a relief."

"However, at dinner, Sir Dunord discreetly informed me of Lord Black's interference with your application to the women's college."

Elena nodded. "It's true. That's why I left Black House, and moved into the dormitory."

Charles swallowed hard. "I believe I've got the perfect solution for you."

"I'd love to hear it." She couldn't imagine what he's suggest. She'd wracked her brain trying to think of a way to get around her guardian's powerful influence, and her future lack of funds, and had come up with nothing.

"Marry me."

"Marry you?" Her mouth fell open.

"Yes, Elena," he answered, moving forward to clasp her hands. "Don't you see? It's the perfect answer for both of us."

"For both of us?"

Dear Dr. Harcourt. Was he looking to make her his personal charity case? She couldn't bear that possibility.

He answered, "If you marry me, he will lose the privilege of guardianship over you. I, of course, would not interfere with your desire to attain your medical degree. Indeed, Elena, I would support your every aspiration."

"Those reasons are all to my benefit. How could marriage to me possibly benefit you?"

Harcourt appeared to work at finding the right words, or perhaps it was simply difficult for him to speak of something so personal. "For so long I believed that I would never marry, that I could never ask any woman to suffer my devotion to medicine, and my commitment to the hospital. I never expected to find someone like you. Elena, you share my passions."

His words echoed through her head, and she stared at him, disbelieving and dizzy. She had not expected this. Not at all.

"Together we could achieve all our dreams."

"Charles . . ."

"Say yes."

She cared for Dr. Harcourt. He had been her physician, and her mentor, and had supported her unfailingly in her quest to become a doctor. Now that he'd proposed marriage, everything felt different. It was as if his confession unleashed a floodgate of honesty in his eyes. He stared at her with unconcealed adoration.

"I can't marry you."

His handsome face darkened, and the smile faded from his lips. "It's him, isn't it? Lord Black."

"No."

"By God, he hasn't compromised you, has he?"

She shook her head, mortified that he might believe such a thing. "No, he has not."

At the same time, she could only wish Archer had.

She wanted him with a passion that defied all bounds of rationale and self-respect. Given his betrayal, that made her a complete fool—a fool who couldn't possibly turn her affections toward someone else, no matter how worthy they might be.

"Quite the opposite," she whispered. "He has attempted at every turn to see me betrothed. I'm certain he would be very pleased to know you offered to marry me."

Charles stormed toward the blazing hearth. He pressed his forearm against the mantel, and stared morosely into the fire. "I saw the way he looked at you tonight."

She shook her head. "You imagine things."

Harcourt appeared unconvinced. He pressed his fist against his handsome lips. Suddenly he turned.

"I'll wait until you are ready, Elena."

"Don't say that. You've no obligation to me."

"I've an obligation to my heart, because, do you see? I love you. I suppose I've known from the start, and I've waited, and . . . God, no time ever seemed right. Now it appears I waited too long."

Moments later, Elena pushed into the small dressing room where she'd left her bag before dinner. She dropped onto a stool, and crossing her arms on the table, lowered her head and cried.

She had just broken the heart of an honorable man.

A tap sounded at the window. She lifted her head to peer in that direction—and nearly screamed, seeing Archer's face floating in the darkness, like some ghoul from a macabre tale.

"Go away," she wailed softly, not wanting anyone to hear.

He tapped again, tersely pointing to the latch. Finally, growing more and more ill-tempered, she crossed the small chamber. After unlocking the window, she pushed out the twin panes.

"I've had the devil finding which room you were in."

She glanced over the ledge and saw his boots planted on the rung of a rickety-looking ladder. He appeared completely out of place in his fine evening clothes.

"I said go away."

He stared hard at her face. "Are you crying?"

He reached for her arm, but she twisted out of reach, returning to the center of the room.

"Tell me what is wrong," he demanded. "Has someone hurt you?"

I have hurt someone, unforgivably. All because of you, she wished to rail.

"Just go away."

"I'm not leaving."

"Well, you're not coming in here."

She rushed toward him again to grasp the windows. With a frown, she swung them closed—

He halted each effortlessly with his hands. "I've a gift for you."

"I don't want a gift. Not from you." She peered at him through the narrow space created by the wood frames.

"I'm afraid you don't have any choice but to accept it. It's not the sort I can return. And if I must say, it was rather expensive."

She released the windows and went to the mantel, where she folded her hands behind her waist. "Leave the bloody present there on the windowsill, then, and go away."

She didn't care about the gift; she just wanted him to go.

"I'll be waiting for you below. Be careful climbing down."

"What?" she sputtered. "I'm not climbing down—"

Elena saw the bundle on the sill—a dark bundle. She went to it and poked at it with her finger. When it didn't growl or bite, she took it up and found it to be a man's coat . . . a shirt . . . and trousers.

Archer leaned against the trunk of a tree in the garden, waiting. Soon, he saw her return to the window, dressed in the clothes he'd left on the sill. Gratification flooded his veins. She dropped down her bag. It bounced on the earth, obviously stuffed tight with her clothing.

He strode across the yard to hold the ladder steady, all the while taking in the arousing sight of Elena's bottom in the trousers as she descended. He did not back away, even when her feet touched upon the bottom rung. When she turned, he effectively held her in a cage formed of the ladder and the brace of his arms.

Her pale hair shone like gold against the shoulders of the man's coat. "I still despise you for what you did."

"As you should." He lowered a top hat onto her head and tapped it down, into place.

"For someone who insists that I settle down into a respectable life and marriage, you seem determined to ruin my reputation."

She was right. His logical mind told him he ought to let her go and allow her to live her own life—but he couldn't force himself to leave things alone. At the same time, he acted with distorted purpose. He needed to get her back to Black House and safety before the predicted Tartarian wave passed over Lon-

don, when Jack the Ripper would act again. Somehow he had known she wouldn't be able to resist the
promise of an adventure.

"Come on." He bent to retrieve her bag.

They quickly rounded the side of the house and
went out to the street.

"Where are you taking me?" she asked in a low,
sardonic voice. She jabbed her curls under the hat.
"Gambling? To a house of ill repute? Are you finally
going to share all your dark secrets with me?"

"Wait and see."

He lifted his hand to summon a hackney. One
veered across the road and rolled to a stop in front
of them. Inside, Elena lowered herself to the bench.
Archer slid in beside her. They traveled in silence for
the better part of a half hour.

At his signal, they disembarked on a narrow thoroughfare lined with sidewalks and neat, middle-class
houses. Although a handful of passersby bustled to
and fro and a carriage clattered by, there was an air
of quiet unknown to the rougher districts of the city.

"Here we are," he said, stopping on the sidewalk.

"At long last," she answered, unimpressed.

The front face of the house inspired no grandiose
expectations—only suspicion on Elena's part. Iron
lamps hung on either side of the door, empty of
flame, and she could see no light through the windows. Why would Archer bring her, dressed as a
man, to an abandoned house? He climbed the front
steps, and knocked. The windowless wooden door
creaked inward, and a gray-bearded face appeared.

Archer announced in a low voice, "Lord Black and
Mr. Flowers."

Elena supposed she was Mr. Flowers. She exhaled
nervously and kept her hat low on her forehead, hop-

ing the wide leg of her trousers continued to conceal
the taffeta bow on the top arch of her shoe.

The bearded man backed into a dark entry hall,
bowing and pulling the door wide for their entrance.
"Welcome, your lordship. We've been expecting you."

Archer set her bag down against the wall. Elena
slipped her hands into the narrow pockets at the
front of her coat and followed her towering companion down a short corridor. Conversation buzzed,
formed of many male voices, but stopped instantly
on their arrival. A room full of faces turned toward
them. All wore respectable vests and suits. Piles of
discarded top and bowler hats littered two side tables. Three huge brass candelabrum blazed, filling
the room with light.

One gentleman, wearing spectacles and a surgeon's
tunic, broke free of the group and came toward Elena
and Lord Black. He wore an open expression of
greeting.

"Gentlemen of the society, please join me in wel-
coming our most recent financial donor, Lord Black.
How pleased we are to have you and your associate,
Mr. Flowers."

Elena touched the brim of her hat but kept it on
her head, and her face tilted low.

"Thank you, Dr. Alcott," said Lord Black.

The man smiled and circled round to address the
gathering. "Now that our special guests have arrived,
we may proceed."

The bearded gentleman who had shown them in
from the door touched Elena's elbow and, with a
gentle nudge, urged her toward the center of the
room.

"You must both move closer, for the best view."

To her amazement, everyone parted to reveal that

which had been laid out on a metal table at the center of the room. Beneath a gleaming white sheet lay the unmistakable outline of a corpse.

Elena glanced toward Archer. He looked ahead, a smile turning the corner of his lips. Tears glazed her eyes, but she quickly blinked them away.

Dr. Alcott said, "The human body is a fantastic and mysterious thing, and as physicians, physicians-in-training, and men of knowledge, we all know how rare it is to have an opportunity to dissect the human body, in its most complete form, at our leisure and for the simple luxury of education."

"Here! Here!" came the response around the room.

"Sir James, who passed away only this morning, arranged that his body be donated to the society for this specific purpose. I hope the rest of you will consider making the same generous sacrifice when your own final decisions are made."

"God bless Sir James," bellowed a gentleman in the back, who then snorted into a handkerchief.

Dr. Alcott stationed himself beside the corpse. "Let us begin."

Several other men in tunics took places beside him, ready to assist. The surgeon pulled back the sheet and picked up a gleaming scalpel.

Archer could not see Elena's reaction below the wide brim of her hat, but from behind, where no one would see, she grasped the cuff of his sleeve and angled for a closer look.

They did not speak as they descended the steps amongst the other attendees of the dissection. In silence, the group dissipated into the shadows of the night.

Gas lamps lined the avenue, hissing softly as they passed. Her mind still couldn't grasp what had just taken place. Her estranged guardian had dressed her in men's clothing, brought her out into the dark London night and gifted her with something so dear to her heart, she could not help but feel they'd grown infinitely closer in the passing of a few short hours—hours in which they hadn't even spoken; they had only stood beside each other, observing the dissection of a dead man. Bizarrely, she found the gesture *achingly* romantic.

"Do you wish to return to the hospital?" he asked quietly.

No, I don't. I want to stay with you.

She nodded. "Yes. The hospital."

"I'll take you there." He raised her bag in the direction of the avenue.

"Thank you."

The fit of the trousers against her body felt foreign and sensual, even though beneath, she'd worn her wool, lace-edged drawers. The idea of him selecting the male garments for her was nearly as illicit as if he'd purchased some piece of diaphanous lingerie.

The cluster of physicians who preceded them on the sidewalk secured the last available hackney parked at the curb. They piled in, and the vehicle clattered down the street.

They stood for a moment, watching the avenue for another. Archer glanced at his watch. "It's not yet midnight. Let's take the train."

They walked a brief distance before coming to the arched-stonework entrance of the railway station, and descended the stairs. Oil lamps lit the walls, providing dim light for the cavernous, subterranean space. The scent of coal dust mixed with sulfur crowded Elena's nose. Archer paid for their tickets, and together they crossed the platform to wait with a handful of other passengers.

Eventually the engine hurtled out of the dark tunnel and screeched to a halt. Elena followed Archer onto the first-class car and sat a respectable distance from him on the leather seat. High, wood-paneled walls surrounded them. The only windows were narrow, and occupied a space along the stamped-tin ceiling. Oil lamps hung from brass chains, giving off a golden glow. The uniformed conductor claimed the tickets and passed through the door to move into the second-class car, leaving them alone.

The train lurched into travel, and the car darkened further going into the tunnel. The bench they sat upon took up a gentle, rocking motion, which, in the company of her silent guardian, resulted in a distinctly seductive effect.

She rested her head back against the leather and considered him. "Why did you take me there tonight?"

For a long moment he stared at her hand, which lay on the bench between them. Finally, he lifted his gaze to hers. "Because despite what I did . . . I wanted you to know—" He faltered, looking away, and laughed low in his throat. "I'm decidedly awkward at subjects like this. Personal subjects."

Elena did not reply, did not try to make the moment easier for him. She waited for him to continue.

He did. "You were wrong when you said I didn't believe in you."

"Then why, Archer?" she asked softly. "Why did you do what you did?"

Slowly his hand covered hers.

"Because nothing else mattered but protecting you. I hated that you wanted to spend your life in Whitechapel. I still do. I thought I could bear your hatred, but I can't."

"I don't hate you." She exhaled shallowly. "I could never hate you."

His fingers wove between hers.

"You hurt me."

"I know." He lifted her hand and closing his eyes, touched his lips against her folded fingers. "I'll fix things. Everything. I realize that I was trying to smother everything in you that I admired. I also realize I've got to let you—"

He exhaled.

"Let me what?"

"Fly, Elena. I've got to let you fly."

His words touched her heart, and at the same time, she realized this night might very well be good-bye. She leaned closer. His hand cupped her chin. His gaze moved from her eyes, to her lips.

Elena trembled, knowing he would kiss her. He angled his head, dipping beneath the brim of her hat to press his warm mouth against hers. Elena clasped her hand against his jaw, wanting to hold him there forever. She spread her fingers round into the thick, cool hair of his nape. With all the passion inside her she returned his kiss.

He growled into her mouth, "Why, Mr. Flowers."

The vibration of the train spread up through her back, and along her buttocks and the undersides of her thighs.

"Touch me, Archer," she begged.

His hand thrust beneath her necktie, invading the slit between the buttons of her shirt to caress the bare upper swell of her breast above her chemise. Her nipples tightened to hard peaks. She couldn't get close enough. She curled her fingers into his coat lapels, and twisted, rising up onto one knee to swing her leg over his hips so that she straddled him.

"Darling . . . ," Archer groaned, deep in his throat.

Face to face, their lips melded, hot and open. Her hat fell to the seat, and her hair tumbled over the shoulders of her greatcoat. Beneath the fine linen of his shirt she felt the hardness of his chest, the heated flex of his stomach. He slid his hands over the tops of her thighs, beneath the tails of her coat to clasp her buttocks. He tilted his hips and seized her against him. Rigid and hot, he pushed against her, spreading her, giving her unimaginable pleasure even through the layers of her woolen trousers and linen underpants.

Suddenly Archer twisted his face aside and dragged her to sit on the bench beside him. She sprawled, dazed with passion.

"The conductor," he rasped, quickly handing over her hat and straightening her tie. He chuckled, a low, hoarse sound, and crossed his legs, and his arms over his chest.

She thrust the hat atop her head and stuffed her hair beneath. Had he heard a footstep? A door? She had heard nothing, but then again, she lost all sensibility in his arms.

As Archer had warned, the porter stepped through from the second-class car and gripped the brass pole. "Aldgate! Last train."

The wheels screeched, and their bodies swayed at the rapid deceleration. Once the train had fully stopped, Elena stood on shaky legs and exited onto the platform. Archer shadowed her just behind, carrying her bag. As they ascended the dark stairwell, he caught her wrist, and laughing huskily, pushed her to the wall. He dropped a brief but fervent kiss to her lips. The illicit excitement of knowing they could be discovered at any moment sent an unexpected thrill of excitement through Elena. She arched against him, holding her hat in place. Between her thighs she felt slick and hot, and ached for something more.

"Return with me to Black House tonight."

Feverish with desire, Elena nodded. "Yes. I want to."

He backed away from her, his eyes vivid and intense, even in the dark shadows. She knew exactly what she agreed to. She would spend the night in Archer's bed, making love to him. He might be gone tomorrow, but the next few hours would be enough to last her a lifetime. It had to be.

When they came out onto the sidewalk, she startled, seeing a familiar town coach parked at the curb. Mr. Leeson perched atop its bench, a cane-whip in his hand. He nodded to her, grinning.

"Don't be angry," Archer murmured. "I had hoped to convince you somewhere along the way to return home—though not in the manner that occurred."

"I'm not angry. I want to go with you." She exhaled excitedly. "Just one thing."

She grasped his sleeve.

"We are just a few moments from the hospital. With the recent murders, they've strict rules about our comings and goings, and we the nursing staff must verify our whereabouts to the dormitory deputy each morning and night. I don't wish her to send the police out when I don't check in as expected."

Archer glowered, a sensual image of impatience, but nodded in agreement. Once inside the carriage, Elena set aside her top hat. Her valise sat on the floor. She bent over to retrieve her long mantle from inside.

"I can't have them see me dressed like this," she chuckled, shaking it out.

Suddenly, from behind, Archer banded his arm around her waist, drawing her back against his chest. "I don't want you in more clothes; I want you in fewer. I'm loath to let you go for even a moment."

He bent his face to her neck, kissing her there, and teasing her skin with his tongue. Everything inside her went warm like melted wax. His hands pressed up along her rib cage to cup the undersides of her breasts. Elena writhed in pleasure.

The carriage rolled to a stop. Archer released her to recline into the corner of the bench into a regal, long-legged sprawl. One glance out the window showed Elena the carriage had pulled alongside the rear entrance to the hospital, the one usually utilized by the staff.

"Hurry."

She quickly drew on the mantle and fastened the buttons down the front. She scooted closer to the door, but hesitated, pressing her hands to her cheeks and rubbing her eyes.

"What are you doing?" Archer asked.

"Trying not to look so *impassioned*. Nurse James will certainly realize I'm in the midst of being seduced."

Archer grinned. "Should I go with you?"

"No," Elena insisted firmly, laughing. "That would only make things worse."

She turned the latch and disappeared into the blue darkness, closing the door behind her.

Instantly the smile slipped from his lips.

With the intrusion of night air came a powerful curl of trace, stinking and fetid.

He jerked the door open. He could still hear her footsteps.

Leeson crouched, preparing to leap from the bench. His daggers glimmered inside his vest. "I sense him too."

"Stay." Archer held up a halting hand. "You may be called upon to take Elena away quickly."

Archer followed the path she'd taken up the stairs. He caught a glimpse of her dark mantle as she swept into the hospital.

Inside the small entrance hall, two weary-faced nurses gossiped and giggled on a bench. Here Jack's trace was stronger.

He was here, in the hospital.

Every muscle in Archer's body drew taut in preparation for battle. His gaze focused on the hall where Elena had gone. He would find her and send her off with Leeson, before beginning the hunt.

Suddenly, something distracted him. The attention of several mortals focused upon him, their thoughts twisted about him. Behind him the door whooshed open.

There he is.

Lord, he's a big gent.

He closed his eyes in anticipation—

A hand clamped down on his forearm.

"Pardon me, sir," a voice inquired. "Is that your town coach waiting at the curb outside?"

"It is," Archer answered, watching the hall and praying for Elena to reemerge.

"Then you are Lord Black."

"I am."

The man stepped in front of him. He was a good half foot shorter than Archer, and his mustache swept low over his jowls to meet up with his sideburns. He drew aside his frock coat to reveal a brass badge pinned to his brace strap.

"First-Class Inspector Abberline of the Metropolitan Police, sir, Home Office. I'm afraid, your lordship, you'll have to come with us for questioning."

Chapter Sixteen

Three more officers closed in, two of them pressing close to grasp his arms above the elbows. The nurses, wide-eyed and whispering, scurried off down the hall.

He could easily throw the men off, but he could not afford to draw attention to himself or his unnatural powers, not with so many witnesses. Shadow Guards, and any Amaranthine for that matter, were forbidden to reveal their extraordinary powers to a mortal audience. Such a display would only draw unwanted attention and lead to the potential discovery of the Inner Realm.

"What is this about?" Archer asked.

Abberline's gaze revealed an appreciation for Archer's relative cordiality. He spoke quietly, discreetly. "You've been implicated in a crime, your lordship."

Word had spread. Patients and hospital staff flowed into the room. They spoke in hushed tones, their eyes wide, amazed that they might be witnessing the apprehension of the Ripper.

The Ripper *was* here, goddamit, somewhere.

Archer swallowed hard and tried to calm his racing heart. He had never before felt this fear. Fear of losing someone. Fear of being alone again. God, Elena, where was she?

The Ripper's trace curled about him, almost taunting in its strength. The urge to quicken into a predator came fiercely upon him.

The police, and everyone who gathered, would believe him a lunatic if he started spouting off. If he did not mind himself, he would find himself not only imprisoned, but whisked to Bedlam. He had to remain rational.

He leveled his gaze on Abberline. "Someone has misinformed you."

Who was that someone? And how would they have known to send the police to the hospital to lie in wait for him?

"Now settle down, your lordship," Abberline assured him in a calm voice. "That may be true, but we can't clear the report until you come with us and offer your testimony, and a supporting witness or two."

Archer responded through clenched teeth, "You must summon my man outside so that he may find my ward, Miss Elena Whitney, and inform her I am being taken into custody."

Abberline answered flatly, "Mr. Leeson has been named your accomplice. He'll be coming to the station as well."

"Archer!"

Elena's voice.

Relief coursed through him, tempered by the knowledge she remained in danger. She raced toward him, her face stark above the high collar of her mantle. One of the detectives intercepted her, catching her by the shoulders.

"What's happening?" she demanded, in a blaze of

white-fire beauty. Even now, in the midst of this, he wanted her still.

Archer snared her gaze. "I'm being taken into custody."

Elena's face fell. "Into custody?"

Abberline assured her, "It's all right, miss. If he's telling the truth, then you've nothing to worry about. Once the appropriate witnesses are provided, and supporting documentation gathered—"

Archer bit down on a curse, hopelessly trapped by the confines of his false mortal identity.

Dr. Harcourt pushed into view. "What is the meaning of this?"

One of the other detectives answered this time. "His lordship has been implicated in the Ripper crimes."

"That's impossible."

Abberline chuckled, "So he maintains. I suppose any suspect would say the same, now wouldn't he? So let us do our work, and if there is no validity to this anonymous report—"

"Anonymous?" Archer gave a caustic laugh. "How many anonymous reports have you received on the Ripper case? Thousands. I am certain you do not act on them all."

Abberline's brows rose high. "They are all not as compelling as this one."

Archer claimed Harcourt's gaze. "Take Elena to Black House. Inform the Countess Pavlenco that I've been taken in for questioning."

"Yes, of course."

Though after midnight, word had spread quickly, and a raucous throng had gathered outside. As Archer was dragged down the hospital stairs, he spied Mark standing in the crowd.

Elena, stunned by the sudden and unexpected loss

of Archer, stared at the door through which the detectives had taken him. All too quickly, the crowd
dispersed, and she was left alone—alone except for
Harcourt.

He stared at her, unsmiling. "After my failed proposal, I came here thinking I would find you. I had
hoped I might still be able to persuade you to
marry me."

Elena did not answer. She clasped her mantle
around her, wanting to weep, yet she refused to give
in to hopelessness. Archer would expose whatever
false allegations had been made against him. He
would return for her, and they would have their
proper good-bye.

Harcourt probed softly, "You weren't with him before. But you're with him now, aren't you?"

She perceived no rancor in his voice, only hurt,
and resignation.

Elena whispered, "Yes."

Even if Archer departed London tomorrow, and
she never saw him again, yes. She belonged to him,
body and soul.

Just then the doors flew open. A crowd of men in
leather aprons, their faces grimy with filth, pushed
through. They carried an unconscious man by his
arms and legs.

"Doctor! Nurse! Help us. There's been an explosion at the brewery."

Archer stared at the dingy gray wall of his cell, his
heartbeat crashing in his ears. He was trapped in the
Whitechapel police substation, while the Ripper was
out there, just a few streets away, stalking Elena.

I could teach her a thing or two about human anatomy,
as I have recently become an expert on the subject—haha!

He thrust his hands into his hair. Acid tore at his

stomach, and he felt as if he would retch on the cell floor. He had only glimpsed Leeson, who'd been confined to a cell around the corner. The detectives of H Division had questioned him about his comings and goings over the previous weeks. He had answered them, referring them foremost to the customs officials for proof he had arrived in England after the murders had begun. He had also glimpsed the handwritten note accusing him of involvement in the Ripper crimes. Though the writer had sought to disguise his writing, Archer easily recognized the strokes as belonging to the Ripper.

He cursed and paced the narrow cell. How long would it be before his release?

The only way he could escape the cell would be to shift into shadow and slip through the metal door. Yet the young sergeant outside his cell watched his every move, and would not only see him, but raise an alarm as to his paranormal abilities. He'd never come close enough for Archer to touch him, to blacken his mind. Rigidly, Archer seated himself on a stool in the middle of the cell. He lowered his head into his hands and steeled himself to wait.

Hours later Elena, numb with exhaustion, sat on a bench with another nurse. After the casualties from the brewery had started flowing in, she'd never found an opportunity to leave for Black House. With Harcourt's authorization, she'd sent one of the hospital couriers with a note informing Selene of Archer's arrest.

Her back ached from hours standing on the hospital's India rubber floor. She untied her apron, which was hopelessly soiled. Sadly, two brewery workers had died from their injuries, but Dr. Harcourt and the three night surgeons had saved the lives of the others.

"I don't know about you, but I'm starving," the ever-cheerful Nurse Braxton exclaimed, sagging beside her against the wall. She too removed her apron and used its corner to scrub a bit of blood from her wrist.

Elena looked at her watch. "It's too early for the dining hall."

Not that she was hungry. Her stomach had been a tangle of knots since Archer had been taken away. Her only saving grace had been the hospital, which had provided constant distraction . . . until now.

Where was Archer now? Why had the detectives taken him and Mr. Leeson, and would they soon be released? Her mind repeated the same questions over and over again.

Nurse Braxton elbowed her. "There's that chandler's shop off Philpot, always open early. Come on. Walk with me. You know we're not supposed to go out on our own."

Harcourt hurried past, obviously in response to some new emergency. One of the day nurses who'd just come on duty—her hair drawn neatly back, and her uniform pristine and starched—followed in his wake.

"All right," Elena agreed.

Anything to keep herself occupied. She wouldn't rest until she knew Archer had been released.

Outside, night lifted into pale blue morning. Behind the hospital she and Nurse Braxton crossed the grass and continued down Philpot, joining a good number of wharf workers and warehouse men on their way to the Thames. Eventually they came to the chandler's. Light glowed from the windows, revealing the movement of other customers inside. They walked beneath the yellow canvas awning, and Nurse Braxton pushed open the door.

"Nurse Whitney!"

Elena paused, searching the space around her. Lizzy stood at the corner of the building, wearing a crooked, apologetic smile. She wore her old clothes, and appeared mussed and weary as if she'd spent the night on the street.

Elena told Nurse Braxton, "You go on in. I'll join you in a moment."

Nurse Braxton glanced curiously at Lizzy and nodded. "All right, then."

A few steps and Elena stood before the girl.

"Lizzy, what's happened? Why aren't you at Black House?"

"It's a telegraph from the queen herself, sir. In no uncertain terms, she commands his lordship be released. Immediately."

Archer sat on the stool at the center of his cell. He heard the words and realized Selene must have telegraphed Her Majesty, but his gaze remained fixed on the narrow window across the room. The sky lightened with each passing moment. He pressed a hand to his mouth and felt the perspiration on his upper lip. All the centuries, all the battles and all the magnificent events to which he had born witness had faded to nothingness in the course of the night. There was only Elena.

If she died—

His heart seized darkly.

If she died, he would die as well. He would shrivel and rot and waste away inside. He could not explain, even to himself, how he had come to be so connected to her, at such a soul-deep level, but he had. He would not survive her loss. Would not want to.

The lock of his cell rattled, and the door swung inward.

"Your lordship—"

He caught up his coat and hat, and brushed past the detective, to race down the corridor. Leeson called out to him from his cell. Outside, on the street, he broke into a run. His desperation carried him all the way to the doors of the London Hospital.

He pushed inside. A crowd filled the small reception room. Jack's trace, of course, had completely disappeared.

Words and thoughts blasted around him.

"Lord Black!"

"He's been released—"

Who will tell him?

Harcourt's face swung round, stricken. Beside him stood a young nurse with a tear-streaked face, and two grim detectives.

Archer growled, emotion deepening his voice, "Where is she?"

Elena awoke to shadows and something damp and hard against her cheek.

Dazedly, she pushed herself up—and screamed.

Beside her sat a dead man, his head and shoulders canted at an awkward angle. No, her panicked mind realized, the thing beside her wasn't a man—it was a life-size effigy, its head and hands formed of wax. The same effigy of Jack the Ripper she'd seen on the street that afternoon after leaving the museum.

Fear, deeper and darker than anything she'd ever experienced before, numbed her arms and legs. Pressing her hand against her mouth, she knelt against the wall and took cover in the darkest of its shadows.

She was imprisoned at the bottom of a pit, at least twelve feet in depth. A metal grate covered the opening, and orange light wavered beyond. Beneath her feet were pottery shards. She squinted, trying to see more. Old clothing and newspapers. Everything smelled old, damp and decayed.

Elena closed her eyes and tried to remember how she had come to be here. She remembered leaving the hospital, and seeing Lizzy, but nothing more. Had Lizzy done this to her? She couldn't believe that.

So who had?

Her head spun, from panic or some narcotic drug? She suspected she'd been subdued with chloroform, a method often employed by the villains of Whitechapel's streets. How long had she been unconscious, and was anyone looking for her?

She stood again, unsteadily, and pressed her hand against the wet stones. More clearheaded now, she examined them. They were too smooth and closely mortared to climb, not to mention completely covered with greenish black slime.

Something rustled above. One shadow in particular took a more solid form.

"You are awake. Delightful. I so wish to introduce myself."

Such an odd, hollow voice. A man or a woman's, she couldn't be sure.

She cleared her throat, and asked in a strong voice, "Who are you?"

"Call me Jack." The voice chuckled evilly. The chill she experienced did not go just down her spine but invaded every inch of her body. "Everyone else does."

Elena's breath rasped in her throat, echoing against the sides of the well.

"You haven't fainted . . . have you, Miss Whit-ney?" the voice asked hopefully.

"How do you know my name?"

"Mmmmmm . . . Lord Black. I strive to keep my-self informed of all his affairs. He likes to be elusive, though, doesn't he? Likes to play the dark . . . silent . . . *shadow*." The voice hissed off into nothing-ness.

Elena circled the perimeter, her mind occupied in equal parts by horror and curiosity. What sort of creature taunted her from above? She felt an irratio-nal, burning desire to see him for herself.

For the first time she wondered if the Ripper might not be altogether human. But if not human, what?

"What are you going to do with me?"

"Entertain myself."

The shadow skimmed along the edge of the well. Something dark and soft fluttered down all around her. Elena gasped, and sidestepped the stuff.

Rose petals. Dark red rose petals.

She realized they were not the first she'd received from this monster.

He growled, sounding more animal now than man. "It's not really you I want, you see. You're not at all to my tastes with your pretty hair and your white teeth. Though I do find you so very interesting . . . the future Dr. Whitney. I don't believe you'd be able to fix what's wrong with me. Nor my lovelies. Like them, when you look inside me, there's nothing left to work with."

"If you don't want me, then why am I here?"

The petals came in handfuls now. "Because he wants you. And you see, I like to play games. My master bids me to do so."

The petals were heavier now, and wet. They smelled rotted. They struck her in the head and shoulders, great stinking gobs. She fended them off, only to realize they stained her hands . . . with blood?

Something clanked onto the stone floor beside her, a rusted metal sphere the size of a croquet ball. Acrid yellow smoke spiraled out from inside. She sank onto her knees, covering the ball with newspaper and clothing. Another came down to hit against a chunk of pottery. *Clank.* And another. The narrow space filled with smoke. Even though she pressed her hands over her nose and mouth, and tried to cover them as well, her throat closed upon the burning stuff. Her eyes watered too greatly to see. Dizzy, she fell back against the wall.

"No," she pleaded softly. *Don't lose consciousness.* The Ripper would certainly do to her what he'd done to Catherine. "No . . . no . . . no."

"Don't worry, my darling," she heard him say. "I've something quite spectacular planned for you. I just don't want to hear you scream."

Stone thumped against the back of her head. Someone gripped her shoulders with painful strength and pinched her cheek. Someone with fingernails. She'd so much rather sleep than be assaulted.

"Ouch," she finally complained.

"She's alive," a woman's voice announced, sounding vaguely disappointed.

"Out of my way, Selene."

Elena opened her eyes.

A face replaced Selene's. Mark. He was so handsome. But not as handsome as Archer. She heard the crush of shards and newspaper as they moved about.

"Miss Whitney, are you all right?"

She felt so weak and out of sorts. She could barely keep her eyes open. Yet she was conscious enough to know she was safe and no longer in the Ripper's vicious clutches.

She mumbled, "I'm feeling better already."

He lifted her, and her head lolled onto his muscular shoulder. At the museum that afternoon, she'd gotten the distinct impression Archer and Mark didn't like each other. Perhaps she ought to show Archer some loyalty, but at this moment she felt nothing but adoration for the man. She wrapped her arms around his neck and squeezed.

Selene gasped. "She's been cut on her throat."

Damn the Ripper. He'd cut her.

Odd. She didn't feel any pain.

Sweet, though, of Selene to care.

Warm fingertips pressed against her skin. "No. It's only paint. The bastard drew a line across her throat to show us what he could have done to her."

In three fantastical steps, Mark carried her up the high well wall. Such a feat was not humanly possible, but obviously, her mind played tricks because of that nasty yellow smoke.

"Thank God we found you." His voice rumbled in his throat. She felt the vibration against her forehead.

"Thank you. Thank you so much," Elena whispered.

"Let's go." Selene hovered near a wooden door. "He wasn't ready for us to find him yet. He's not gained his full strength. We can catch him if we hurry."

"We can't leave her here." Mark lowered Elena onto a sagging chair. Darkness surrounded them. From what she could see in the weak glow from the fire grate, they were in a basement. She had not heard the sound of carriages passing by while she was in the pit, but she did now. The place stank of roses. They were everywhere, layer upon layer of blooms and broken stems. She never wanted to smell another again.

Mark knelt beside her, and taking a handkerchief from his trouser pocket, scrubbed at Elena's neck until she pushed him away.

The countess growled, "Fine. I'm going alone."

"Damn you, Selene."

Her mind slowly cleared and presented a host of questions, the foremost being why the countess would be itching to engage Jack the Ripper. Why had the Ripper talked about Archer? Her mind was like a thousand puzzle pieces, none of them seeming to fit.

"Damn you both," came a guttural curse. Archer materialized from beneath the door, like a towering wraith—something her mind *again* pronounced impossible.

With a sudden flailing of arms and legs, Mark slammed back against the stone wall with such force that a cloud of dust sprang out to dirty the air around him. He grimaced, groaning, and threw a furious look at Archer.

Archer raged to the center of the low-ceiling room. Fury contorted his handsome features along with some other emotion she couldn't put her finger on. He wore no coat, no hat. Though he wore braces, his shirttail had slipped free of his trousers. She had never seen him in such disarray.

"I thought she was dead." Suddenly, his voice cracked into a whisper. "She was here with you."

He sank to his knees, seizing her about the waist and drawing her fiercely toward him. He buried his face in her bodice and let out a ragged breath.

Stunned by the ferocity of his emotion, Elena clasped her arms around him. His muscular shoulders shook. He trembled. Out of fear for her?

Selene said in a sullen voice, "We only just arrived

ourselves. The Ripper was here. He had her imprisoned in that pit. No telling what violence he had planned for her."

He drew back. Elena gazed into his eyes.

She nodded. "I'm sure they saved my life."

Archer's brows furrowed. "But I followed Elena's trace here. Why is there nothing of the Ripper?"

Mark kneaded one shoulder, as if injured. "Last night, after you were taken into custody—and don't even *think* to accuse me of instigating that, Archer, because I did not—I tracked the Ripper from the hospital, but it's as if he evaporated. He must have come here. His sudden disappearance may have something to do with all these stinking roses."

Selene said, "It's odd, but they somehow muddy his stench."

Her twin surmised, "His tactics are ever changing. If I didn't want to cut him to shreds so badly, I might find the whole thing very interesting. We found this place by latching on to Elena's trace as well."

Archer's jaw flexed, and with great apparent effort he said, "I owe you both my deepest gratitude for saving her."

From behind, Archer heard Selene say, "He's close, Archer, and because he came out of hiding early, before the next wave from Tartarus, he's not strong enough to fight us if we catch him now."

Mark added, "It's almost time, Archer. We can stop him before he turns *brotoi*. Selene and I can handle him."

Archer's pride shouted that he must go, that he must be the one to claim this matchless soul and punish him for having used Elena against him at the threat of her life. But suddenly his pride did not hold all influence over him.

"Go after him." Archer thrust his arms beneath

Elena and lifted her from the chair. "Reclaim the bastard and accept, with my gratitude, whatever acclaim
you receive from the Guard. I am taking Elena
home."

Elena clung to Archer as he kicked open the door
and bent his head low. He carried her toward a carriage. On the perch, Leeson tipped his head against
clasped hands, as if thankful for her being brought
out alive. His eye glistened with moisture. He leapt
down, opened the carriage door and quickly laid
down the stairs. Archer clambered up.

Holding her tight against him, like some priceless
treasure, he fell back onto the leather seat. The door
closed behind them.

Archer's hands moved over her, frantically touching her everywhere—her breasts, her stomach, her
legs—as if satisfying himself she were not cut or
missing a limb. He growled, drawing his thumb
across the place where the Ripper had painted the
line on her neck. Suddenly his hands were twisted
in her hair and his lips crushed her mouth.

Elena gasped, overwhelmed.

He drew back, still cradling her in his arms, and
stared into her wide eyes.

"What is it?" he asked.

"Your eyes," she whispered. "Your skin—"

Realization swept through Archer. He had been so
frantic over her safety he'd spoken and acted rashly,
right in front of Elena. She had heard everything he
and the other two Shadow Guards had discussed.
Worst of all, he'd revealed himself to her, in all his
monstrous splendor.

He gripped her by the shoulders and pushed her
from him. With nothing to shield himself, no hat, no
dark glasses, he covered his eyes with his palms.

"Don't look at me."

With excruciating effort he forced himself to detach emotionally from the moment. From Elena. He had allowed himself to get too close. The world shattered around him. How could he have failed her so greatly and brought her back to this? It was as if they again stood on that dilapidated tenement roof, the past two years—and especially the last six weeks—ripped into a thousand shreds.

She gripped his wrists.

"Don't do that. Don't hide from me," she insisted, but he heard the fear in her voice.

He *frightened* Elena, and she had not seen half of what he was capable. He allowed her to pry away his hands.

Last night they had been a man and a woman, almost lovers. Now, in the cold light of day, she was mortal—and he was an immortal monster.

"I will make you forget," he vowed.

"Why?" she gasped, hearing his words. "Why? Did you make me forget before?"

A slow understanding spread over her features.

"You did, didn't you? You're the reason I don't have my memories."

Suddenly she struck his shoulder with her balled fist. "Don't you dare. Don't you dare make me forget." She struck him again. "Give me back my memories, damn you!"

"I can't. I won't."

Her despair washed over him.

"What are you, Archer?" she demanded suddenly. "Angel or devil?"

A tortured smile lifted the edge of his lips. He laughed hollowly. "I don't know any more."

"This is me, Archer. Me, Elena. I don't care what you are. Just talk to me. Don't pretend I matter nothing to you."

"It is done between us."

Tears glazed Elena's eyes. "After having come so far? Because I have seen you like this? Because I have heard your secrets?"

She blinked them away, and hardness claimed her features.

"I'm not doing this anymore. It hurts too much. I surrender." She drew as far away from him as the bench would allow, her breasts rising and falling with emotion beneath her uniform bodice. "But you will not take away my memories of you. I want to remember you when I marry Harcourt. I want to remember you when I sleep in his bed—" Her voice thickened with emotion. "And make love to him every night, and have his children—"

"Be silent, Elena." Archer clenched his eyes shut.

He had always pitied humans for the brevity of their lives. Now he realized he'd been wrong. The very brevity of their existence imbued every moment with such intense meaning.

Her words tortured him with everything he could never have.

"I want to remember you, every moment of every day—"

"Don't say it."

"—and wish that he was you."

He didn't understand how she could look at him and still want him. Archer seized her around the waist, pressing his cheek against her breast. Her arms came round him, her hands staving through his hair, and she pressed a fervent kiss against his bowed head.

"Just love me Archer," she whispered. "Just once. I promise it will be enough to last me forever when you've gone."

Suddenly, her arms were empty.

Chapter Seventeen

Elena leapt out of the carriage and ran up the steps of Black House, seeing everything through tear-glazed eyes. Leeson called after her, but she wouldn't stop, not until she got to her room where she would wail and cry and throw every last blasted thing against the wall. A startled footman held the door for her.

Archer was gone. He had disappeared from her arms, and she knew she would never see him again. She grieved him and hated him all at once. Her skirts bunched in her hand, she raced past Mary Alice on the stairs.

"Oh dear, miss!" The maid frowned in concern. "What is wrong?"

"Please," Elena answered, pleading. "I just need to be alone."

On the second-floor landing, she grasped the decorative pommel and veered up toward the third.

Halfway up, something seized her ankle—

She twisted round but fell, sprawling back—only to be caught by some invisible force and spared the pain of a fall.

A shadow, barely visible to the eye, curled up from

her feet . . . twining round her skirts . . . and her
shoulders.

She recognized the spice of Archer's skin.

She felt heat and pressure, which she easily interpreted as his body. Skillful, unseen hands greedily
claimed her breasts and squeezed her buttocks, sending a blaze of pleasure through her limbs. The buttons of her bodice sprang free to ping against the
marble banister.

"Miss Whitney?" Mary Alice's voice echoed up
from below.

The shadow ceased its pleasurable onslaught, retreating into nothingness.

"Ah . . . I'm fine!" Elena shouted.

She twisted over on the stairs and clambered up
the remaining steps, not stopping until she got to
her room. There she frantically locked the door, then
yanked the key free to hurl it into the far corner—
not because she wanted to keep Archer out, but because she wanted to watch him break through.

She gasped for air, out of breath.

Long moments passed . . . and Archer didn't appear, not like she'd expected. She twisted around,
bereft, only for him to brush against her.

Darling.

Archer's voice. Only darker and more mysterious.
Anticipation seized her.

"Where are you?" She whirled, searching the space
about her.

Sudden friction, formed of heat and power, moved
up her stomach and over both breasts in a possessive
caress. She stood helpless, tortured by pleasure,
yearning to embrace him. His heat spread like honey
beneath her uniform, over her skin. Her nipples
hardened, and instinctively she crossed her arms
over herself.

I want you.

Elena wasn't frightened. Not really. More excited. After all, this was Archer.

Afraid?

Her cheeks burned. *Everything* burned. "No."

Good.

She glimpsed a sudden flash, flame or metal.

Her uniform, and everything beneath, split cleanly down the center. She gasped and caught the gaping edges against her naked skin, but Archer, unseen, tugged and pulled—his warmth touching against her skin—until the muslin shifted and slid away.

"Archer!"

When he was finished, she stood in her shoes and her black stockings, tied with ribbons at her thighs.

Invisible hands tipped her off balance, and she dropped back, on her naked bottom, onto the dressing table bench. Unseen hands stroked her along her knees and upward, coaxing her thighs, with gentle pressure, to open.

Elena laughed nervously. Instinctively she dropped both hands between her legs to cover herself. But as she defended the center of her femininity, he eased her back onto the bench. She felt the glow of his tenderness, the intensity of his adoration.

His tongue laved her nipple. She watched it stiffen into a wet peak.

"Oh my . . . ," she gasped from low in her throat.

The sensation was too intense. She slid her hands over her breasts, only to feel an immediate pressure between her thighs. His hands . . . his fingers . . . massaging her there. She grew slick and wet, and writhed with pleasure. Her eyes rolled back in delight.

"Yes," she cried out, only to freeze.

Most definitely a tongue. A long, muscular tongue,

exquisitely skilled. Her shoes fell from where they dangled off her toes, to the floor.

She melted just as quickly. "Archer, please—"

Please what?

"Let me see you."

She tossed her head in ecstasy, gripping the edge of the narrow bench just above her shoulders to keep from falling off. When her eyes opened again, his dark head arose from her thighs, his gaze intense, and his expression passionate. No more a shadow, but a man. She flushed wildly that he was still fully dressed, while she wore nothing but stockings.

"Come on, darling." He seized her by the waist, easily lifting her against him. She held on to his shoulders. Her hair had fallen free. The lengthy mass trailed down his back. Just a few steps and he tossed her to the mattress.

"We should be in my bed, you know." He chuckled, a harsh, very male sound. "Yours is too small, and probably squeaks."

She rose up onto her knees, watching as he dropped his braces, tore his shirt over his head and unfastened his trousers to reveal himself.

She whispered, "We'll go to yours next."

Her mouth went dry as he solemnly drew his hand down the length of his long, swollen shaft.

"Lie back, Elena." His voice was tense with leashed desire.

She did as he told her, dropping back onto the velvet coverlet to prop herself on both elbows. She didn't want to take her eyes off him. She loved the firm, swarthy perfection of his skin, and the powerful ripples his muscles made with the slightest movement. He was beautiful, and she could tell by the way his gaze moved over her, he thought she was beautiful too. After bending at the waist to discard his boots, he pushed his trousers over sinewed hips, dropping them to the floor.

Kicking them off, he finally touched her again, starting at her stocking-covered feet. Her belly fluttered with excitement. His hands, large and competent, smoothed over her skin, up over her ankles . . . her knees . . . and her thighs.

Just there his thumbs dipped low, grazing against her in long, unison strokes. He boldly spread her. She gasped, instinctively opening for him. His knees took advantage, bunching the velvet as he braced her legs wide. He eased down, nudging her until his rigid shaft settled lengthwise against her damp flesh. One hand swept up over her rib cage to capture her breast. His thumb pressed over her puckered nipple.

Suddenly he evaporated to shadow. Elena's arms caved in upon themselves, and his warmth disappeared.

Certain you still want me?

She let out a desperate cry. With a deep, husky laugh, he grew solid again, dipping his head to suckle the peak of her breast with his tongue and lips, a long purposeful draw. The pleasure coursed, in massive waves, all the way to her pointed toes.

"Don't do that again." She threw her arms around his shoulders. "Please."

He tilted his hips, pressing his thickness along against the slick channel between her legs. "I'm going to come inside you now."

"I want you to."

He lifted slightly. The cool air of her room swept between them, and her nipples hardened. She watched between them, as he grasped his shaft. His stomach flexed, a defined grid. He prodded his swollen pink tip against the center of her, moistening himself with the evidence of her pleasure.

"Now, Archer." She clenched her hands on his shoulders, and moaned, her body, her passion, demanding everything. Slowly, he eased into her.

Her body stretched tight, accepting him.

"So good," he hissed through his teeth, drawing out, only to test her again. "Better than I dreamed. I don't want to hurt you."

"You can't hurt me. I want you too much."

"Good, because . . ." His breath caught in his throat. "I can't wait."

He speared into her tight, wet perfection, only to gasp, deep in his throat, at the resistance of her body—resistance he, with one powerful thrust, had destroyed.

Elena, a virgin.

He stared down into her passion-glazed eyes, and her tears.

"I'm sorry," he uttered, feeling regret to the bottom of his soul.

"Why?" She writhed beneath him, embracing him tighter, drawing him closer until he shook with need. "Don't be sorry. I love you."

Archer's heart swelled and shattered all at once. He closed his eyes, sinking into her, and pressed his face to her neck, never wanting to leave, never wanting to forget.

Elena moved against him, the pain of her lost virginity faint compared with the enormity of her love for him. So close. So close. She'd never felt closer to anyone.

"Elena," he rasped, his rhythm suddenly and intensely urgent. She touched his chest, his face, memorizing him, accepting each thrust with one of her own. She felt the coverlet scoot beneath her, and his skin against her, and the vague pressure of the headboard.

Suddenly, an intense, indefinable wave of joy rolled through her, out from the place where their bodies joined, blazing outward as pure and white-hot as a sudden explosion of naptha light.

Archer, feeling her body pulse against him, instantly lost himself. He cursed, and praised her, and cursed again. He gripped her hips and spilled his release.

He fell over her, surrounding her in the cage of his arms and his legs, adoring her loving eyes and her dazed smile. Precious Elena. He wove his arms beneath her, between her silky skin and the velvet, embracing her, whispering at last, "I love you too."

She awoke to Archer's kisses against her neck. "I know you are tired, darling, but you've got to wake up."

He lay beside her, muscular and warm against her back. His large, heavy leg cambered over both of hers. She felt small, treasured and protected.

She shifted to her back so they lay face-to-face.

"For just a moment there, when I woke up, I feared this had all been a dream."

"Perhaps when you fell asleep I should have dressed you and pretended the same?" Archer laughed in gentle cynicism.

"No." She shook her head, unsmiling. "I don't ever want to forget this day. By the way, where's your tattoo?"

"Pardon?"

"It's not there."

"Sorry, love," he murmured intimately. "I just wanted to make you happy. Ink doesn't take on Amaranthine skin."

"*Amaranthine*," she repeated.

"My body rejects anything foreign. That's why,

when you cut me with the scissors I healed so quickly. My body rejected the steel."

"Really."

He saw her medical mind working, trying to determine the science of how that might be possible.

"Mind you, I'm not invincible. A gunshot or any other deep wound could do a nasty bit of damage, but only temporarily. What might be instantly fatal to a mortal might put me out of service for a day or two. Or five to seven in the case of . . . you know."

He drew a finger across his neck.

Elena shuddered. *"Decapitation?"*

"Mark can tell you from experience, there's no pleasure in that. But only an immortal can kill an immortal."

She shook her head, marveling. "Just to think, all this time my guardian was a—"

He stared at her.

Her smile faded. "What exactly are you, Archer?"

"You asked if I was an angel or a demon." He scrutinized her face, as if trying to decide how much she could take. "I'm neither of those things."

She lifted her hand to his cheek. "Tell me, then, what you are. I want to know."

"I am an Amaranthine. I'm an immortal."

She closed her eyes for a moment. "I still can't believe all this. If I hadn't seen those things myself—" She bit her bottom lip. "It's like something from a fantasy, but you say you are immortal as if it's the most normal thing in the world."

"It is normal. For me and those of my kind." He shrugged. "I suppose we've had plenty of time to get used to the idea."

She nodded, trying to understand. "I guess it would be. Have you always been so?"

He rose up onto an elbow and, solemn now,

peered down into her face. "I'm very old, Elena. This might be difficult for you to understand, but I have walked this earth from almost the beginning of time."

"What about Selene and Mark?"

"They were born mortal, and later transformed. Some mortals have that disposition, to become immortal. It's a rare thing, though, and even more rare in recent centuries. We don't know why."

He ran his fingertips along her cheek. "It feels so strange to confess these things to you."

Elena ruminated over everything she remembered from the basement. "You and the twins are some sort of hunters, aren't you? You're hunting Jack the Ripper."

"Yes," he acknowledged quietly.

"Why the Ripper? Why not all the other villains of the world?"

"We are members of the ancient Order of the Shadow Guards. We're tasked with the elimination— what we call the Reclamation—of exceedingly corrupt mortal souls. Souls so wicked they approach a supernatural state called Transcension, where they become dangerously powerful, and gain the ability to cross over into the Inner Realm."

"The Inner Realm . . . ," Elena murmured.

"A beautiful place, with endless green hills and air so clean you grow more alive just breathing. Or at least that's what I remember. I've not returned there in a very long time."

A knock sounded on the door. Elena pushed herself up, holding the sheet.

A frown turned Archer's lips.

"It's your girl, Lizzy," he said. "You'd better answer."

"Lizzy?" Elena repeated, a bit panicked. "Lizzy's

the last person I saw before I awoke in Jack the Ripper's pit."

"What you saw wasn't Lizzy, but an apparition created by Jack to gain your trust and lure you close enough to seize. Your Lizzy never left the premises of Black House."

"What a relief," Elena exhaled. She stared at the door. "Still . . . I'm not ready. I need more time with you."

"I know. But we've got a visitor downstairs, and it could be something important."

Elena nodded. Even though she wished they could hide away in her room forever, they couldn't forget everything that had happened leading up to this moment. There might be a battle going on, at this very moment, involving Selene, Mark and Jack the Ripper. Pushing the hair from her shoulders, she quickly pulled a dressing gown from her wardrobe. A moment later she peered through the cracked door.

"Lizzy."

"Good afternoon, miss." The young maid eyed the narrow opening with suspicion. "It's after two and you're not dressed? I hope you're not ill."

"I had a very long night."

"You've got a visitor. Should I tell him you are not receiving?"

"Who is it?"

"It's that handsome Dr. Harcourt from the hospital. He appears quite agitated, miss. He asked to see you and Lord Black, but we've not located his lordship."

"I'll be right down."

"Do you need help dressing?"

"No, thank you. I believe you may find his lordship in his study."

"I already looked there, miss."

"Try looking again." Elena started to shut the door.

"Wait, miss," Lizzy whispered, pressing her face into the crack.

"Yes, Lizzy?"

The girl grasped her hand and pressed something smooth and cool against her palm. Elena glanced down. Her buttons. A rush of heat scalded her cheeks.

Lizzy grinned, and scampered down the hallway.

Elena quickly shut the door again. Archer swung his legs over the side of the bed. The sheet barely covered his hips. He reached for his trousers. Her gaze swept in appreciation over the heavy muscle of his shoulders. Her heartbeat raced unevenly as she remembered the passion they'd shared just hours before.

"Do you think they got him?"

Archer paused. "Once we find out what Harcourt's got to say, I'll leave you here with Leeson and go find out."

She said, "You go downstairs first. I'll follow you in a few moments."

Tugging his shirt up his arms, he bent to kiss her nose. "You and I still have much to discuss."

"Yes, we do, but Archer—everything is good. Between you and me—whatever happens. I just want you to know that. I understand better now."

A quarter hour later, after having dressed and repaired her hair, Elena joined Archer and Dr. Harcourt in the study. Archer sat behind his desk. Harcourt sat in the wing chair. Both sat quietly. Rigidly. She wondered if they had spoken two words to each other before she came into the room.

Seeing her, they both stood, Archer coming round the desk to tower beside her.

Harcourt gripped the brim of his bowler in both hands. "I received word you were safe, Miss Whitney, but I feel immensely better now that I've seen you with my own eyes." Agitation brightened his features. "Lord Black told me of your ordeal. I can blame only myself. If I had brought you back to Black House immediately, as Lord Black instructed—"

Elena glanced to Archer, hoping he had not taken the man to task over that detail. His stony expression gave her no reassurance.

Looking back to Harcourt she said, "You must not blame yourself. Like you, when the casualties from the brewery arrived, I thought it better to stay and assist. I'm safe now." She smiled to reassure him. "That's what matters."

His normally golden skin grew very pale. "I'm not altogether convinced of that."

"Why do you say that?"

"Have you ever met a woman by the name of Mary Kelly?"

Mary Kelly. What a familiar name. She scoured her memory.

"Yes." The woman she had met at the Ten Bells with Mrs. Scott. "I believe I have, if it's the same girl. I cannot say we shared more than a few words, but someone remarked how we looked like each other." Elena's smile faded. "Why?"

"This morning I received a summons from the police surgeon, asking that I accompany him to a crime scene at Miller's Court."

Elena experienced a sudden premonition of what he would say. "Don't say it."

Harcourt nodded. "It's true, I'm afraid. Last night Mary Kelly was murdered in her bed."

Elena gasped, "No."

Harcourt continued in a gravelly voice. "That's a

kind word for what he did to her. I say 'he' because
there is no mistaking who committed the crime."

She glanced at Archer, and found him standing
rigid and emotionless beside his desk.

"I found this in her room." He pulled an envelope
from his hip pocket and held it out to Archer. "It's
addressed to you, Lord Black."

Archer's gaze burned upon the envelope with such
intense hatred that Elena feared the contents would
burst into flames in Harcourt's hand before they had
a chance to read them.

"Don't tell anyone where you obtained the letter,
I beg you. I risk my professional reputation in not
turning it over to the authorities, but when I saw
what was written inside, I could do nothing but bring
it directly to you."

"Open it, Archer," Elena urged. "Read what it says."

Archer seized the envelope and opened its flap.

"What does it say?" she asked.

He read in a quiet voice. *"It seems that like you . . .
I am developing a preference for pretty girls."* He closed
the letter. "There's more vile stuff. I will not read the
rest aloud in Miss Whitney's presence."

The blood drained from Elena's face, and she
quickly seated herself into a nearby chair. "He's
threatened me again, hasn't he?"

Just then she startled, seeing a shadow move out
of the corner of her eye. And another.

Harcourt strode past her to stand before Archer.
"Your lordship, Miss Whitney is in further danger.
Protect her. I beg you. Do what you must to keep
her safe. My God, take her out of the city if you
must. As for me, I must return immediately to the
scene of the crime."

With that the doctor took up his hat from the chair
and vacated the room.

A long, silent moment passed.

Elena whispered, "They are here, aren't they?"

Archer nodded.

Selene and Mark materialized from shadow.

"So you've heard the latest news from the East End." Mark paced before the fire.

Elena whispered, "He killed that girl while I was down in that pit."

Selene threw her mantle over the back of the empty chair. Glaring at Archer, she seethed, "He used your lover against not only you, Archer, but all of us. As a distraction."

Elena pushed herself up from her chair. "Tell them about the letter, Archer. He wants me, if only to get to the rest of you. So let him have me. Use me as bait and lure him out."

"I won't put you in danger."

She came closer, placing her hand on his arm. "You wouldn't let him hurt me, I know you wouldn't. I have every faith in you."

"Elena," he said quietly. "I've got to ask that you leave us now. I must speak with Mark and Selene privately."

Elena went stiff. She nodded, her plan obviously rejected. She wanted to stay with him, to be included in everything, no matter how dangerous the outcome.

But she couldn't forget what he was, and what she wasn't.

Archer watched Elena go. At the door, she paused.

Love you.

Her shoulders straightened but she didn't look back. Instead, she pulled the tall wooden door shut behind her.

Good girl.

He gave his full attention to the twin Guards who

awaited him. "The wave is upon us. Jack has turned *brotoi*."

Mark crossed his arms over his chest. "Let's go get him then, the three of us, together. We won't allow ourselves to be divided again."

Selene grasped up her mantle.

Archer slowly shook his head. "Things have gone too far. This *brotoi* has made fools of us, while we've struggled to find our bearings. I won't take any more chances."

Mark asked, "What are you saying?"

Peace spread through Archer, calming the beat of his heart. He was ready. Content. He had taken his existence as far as he wished to go. He could not share this earth with Elena knowing each moment brought her closer to death, to a place where, because of his immortal spirit, he could not follow.

The mantle slipped from Selene's hands. "You're going to Transcend."

"Yes." Archer stared into Mark's eyes. "And after I've Reclaimed Jack, you, Mark, are going to kill me."

Elena lay on her bed, staring at the ceiling, while trying to grasp the enormity of everything she'd seen and heard and learned that day. She closed her eyes.

Too much. She couldn't imagine how any of it would work out. She pressed her fists against her forehead, trying to stave off the hopelessness.

"He's going to sacrifice himself, you know. For you."

She gasped and sat up. Mark sat on the window seat, his long legs extended before him.

"He's going to Transcend in order to slay the Ripper."

"I thought Transcension was something only deteriorated souls could do."

"Shadow Guards can employ Transcension as a sort of strategy, but only as a last-ditch effort to defeat our foe. It's the greatest sacrifice a Guard can make."

"You keep using the word 'sacrifice'. Why?"

"Because once he's Transcended, he'll defeat the Ripper, no doubt about that. But afterward he'll go mad. Become unstable. A loose cannon. The Primordials will order him hunted down and killed, for the protection of the Inner Realm."

"He is one of their own."

"He wouldn't be one of their own anymore. He'd be a threat."

Elena pushed herself off the bed and slowly crossed the room toward the pale-haired Shadow Guard. "What is your motive for telling me this, Mark?"

His gaze, his expression, remained guarded. "It's not important for you to know my motive. Do you want Archer to live or die? That's it. There are only two possible outcomes to this scenario."

Chapter Eighteen

Elena drew a shaky breath. "Of course I want him to live."

He held her gaze. "Then say you'll help me. I shall bear the only consequence."

Elena pondered his words for a long, tortuous moment. Did she betray Archer by even considering Mark's words?

Do you want Archer to live or die?

"Tell me what you want me to do."

He sat straighter now, and his eyes glowed with some secret ambition. "It's no different than the plan you proposed, really. Tonight, after dark, I want you to take a hackney and meet me at the Ten Bells. That's it. Plain and simple."

"The Ripper will find me," she whispered.

"You won't so much as see him. You won't be harmed."

Elena closed her eyes. She couldn't believe she was agreeing to this. She didn't even know if she could trust Mark.

"One more thing. He has ordered Selene to see to your protection, here at Black House."

"How am I supposed to escape her long enough to meet you?"

"Give her this." He handed her a slim package, wrapped in brown paper. "She'll be drunk on it for hours. It's important you don't tell her of our plan. She would do everything to thwart us."

"She loves Archer too," Elena countered softly. "She supports his decision to Transcend?"

"Over mine, yes. Because, you see, I am her blood. Her twin. You'd have to be one of us to understand."

In a blink, she found herself alone in her room again. Her gaze went to the window. Already the day began to fade. Her heart beat an anxious, erratic tempo. She knew full well this plan of Mark's was no sure success. So many things could go wrong.

Knowing Archer would leave soon, she went downstairs to the study. He and Leeson stood amidst an array of open cases. Leeson, upon seeing her, seized the nearest lid, as if he would hide whatever was contained therein.

Archer said, "It's all right, Leeson."

Elena drew near, and saw the white gleam of metal. Weapons. Swords, daggers, and others she couldn't exactly define.

Lesson murmured, "Just don't touch them, child. They are . . . very sharp."

Elena nodded, her gaze having lifted to Archer. "You'll be leaving soon, won't you?"

He avoided her gaze. "Yes."

"Were you planning to say good-bye?"

Archer stilled. After a long moment he spoke.

"Leeson, if you could go now and tell Mr. Jarvis the staff, himself included, may enjoy the remainder of the weekend with their families, or doing whatever they wish as a paid holiday. I do believe it would be simpler to have them away from the house while we make our preparations."

"Very well, sir."

Once his secretary had gone, Archer stood silent, staring at her. Finally, when Elena could bear their separation no more, she ran to him. His arms enfolded her so fiercely she lost all breath.

His jaw moved against the top of her head. "I don't ever want to say good-bye to you."

"This is it, isn't it? You might not return. I might not ever see you again."

"That's right."

"I love you, Archer."

His embrace grew stronger.

"I love you too."

"I've loved every moment spent with you. Even the unhappy ones."

He laughed, with a deep, rumbling sound.

"And your gifts to me." A tear ran down her cheek. "I will treasure the memory of them forever."

"I've one more gift for you."

The emotion she felt burned too intensely. She wouldn't be able to look at him without sobbing like a child. "I can't, Archer. I can't look at you."

He forced her chin up. "You must."

She did as he asked. Unencumbered, tears flowed down her cheeks.

"Don't close your eyes, darling."

He bent his head to press his lips against hers.

Elena stared into his silver eyes. His pupils dilated. The world spiraled.

Now she did close her eyes. She gasped, the images, the emotions, flashing across her mind in wild, colorful profusion. He caught her against him and held her tight.

"There they are," she marveled. "My memories. Every last one—"

Archer waited. As he had known she would, she suddenly stiffened. Her face went white, and she grew rigid in his arms.

After a long moment, her eyes finally opened.

"Dr. Philip Whitney, my father. A missionary physician on the Ivory Coast. It's all true."

Archer caressed her cheek. "I knew only the barest details. It's very difficult to gain particulars on a mortal soul who has passed over. Most are outside my domain."

"I'm sorry." She pulled away. Despite the moment, she laughed low in her throat. "I have made your shirt hopelessly wet. Do you have a handkerchief?"

Archer retrieved one from his desk.

She wiped her eyes. "My father and I had a wonderful life there, but he passed away. I had always assisted him in his practice and wished to continue in the occupation. I came to London to attend to the formalities of medical school and acquire my license, but my first day here, there was an accident. It is all as you explained in your letter to me, only I wasn't injured. I was left destitute when everything was stolen from me."

"That was the extent of my knowledge of you, Elena. I took license with all the rest."

She nodded, her expression brave. "I went to the address of the man who was to have been my guardian, only to find he too had recently passed away. His stepdaughter wanted nothing to do with the expense of taking in a penniless stranger, and she sent me back to the streets. Without food, or a place to stay, I had no other choice but to take work in a factory. Mrs. Eddowes thought she remembered me from a Berner Street boardinghouse. That hovel was one of many such places where I spent my nights."

Archer came close again, a silent, comforting presence. "You did what you had to do to survive, Elena."

"Yes." Her voice quieted to a whisper. "I cut shoe leather. Winslow was my foreman."

Her mouth trembled. Again, Archer pulled her into his arms but did not interrupt.

"He abused so many girls. I managed to escape his notice until that night." She pressed a hand against her mouth, remembering. "He forced me to . . . *touch him* . . . but you stopped him before he could . . ."

She swallowed hard, trying to calm herself. He pressed a kiss against her temple.

"I thought he had succeeded. I did not know differently until we made love."

"We fell. He killed me—or almost did."

"Yes."

"You gave me a second chance." She looked up into his eyes. "Why?"

"Because I loved you." Archer stroked her hair and touched her face. "My beautiful Elena, I loved you even then."

Elena was still sobbing an hour later. "And so your mother, even though she could have made herself immortal, killed herself upon learning of Antony's death?"

She and Selene lay side by side on the countess's bed, with every one of Selene's serpents slithering and twisting either atop or beside them.

Selene nodded, completely dry-eyed. "She made Mark and me immortal instead. We were to be her revenge against Octavian—and the world—I suppose."

Elena sniffled, "That's the most tragic story I've ever heard."

Selene rested back upon the pillows, her hands behind her head. "This is so lovely, us being here together and talking. I haven't had a woman friend in so very long. Not since that mob flayed dear Hypatia to death."

Elena dabbed a fresh handkerchief to her eyes. "Flayed. That sounds horrible."

"Do you remember the first night when you found me in your room? The night I told you I needed a night rail?"

"Yes."

"I didn't need anything to sleep in."

"Why were you in my room?"

Selene rolled and grasped a jeweled box from beside her bed. She opened the lid and from inside pulled a crudely formed little doll. It appeared to be made of wax and boasted an unruly wad of pale hair on its head.

"What is that?"

"It's *you*," Selene giggled, waggling the doll. "Or the *kolossoi* I made with the hair I pulled out of your brush that night. And see these other little threads and scraps from your clothes?"

"Why would you make something like that?"

"I so wanted to stab a pin into your stomach, or cut off your head. I'm glad I didn't. I really like you now, even if Archer does love you."

"Surely I'm not the only woman he has cared for."

Selene lay back, twirling the doll between her fingers. "He did love someone once, very long ago."

"Tell me about her."

"I don't know much, and as you know, Archer isn't the sort to share his *feelings*." Selene shrugged lackadaisically. "From what I understand they were mad for each other, but her mother forbade the match."

"What happened? How did things end?"

"From what I've been told, one afternoon she was in a field picking flowers, waiting to tryst with Archer, when a Transcended soul abducted and killed her."

"That's horrible," Elena gasped.

"This was back when civilization first began to show signs of deterioration along its outer fringe. Long before my time. Even before the Primordials decided to close the Inner Realm off from human intrusion. That's right. Mortals and Immortals once lived in peace alongside one another. Archer tracked the soul, of course, and cast it down into Tartarus."

"Tartarus?"

Selene nodded. "The Eternal Pit of Darkness."

"There's an Eternal Pit of Darkness?"

"Oh, yes." Selene's eyes widened dramatically. "Very dark and very eternal. You wouldn't want to be cast down there. That's where the nastiest of souls are imprisoned. That's where Reclaimed souls are interred forever, after we Reclaim them."

"At least Archer punished the villain."

Though the tragedy had taken place ages before, Elena had seen glimpses of pain hidden in the recesses of Archer's eyes. Now she knew why. She said a prayer for the girl.

Selene reached out to lay the doll on the table beside her. "Can you believe her mother blamed Archer for everything? Centuries later, mortals put their own spin on the story and voilà. It's his fault we've had terrible winters ever since. Her death is why Archer became the first of the Shadow Guards, so that no other Amaranthine would suffer the same loss."

For the first time, emotion moistened Selene's eyes. "I'm going to miss him."

"Ooo-*ooh*!" Elena jerked.

"What is it?"

"Jezebel just went up my skirt."

Elena sat up, careful not to crush any of the countess's favored pets. She fished the serpent out from her underskirt and sent her slithering toward Selene.

"Where are you going?" Selene asked sharply.

"I just remembered something. . . ."

"Oh, no you don't." Selene leapt from the bed with the grace of a leopard. "Don't even think of trying to escape. Archer left me responsible for you."

"I'm not trying to escape. I've got a gift for you."

"Really? A present?" Selene softened. "I love presents."

"I hope you'll love this one." Elena went to a table beside the door where earlier, she'd laid the parcel. Returning to where Selene stood, she carefully tore off the paper. A musty scent struck her full in the face. Seeing the book for the first time herself, she read the title aloud.

"Le Morte d'Arthur."

Selene gasped, reaching. Elena quickly delivered the tome into the countess's greedy hands.

The countess held the book level to her nose, gently fanning the pages into her face. She inhaled deeply, and murmured, "Excellent bouquet."

"You really like to eat . . . paper?" Elena inquired doubtfully. Hopefully.

"Not all paper. Just the interesting stuff. Once I eat the pages, I remember their contents."

"That's amazing."

Selene drew her fingertip along the gilt-stamped border of the volume. "I'm quite the expert on many subjects. Don't ask me to explain how it works, because I don't know. It started as a nervous habit, I suppose, after the Royal Library of Alexandria burned. All that history and knowledge, so much of it lost forever. I started nibbling on what remained, and have never been able to stop. I crave finer selections such as this."

"Then go on. Rip a strip," Elena encouraged, slyly stealing a glance at the mantel clock.

"It's too fine a gift. I couldn't." Selene bit her bottom lip; yet her eyes lit up, twin bonfires of desire.

Elena winked. "Please. You'll hurt my feelings if you don't."

"Perhaps just a taste off one of these blank pages at the back."

Soon, Selene dropped to a nearby chaise.

"Mmmm." She lay back, eyes glazed, and dropped several tangled strips between ravenous, parted lips. "So good."

Elena quietly turned the doorknob and backed into the hall. After closing the door behind her, she raced to the far wing. From her wardrobe, she frantically selected her shabby clothing, more appropriate for an evening at the Ten Bells. She quickly changed.

After snatching up her bag and a wide-brimmed black hat, she hurried back to Selene's room and peered inside. Selene lay senseless and snoring on the chaise.

Satisfied her keeper would remain thusly incapacitated, Elena slipped downstairs. One final stop. She went to the study. Mark had told her she wouldn't so much as see the Ripper, that she'd be safe. However, as he was a mercenary rake, she wasn't about to take his word. No, she wasn't an immortal Reclaimer, and no, her feeble attempts to defend herself would certainly fail in the face of a Transcended soul like the Ripper. Even so, she'd feel better carrying a weapon of some sort.

In the darkness she found the cases. She opened one. Two. Three. All empty. Four.

Daggers. So pale and beautiful. She'd never seen anything like them. She grasped them up by their hilts and tucked them securely into the band of her skirt. A moment later and she was racing over the night-darkened grass, toward the road. All she could think of was Archer, and pray Mark's plan would work.

Suddenly, her feet flew out from under her. She stumbled. *The daggers.* She fell hard, but managed not to impale herself. Slowly, carefully, she stood, brushing the grass from her skirts.

Selene shouted, "What the hell is going on?"

Towering above Elena, the countess advanced.

"I was . . ." Why lie? Her intent was obvious. The confession spilled from her lips. "I was going to try and save Archer."

"By yourself?"

"Yes."

"Now you are lying," the tall Reclaimer hissed. "The paper used to wrap that book was the same paper I used to wrap the scroll at the museum—believe you me, I know my paper. It came from Mark's room at the Savoy. What has he convinced you to do?"

Selene snapped the reins. Elena clenched the leather bench beneath her, holding on as they raced along the narrow avenue toward the Ten Bells Pub. Obviously the details of Mary Kelly's horrific murder had spread. The streets were mostly abandoned, leaving their way free and clear.

Elena grasped Selene's arm. "Look out. There's someone in the road."

"It's just a girl. I'll go around her."

Elena squinted, her eyes narrowing. Lizzy stood in the center of the road, waving her hands for them to stop.

"Turn the carriage around."

"I'll just go around her."

"Turn the carriage around," Elena screamed, reaching for the reins.

Selene elbowed her away and steered the vehicle down a side street, lined with tall, dark buildings. Scowling, she demanded, "Why did you do that?"

Elena twisted, looking over her shoulder. "He's here."

Metal and wood crashed.

The night sky tilted wildly.

The force of the Victoria overturning hurled Elena to the road. Dazed, she lay for a long moment, her palms bleeding, and her skirts tangled around her knees. Her shoulder ached and her head throbbed.

The Ripper.

Elena pushed herself up from the ground. Standing, she struggled to regain her bearings. She saw Selene on the far side of the overturned carriage, laboring to rise from her hands and knees. Snorting and neighing, the horses righted themselves, then raced down the street, their harnesses jangling along behind them.

Then she heard a sound—a horrible, low laughter, laughter she'd heard before, from the bottom of a dark pit. Something shadowy raced along the edge of her vision. She whirled, following its course. The shadow leapt onto Selene.

Blood thundered in Elena's ears. The Ripper crouched over Selene, his mantle flowing out like bat wings on a nonexistent wind. His tall top hat shone darkly in the night.

His powerful arm swung up, a small blade gleaming in his fist. Without hesitation, Elena clenched her hands around the dagger hilts at her waist, and she yanked them free. She raced toward the two grappling figures, raising the blades high.

She plunged them into Jack's back and felt the revolting reverberation of the blades as they tore through muscle and bone.

He screamed, an inhuman, high-pitched sound, and with a blow of his arm, cast Elena across the pavement. She landed just beside the carriage, so close she almost struck her head upon it.

"*Run,*" commanded a voice. It was Selene, slowly arising from the pavement.

The Ripper crouched nearby, raging in a language Elena did not understand. Two silver hilts jutted out from each shoulder. He reached behind his head, gripping one in his black glove.

"Do as I say, Elena," Selene ordered. Her eyes glittered, never leaving the Ripper. Her hair had fallen from its elegant style, and her bodice sagged, slightly torn, to reveal the lace edge of her chemise. She jerked the bodice up and straightened her shoulders imperiously.

"I don't want to leave you."

Having ripped one blade free, the Ripper unfolded again to his full height.

"He'll only use you against me," Selene hissed, eyeing him like a ravenous jaguar, inhaling deeply as if she prepared for attack.

Elena exhaled in frustration, realizing the truth of Selene's words. Grasping her skirts, she raced along the sidewalk, away from the Ripper. He materialized in front of her.

She screamed and veered into an open doorway. Just as she slammed the door shut, a Valkyrie's battle scream pierced her ears. A huge, rattling crash shook the door and the wall of the tenement. Dust and fragments jarred loose to litter the air and floor of the dark, interior room where she'd taken shelter.

She shoved her back to the door and clasped her

hands against the sides of her head, trying to think. Staring into the black darkness around her, she made out the shapes of shredded mattresses and destroyed furniture. Another crash. She braced herself. Near her feet she found the bar to the door. Retrieving it, she quickly forced the bolt into place—knowing it would not save her if the Ripper turned his attention to her.

Elena took to the sagging stairs, careful to keep to the sturdier edges. She quickly maneuvered up the five flights. Once on the roof, she raced to the edge and crouched to peer down on the street.

Unease trickled through her. There was no one below.

Chapter Nineteen

Elena's mind produced an image of Selene, slashed to ribbons below.

Something creaked and slammed.

A door.

She whirled, scanned the rooftop, but saw no one. Had there been a door at the top of the stairs? Her blood surged through her heart so fast and hard that she could scarcely catch a breath.

Moving closer she saw that yes, there was indeed a door—and someone had shut it. Fear rippled beneath her skin. Someone likely watched her from the shadows even now.

Sensing something malevolent behind her, she spun around.

A tall, thin man wearing a cape stood close enough to have seized her if he had so wished.

"Good evening, Miss Whitney."

She backed away, almost stumbling.

"I hadn't expected you here tonight. I'd rather thought we'd had our bit of fun." He stepped toward her, his feet crunching against the tar paper. "You shouldn't have stabbed me with those awful blades. You hurt me. And now I shall have to hurt you."

"What are you?" She veered backward, never taking her eyes from him.

She could not, for the life of her, make out his face. Yes, there were eyes. Yes, there was a mouth. She could discern no distinguishing features beyond those. She saw his teeth gleam as his lips spread into a wide smile.

"What are you?" she shouted.

"I am the first of many. I am *brotoi*."

"Get away from her," a voice commanded ferociously.

Elena covered her mouth with her hand to silence a sob. Archer stood on the ledge, a shadow transitioning into immortal hunter, as beautiful and deadly as the night she'd first seen him on the roof of the Spitalfields tenement.

His black-silver gaze touched upon her only fleetingly.

As he flung his arms to his sides, heavy twin blades slashed out. He hissed a spate of words in a language she did not understand.

Suddenly his skin began to alter, and his black eyes flickered bronze.

Oh, God. She knew what was happening. He was Transcending.

Desperation and grief seized her; she knew he gave his immortal existence to save her and to stop the Ripper.

"Too late, Reclaimer. You're too late to stop me." Jack lunged, shoving Elena to the ground. He raced across the rooftop to the ledge, from where he leapt, cloak spread, into the night—

Only to be hurled back.

He crashed down against the weakened boards. Wood splintered; bricks flew. His hat rolled to the side.

Mark veered out of the darkness, his eyes gleaming bronze. He clenched a sword with a wickedly curved blade.

Instantly, Archer ceased the process of his Transcension. The poison beneath his skin ebbed.

Of Mark he demanded, "What have you done?"

"And to think I expected a thank-you," Mark responded in a hollow, dead-sounding voice.

Jack scrambled over the boards, an attempt at escape.

Bronze eyes turned on him with almost leisurely malice. "Where do you think you're going, little man?" Mark tapped the flat of his sword across the back of Jack's head. Jack keened in pain.

"Elena's been cut."

Archer pivoted to find Selene rushing from the ledge toward Elena, who clasped both hands against her bodice. His soul caved in, seeing the blood.

"I'm all right," she whispered, her eyes glazed.

She swayed and sagged. Archer lunged, catching her in his arms.

The Ripper's laughter echoed in the night, a wicked, inhuman sound. "I got you. I got you before you could get me. She'll die. Too bad, though, I couldn't cut her more. I am a son of Tantalus. Others will follow me. They already hear my call. Can you imagine? Soon there will be thousands—thousands upon thousands of banished souls wanting revenge on you and your kind."

"Such a bad little *brotoi*," Mark hissed. "One who doesn't know when to shut his mouth."

The Ripper screamed, punished again by a shallow slash of Mark's blade.

Selene dropped beside Elena, dragging her from Archer's embrace. "Go, Archer. End this now."

Mark called. "Much as I hate it, you've earned the

honor. But you've got to hurry." Effort strained his voice.

"Go," whispered Elena. "Stop him."

Archer pressed his mouth to Elena's alarmingly cool palm and prayed the kiss wouldn't be their last before life abandoned her.

Mark growled, "I can't bind him much longer."

Archer strode toward Jack.

His eyes gleamed hot, and his blood thundered with murderous rage. His blades hissed from his hands.

"Time to die, Jack."

"Never," the *brotoi* growled. Suddenly, his cloak flew out beside him, and like a great, dark bat, he leapt up, his face a demonic mask.

Archer kicked him in the center of the chest. His blades flashed, and his arms swung round in a double blow.

Jack's head parted from his neck, and a flash-second later his entire body disintegrated into thousands of tiny fragments. For a long moment, there was nothing but the sound of the small particles falling against the roof.

"*That's* never happened before," Mark muttered. He moved closer to where the Ripper had stood and ground his boot into a small pile of the black stuff. Bending, he touched the shining grains and smelled their residue. "Volcanic sand."

Archer wasn't listening. He drew in his blades.

Selene looked up. "She's still alive."

But Elena had lost consciousness. Archer crouched, gently gauging the pulse of her neck. Grief spread through him like a plague, devouring anything good within him. She was beyond his help. He had spared her life once, and could not do it again. There were no second chances.

He stared, stricken, into Selene's eyes. "Why did you bring her here?"

"Damn you, Mark!" Selene raged, tears sliding over her cheeks. "If not for your reckless ambition, I would still have—" Her voice broke. "I would still have my friend, and I would still have my brother."

Archer turned. "You brought Elena into this?"

Mark stared back at him, his bronze eyes unwavering.

With a roar, Archer again extended his blades.

Mark backed away. "If I can come back from this, Archer, I'll be a legend amongst legends."

"Come back from this?" Archer stalked the Reclaimer. "You can't come back from this. I've got to slay you now."

Selene sobbed, "*Mark.*"

"Break the rule."

"I can't."

"You will. In exchange for what I can offer you."

"Glory no longer appeals. There's nothing you can promise me."

Archer trembled, consumed by hatred and grief. He would slay Mark and then hold Elena until she died.

"I can save her."

Archer slashed his blades. "Just shut your mouth and die."

"I saw her on the street below," Mark hissed. "She wielded blades. *Amaranthine silver.*"

Selene wiped at her eyes. "My God. That's right. She had daggers on her. *Your* daggers. She stabbed them into Jack."

"What?" Archer whispered, disbelieving.

Just a touch of primordial silver would blister a human hand.

Mark moved closer, daring to come within range

of Archer's blades. "She could cross over, Archer. Like Selene and I did. She's a mortal, capable of becoming immortal."

"Hurry," Selene pleaded. "We've got to get her to the portal."

Archer rushed to claim Elena from Selene's arms. He lifted her limp body against his chest. Clenching her tight he felt her blood seep through his shirt, warming his skin. Desperation closed his throat. He felt as if he could barely breathe, as if his heart would burst. He had but one chance to save her.

The stairs creaked beneath their combined weight. Soon, he was racing with her toward the street. Mark and Selene, having descended from the ledge above, already climbed into the carriage.

Archer commanded Leeson, "Drive!"

The vehicle lurched forward. Archer cradled Elena in silence. After an eternity, the carriage clattered to a stop before Black House's steps. He raised his face from the tangled splendor of her hair.

Selene leapt down, racing up the steps to hold the door for Archer. His heart pounded with the enormity of what he intended to do. He carried Elena through the hall and into his study. Mark and Leeson's footsteps sounded on the marble floor behind him.

Orange light flickered off the ceiling and the walls. A huge fire blazed upon the massive hearth—as if the portals had blasted wide-open with news of the Ripper's Reclamation.

Selene waited off to the side. "I've unfinished business here. Send word, Archer. Tell us if she survives."

Archer stared at Mark. "They will send me as your assassin."

Mark's voice echoed hollowly. "All I need is a

good lead start. I'm gone as soon as you disappear into those flames. Watch me, Archer. I'll be the first to return from Transcension."

"Hurry, your lordship," urged Leeson.

Archer paused for a moment to press his lips against Elena's forehead. She was still alive—he could sense the faint flutter of life within her.

"Be strong for me, darling," he rasped, knowing the passage alone could kill her.

Shoulders back, he strode into the fire.

A great roar filled his ears. He gritted his teeth. The flames bore against him, a mighty, scorching wind threatening to tear Elena from his arms. He groaned with the effort. He shouted, giving every last bit of strength within him.

He broke through.

The vivid color—

The purity of the air—

He staggered, collapsing to his knees. Gasping for breath, he gently lowered Elena to the grass.

She blinked. "Archer?"

Before his eyes, she grew radiant. Her cheeks flushed pink with life. Even her hair gleamed with ethereal brightness.

"You look so different," she whispered, staring up at him.

"I couldn't let you go. Not like that, Elena. I hope you do not hate me for taking the decision from you."

"This is your true home?"

"Yes."

"Then I have no regrets." Her eyes shone, intense with love.

"Welcome home, Ancient."

Archer looked up. The three Primordials descended the slope of a green hill, their long white tunics carried on the wind behind them. Countless Amaranthines followed—faces Archer had not seen since he abandoned the Inner Realm thousands of years before. They peered with curiosity at Elena. Aitha crouched beside her and gently touched her cheek.

"Welcome, child."

The tension in Archer's muscles eased.

Hydros, tall and powerful, placed his hand on Archer's shoulder. "A job well-done."

Khaos, whose long black hair swept the grass, took Elena's hand and helped her stand. "Your mortal talents are not forgotten here."

"My talents?" She stared at her, showing no fear.

"Your desire to heal."

Aitha announced, "We cannot lose our most powerful Shadow Guard. But we can strengthen him by enabling you, as his mate, to be an Intervenor."

Archer exhaled at the enormity of their gift. He took Elena by the shoulders and stared into her beautiful eyes, never having believed his eternal existence could have taken such a sudden turn.

"An Intervenor, Elena. You will spare innocent lives not meant to end just yet."

Elena's eyes brightened with tears.

"But you must rest, child, and complete your transition." Aitha smiled benevolently. "Go to your lands, Archer, and share them with your bride."

Archer peered down at Elena. She touched his cheek. "I always knew I'd love you forever."

Suddenly, Archer remembered. He turned to the Primordials. "But what of Mark?"

Read on for a special preview of
the next Novel of the Shadow Guard,

SO STILL THE NIGHT

Coming in May 2009 from Signet Eclipse

Willomina Limpett tilted her face toward the voice.

A man stood there, just off to the side, tall and elegant, against the lush backdrop of the steep, grassy hill. The afternoon grew late, and the shadows long, but how could she not have seen him before? A shadowy thrill rippled through Mina, from the top of her crape-trimmed bonnet to the square point of her black leather shoes. It was a highly inappropriate response, given the event of the moment . . . but no one else needed to know.

"Miss Limpett," he repeated, approaching in measured steps.

He wore a precisely cut suit of rich cloth, the sort only the wealthiest of gentlemen could command from the tailors of London's famed Savile Row. His silk top hat rose high and gleaming. Opaque, blue-lensed spectacles prevented her from directly meeting his gaze.

She glanced toward her uncle, Lord Trafford, who stood just a few paces away, speaking to one of the funeral guests. Moments before she'd politely excused herself from the conversation and wandered off the path to view the striking beauty of Highgate Cemetery.

"Have we been introduced?" Mina inquired. She knew they had not. He was not someone she would forget.

"Forgive my breach of etiquette." His voice was rich, and warm. He deftly removed his hat to reveal jaw-length blond hair, streaked an even paler shade of moonlight. "I am . . . Alexander. I saw the newspaper announcement and knew I must come to offer my condolences."

"You knew my father?" The gravel shifted and crunched beneath her soles.

Not a single one of the professor's professional or academic peers had seen fit to attend his funeral service. The guests, who presently made their way toward the rows of waiting coaches, were society acquaintances of Lord and Lady Trafford, all strangers to Mina. They would have been strangers to her father as well.

"I dabble in languages. A personal interest, really. Nothing on the level of your father's expertise."

"Alexander . . . ," she murmured. Had her father ever mentioned the name?

"I've found myself in possession of something and wanted you to have it."

"Oh, yes? What is it?"

Again she looked toward her uncle, who remained engrossed in conversation. Her aunt and cousins had disappeared into the funeral carriage.

Mina returned her attention to Alexander, who produced a dark, rectangular object from his hip pocket. He solemnly offered his gift. Their gloved hands briefly touched. A rush of heat coursed high into her cheeks. She lowered her chin, purposefully retreating into the shadow of her bonnet, at the same time, considering the leather case in her hand. She slid her thumb against the clasp and inside found a tintype of two men crouched side by side atop an immense slab of stone.

Her breath caught in her throat. For the first time since her father's coffin had been sealed in Bangladesh, tears rushed against her lashes. They blurred her vision of the photograph—an image of her father as a young man, his hat cocked aside, and his face beaming with excitement. He had never lost that fervor, that zeal for adventure. Not even in the final moments, when they had said their good-byes.

Lord Alexander murmured, "The photograph was taken at the ruins at—"

"Petra. Yes. He took me there, once. Who is this man with him?" She pointed, lifting the frame for a closer look. "His face is blurred. . . ."

"Unfortunately."

"He favors you though. He is your father, is he not?"

Alexander cocked his head.

"Thank you," Mina whispered. "We traveled so much, from place to place. By necessity, I collected few mementoes. I shall treasure this always."

"I am glad." He pressed his lips together, as if pondering the words he would speak next. "Miss Limpett . . ."

"Yes?"

"I hope I do not overstep the bounds of propriety in choosing this moment to broach a particular subject, when the pain of your loss must still be so fresh."

In that moment, she wanted nothing more than to reach up and pull the spectacles from his face. She wanted very badly to know the color of his eyes.

"Please speak freely."

He nodded. "The professor, I know, possessed an extensive personal collection above and beyond the one he curated at the museum. In particular, I know he owned two very rare Akkadian scrolls."

Unease, feather-soft, spiraled up Mina's spine. She stared down into the case, into her father's eyes.

"Perhaps now that your father has passed, you might be willing to part with them?"

She shut the case. "I'm afraid that's not possible."

"I'm prepared to pay handsomely for them."

She shook her head, and attempted a polite, easy smile, while her mind threw out options for quickly extricating herself from his company—a necessary reversal, given his line of questioning. "The scrolls are not available for purchase."

"Perhaps you have already sold the scrolls to someone else?"

He edged closer—so close she could hardly breathe for the magnitude of his presence. The boning of Mina's tightly laced corset pressed uncomfortably against the undersides of her breasts.

His voice lowered and grew almost hushed. "If you could simply provide a name, I would be more than happy to approach them myself."

Mina's heart pounded. There had, indeed, been offers. There had also been a few very nasty threats—which was why a pistol presently weighted the tasseled, jet-beaded bag on her wrist.

"I can give you no such name."

She could not see his eyes, but knew they narrowed by the crinkling of lines that formed at his temples. Her thoughts veered around inside her head, as if he prodded inside her mind—no doubt an unfortunate result of her tortured conscience. She experienced a sudden, overwhelming desire to confess everything.

"Where are the scrolls, Miss Limpett?"

Yet she could not confess.

Instead, she blurted, "With Father."

The smile dropped from his lips, and suddenly she felt as if she were being considered by an emotionless, flat-eyed wolf. "What do you mean, *with Father?*"

She looked pointedly toward the Street of the Dead, where it disappeared into the shadowed corridor of evergreens. By now, the coffin would have been lowered on its hydraulic bier, into the tunnel below, and transported by unseen cemetery workers to the catacombs.

Even in the dimming light, his skin appeared to blanch a shade lighter. "You can't be serious. The scrolls were . . . *interred* with your father?"

"In the end, they were his most treasured possessions."

"We are talking about ancient papyri, never translated or transcribed, and you mean to tell me"—he laughed, a deep, incredulous sound—"that they are lost forever?"

"I'm afraid so." She twisted her hand in the velvet cording of her bag. "It's been four long months, you see."

"Oh, now that's *stellar.*"

She glanced out from beneath her bonnet's brim. "I suppose you'd like your photograph returned?"

He responded with a rueful chuckle, but the smile he wore—though a bit tight—appeared surprisingly genuine.

"No, Miss Limpett, I do not wish to have my photograph returned." As he repeated her words, he imitated her cadence and tone, a light flirtation that even now, sent a pleasurable tremor through her. "I am disappointed, of course, but who am I to object to the last wishes of a dying man? I should have antici-pated the same. William always was rather eccentric. Or so I've been told."

Mina nodded. Her father's eccentricity had been the bane of her existence, yet she had adored him completely, through and through.

"I must take my leave of you now, Miss Limpett."

"Thank you for coming," she said quietly, both relieved and disappointed. "Your attendance would have meant so much to Father."

The edge of his mouth quirked upward, and he returned his hat to his head. "I'd like to think so."

She watched him stride toward the gatehouse, and eventually disappear through the shadowed arch-way, toward the main road where additional coaches waited to convey guests away from the cemetery.

"Who was that you were speaking to?" Her uncle approached, black cane in hand.

"I'm not exactly sure. He introduced himself as Alexander."

Lord Trafford grinned. "I *thought* I recognized him."

"You know him?"

"The Viscount Alexander. Haven't seen him at the club in months." His gaze wandered toward the gatehouse. "Wonder if I could catch up to him?"

He escorted her past the glass-sided hearse, where six ostrich-plumed horses stamped their hooves, im-patient in their harnesses.

When they came alongside the carriage, he said, "Dear Mina, do go on to the house with the ladies. Tell her ladyship I'll follow shortly behind."

One of the Trafford footmen, arrayed completely in black, rushed forward to open the door and pull down the steps. Lord Trafford tipped his hat and hurried off in pursuit of the viscount.

Mina looked into the carriage. Three feminine faces, framed by glossy black fur and feathers, peered out from the shadowed interior. She wondered if anyone had ever drowned in black silk. She couldn't quite bring herself to climb the steps.

The cemetery called to her . . . a keeper of secrets. Her secrets. Her conversation with Lord Alexander left her uneasy. How could she eat? How could she sleep, until she was sure? Sure that her father's coffin had been interred in its final resting place, behind a locked iron door . . . *forever.*

She stepped back from the carriage. "Do go on without me."

"Go on?" Lady Trafford repeated, her blue eyes wide with incredulity.

"I just need a bit more time with Father."

"Astrid. Evangeline. Accompany your cousin—" A chorus of petulant refusals sounded from within.

"I'd prefer to be alone. I can walk back to the house when I'm finished. It's not far."

"Don't be ridiculous, dear. There are *Gypsies* camped in the field just across the way." Her ladyship peered into the darkening sky and grasped a gloved hand against the fur at her throat. "And it's getting dark."

"If we stay another moment, it will be *I* who expires next," muttered Astrid in a dour tone.

"Please," Mina entreated. She lifted her handkerchief to her nose for dramatic effect, acting upon lessons she'd learned observing her cousins. "I'm simply not ready to leave him just yet."

"Oh, dear. Very well, then," her aunt ceded, faced with the threat of tears. "We'll collect Trafford and leave the second coach and two footmen to attend you. I must insist you don't stay past dark."

Moments later, after instructing the footmen to remain behind at the carriage, Mina hurried along the tree-shadowed lane. She knew the way. She had walked the path the day before when her uncle had shown her where her father's coffin would be interred. Only then the sun had hung high in the sky, and the cemetery had been crowded with visitors. Now darkness seeped up from the earth, along with low, curling wisps of fog. A stone angel appeared to ward her away with open palms. Only the sound of her shoes on the path, and the furtive scratching of birds and other unseen creatures in the trees and underbrush, broke the silence.

Mina paused for only a moment outside the arched entrance to the Egyptian Avenue, braced on either side by twin columns and matching obelisks. A dense veil of ivy tumbled down from above. She swept beneath, into the darkness. Immense, Etruscan-style crypts lined the avenue, each bearing a massive iron door and two inverted torches symbolizing lives extinguished. She quickly broke free of the smothering tunnel and emerged into Lebanon Circle, where two rows of mausolea surrounded a towering cedar.

Although the Traffords owned a centerpiece crypt for the interment of their titled members, her father, who had married into the family, was to be placed beside her mother in the less-exclusive Terrace Catacomb above. Mina grasped her skirts and ascended the stone steps. A sudden gust of wind lifted the boughs of the evergreens all around, filling the circle with a thousand unintelligible whispers.

In the subsequent silence came the repetitive chink of metal striking against metal.

Chink. Chink. Chink.

Fear twisted in her throat, and deeper, into her chest, but she swallowed it away. Over the past year, she had faced far worse than evening shadows and imaginary phantoms. The sounds she heard were likely created by the cemetery workers doing their final bit of work for the day.

Chink. Chink.

Her lip, where she bit into her flesh, throbbed dully. What task could possibly require such repetitive blows? She arrived at the catacomb where her father's coffin was to have been deposited. The door featured a small, square opening, scored with iron bars and banded with decorative rivets. Shuffling sounds came from within.

Chink.

She launched herself onto the tips of her toes and grasped the edge, peering inside. In the darkness, she could barely perceive coffins, stacked on shelves . . . and a shadow that moved.

"You! *You there.* What are you doing? *Stop!*"

Mina grasped the handle and tugged, but to no avail. The door was locked. To her horror, the sound of splintering wood emanated from inside.

She whirled, returning to the edge of the circle, searching for any worker, any guest, to whom she could shout out her accusations of grave desecration. She saw no one. Again she returned to the door, pressing her fingertips against her mouth, suppressing the urge to scream. She twisted the ball clasp on her bag and snatched out her pistol.

"I'm warning you. Come out of there!" she bellowed.

Desperate to stop the shadow, desperate to protect her secret, she thrust her arm between the metal bars, gun in hand. She would merely fire a warning shot, and flush the person out—at least then she would know with whom she dealt.

A large stone hurtled from the darkness to strike the door beside her head.

The shadow grew larger. Bronze eyes blinked . . . and *glowed*.

Mina screamed. The creature roared and twisted toward her.

She fired.

COLLEEN GLEASON

THE REST FALLS AWAY

In every generation, a Gardella is called to accept the family legacy of vampire slaying, and this time, Victoria Gardella Grantworth de Lacy is chosen, on the eve of her debut, to carry the stake. But as she moves between the crush of ballrooms and dangerous, moonlit streets, Victoria's heart is torn between London's most eligible bachelor, the Marquess of Rockley, and her enigmatic ally, Sebastian Vioget. And when she comes face to face with the most powerful vampire in history, Victoria must ultimately make the choice between duty and love.

"Sophisticated, sexy, surprising!"
—#1 *New York Times* bestselling author
J.R. Ward

Available wherever books are sold or at
penguin.com

ALLISON CHASE

DARK OBSESSION
A Novel of Blackheath Moor

They wed in haste—Nora Thorngoode, to save her
ruined reputation, and Grayson Lowell, to rescue his
estate from foreclosure for unpaid debts. Each resents the
necessity to exchange vows that will bind them for all
time, and yet from the first, passion flames between
them—quickly engulfing them in a sensual obsession.

But soon the lover that Nora married becomes a dark
stranger to her, a man torn apart by guilt over his
brother's recent, mysterious death—and driven half-mad
by ghostly specters who demand that Grayson expose the
truth. Has Nora married a murderer whose wicked deeds
blacken everything around them? Or, together, in the
secret passageways of Blackheath Grange and along
Cornwall's remote coastline, can Grayson and Nora
discover what really happened that terrible night—and in
setting free the troubled ghosts, free themselves as well?

**Available wherever books are sold or at
penguin.com**

Penguin Group (USA) Online

What will you be reading tomorrow?

Tom Clancy, Patricia Cornwell, W.E.B. Griffin,
Nora Roberts, William Gibson, Robin Cook,
Brian Jacques, Catherine Coulter, Stephen King,
Dean Koontz, Ken Follett, Clive Cussler,
Eric Jerome Dickey, John Sandford,
Terry McMillan, Sue Monk Kidd, Amy Tan,
John Berendt…

You'll find them all at
penguin.com

Read excerpts and newsletters,
find tour schedules and reading group guides,
and enter contests.

Subscribe to Penguin Group (USA) newsletters
and get an exclusive inside look
at exciting new titles and the authors you love
long before everyone else does.

PENGUIN GROUP (USA)
us.penguingroup.com